BEFORE AGAIN

THE SHADOW CITY

BOOK ONE

CLAIRE S DUFFY

To Aidan and Brennan, whose imaginations are nearly as ridiculous as mine (you can read this in a few years) Love Aunty Claire xxx

ONE
1968

T he man touched Morag's elbow to steer her across the Gallowgate. She glanced at him, and her stomach twisted with nerves and excitement. She couldn't quite believe this was really happening.

Frost twinkled on the pavement on the January night, but Morag was toasty in her brand-new coat. The fur trim was exactly the sort of thing Audrey Hepburn would wear. Her feet were freezing in her good dancing shoes, but she would be on the bus soon enough and could change into the furry boots she'd worn out. She had thought about putting the boots on when they left the Barrowland Ballroom, but he seemed in a bit of a hurry. Her legs look better in heels, anyway.

She had the time of her life tonight. When the latest Beatles number came on, she'd hopped on a table, and a crowd had gathered. Her flaming auburn curls in a short pixie cut that her mother hated and her brand new green dress barely skimming her bum made her feel like Lulu on Top of the Pops. She did the routine that she'd painstakingly learned off the telly, wishing there was a magic way you could freeze or rewind the picture to watch the tricky bits again. Luckily, the song had been in the charts for weeks, so she'd had plenty of chances to practice.

'I wouldn't want to take you out your way.' She shivered as an icy wind slithered under her collar. She hadn't felt her toes since Glasgow Cross and regretted carrying her boots in her bag. 'If you could just see me to the bus station, that will be quite... sufficient,' she added, hoping against hope that 'sufficient' meant what she thought.

'I wouldn't hear of it,' the man replied.

His voice was posh. The voice of leafy gardens, indoor toilets and being sent away to schools that looked like castles. His family probably played board games.

'I wouldn't have you on a bus on your own at this time of night,' he continued. 'Not a pretty girl like you.'

Morag smiled. He was lying. Glamorous, yes. Striking, maybe. Pretty? Nah.

'Especially not with that madman on the loose.'

'The what?' Nerves shot through Morag's stomach.

'The madman that's been killing lassies at the Barrowland Ballroom.'

There was a funny tremor in his voice.

'Oh, that,' Morag laughed. 'I don't believe in all that boogeyman nonsense. Lassies get hurt all the time. Some enterprising reporter is just getting folk riled up to sell papers.'

'Is that right?'

Morag shrugged. 'Aye, it is right.'

As they approached St Enoch's Square, her bus was already at the stand. She saw the glow of the driver's cigarette as he sat leafing through the evening paper.

'You know they call him The Shadow?'

'What?'

'The madman terrorising the city. They're calling him The Shadow.'

'Terrorising? Who's terrorised?' Morag laughed.

The man's expression changed. It was nothing but the tiniest flicker of something in his eyes, but Morag felt it. She took half a step backwards.

'Anyway, my bus is leaving, so I'd better—'

He moved forward, so close she could smell stale cigarettes on his breath. She glanced behind her. The bus was at the other end of the square. The driver coughed as he turned the page of his newspaper.

'Maybe you'll get a dance next week if you play your cards right,' she said, raising her voice a bit. 'I need to get this bus. My da'll be waiting up, and he'll be raging if I'm late.'

Morag had never met her da. She was conceived amid a lively VE Day celebration in a wee lane round the back of George Square. The American G.I. had melted into the crowd with nothing but a cheery wink and was never seen again. Knowing her mother, Morag didn't blame him for a second.

'You've got such a pretty face.' The man's eyes seemed to glitter as he drank her in, his voice soft and intimate.

She was almost backed against the wall. It was so quiet all of a sudden, even though they were in the city centre. The bus was so far away.

'You could make me very happy.'

She forced a laugh. 'I don't think so, pal. I can burn tea, and the only time I tried to hem a pair of trousers, I sewed the leg holes shut. I'm a lot of things, but no' wife material.'

He chuckled softly. Lead settled in her guts as he stroked the side of her face and it took everything in her not to flinch. Those strong hands had guided her around the dance floor. She'd stumbled at one point, tripping over her own two feet, and he had righted her as though she weighed nothing.

'I don't know if you know who I am, but you should know if anything happens to me, it won't be the polis that comes after you,' she said, trying to ignore the pounding in her ears. 'I'm giving you fair warning.'

The man's smile didn't falter. He reached out and ran his finger gently down the side of her face and across her throat. 'Pretty, pretty girl,' he murmured. Ice slid down Morag's spine.

She had made a terrible mistake.

A piercing scream cut across the square. It reverberated in Morag's ears, distorted and sharp. The man glanced up, his focus lost for an instant, but it was all Morag needed. She kicked him in the shins with the sharp toe of her good dancing shoes and ran like hell.

Two

The taxi rumbled away. Kirsty resisted the urge to wave it down again and tell the grouchy driver to take her right back to the airport.

Wind shrieked and whistled, yanked great trees to and fro and teased loose tiles. Branches creaked, wheely bins thudded, and at least one trampoline would be flying merrily across the city.

Kirsty didn't have to be here. No one was making her. No one even knew she was here.

Horizontal rain plastered her hair against the side of her face and dripped icy needles down the back of her neck as the taxi's brake lights disappeared into the gloom. She could be sipping a cocktail on a beach or watching the Northern lights dance across Arctic skies long before anyone noticed she didn't show up.

She trudged up the muddy path towards the huge, dilapidated house. This kind of storm was so ubiquitous to Glasgow that for a strange second, she felt a stab of homesickness. She had felt nostalgia for these kinds of storms in Nebraska and Nicaragua, Sydney and Shanghai, where wind and rain battered with a ferocity that tried and failed to match that particular mischievous destruction of their Glaswegian sisters.

This path was gravel, once upon a time. She could remember running helter-skelter down it one summer's evening. She skidded and scraped her knee and her dad picked her up and tickled her to stop her crying.

The gravel was long gone now, skittered away over decades of storms like this. Mud squelched and clung to Kirsty's trainers as she made her way towards the house. Or what was left of it, at least. The blond sandstone mainly seemed intact, but almost every upstairs window was a gaping, jagged hole. Several chimneys sagged precariously, and judging by the racket she could hear even over the wind, an army of furious birds had taken up residence in the attic.

Home sweet home.

It appeared that the garden had been slowly reclaiming the house for years. Twisted vines with thick leaves crept up walls and over windows, weighing on the imposing front entryway as though trying to drag the house back into the earth. Kirsty would have no chance of getting to the front door without an axe, and as she didn't happen to have one in her backpack, she made her way around the side path towards the back. She clambered through an aggressive rhododendron, jaggy branches scraping her shins through her joggers, before coming face to face with a gigantic mint plant that—

Not the one she planted with her mum?

She'd been about six. It was the last summer they lived in this house as a family. She'd become obsessed with making mint sweeties from scratch, presumably after reading a story about kids who solved mysteries while making their own sweeties. She banged on and on about it for days. Finally, her mum took her down to a greengrocers on Pollokshaws Road, where they bought a scraggly mint plant and ceremoniously planted it next to the kitchen door. Kirsty faithfully watered it daily for months and months until—

Until she didn't live here anymore.

It couldn't be the same plant. That was thirty years ago, for goodness sake.

A gust of wind splattered her with icy rain as she fumbled in the side pocket of her giant backpack for the keys. Then she noticed the lock was so rusted that no key had a snowball's chance. She stepped back, steadying herself against a rhododendron branch and aimed a sharp kick at the lock. It shattered instantly, and the door flew open in a cloud of dust.

Not ideal for security, but at least she was in.

A pile of beer cans and cigarette ends in one corner suggested she wasn't the first person to break in over the decades. At least the thick layer of dust covering them confirmed it had been a while since the last intruders. The one good thing about creepy abandoned houses. After a while, they become their own Keep Out sign. She bet the local kids told ghost stories about the house, dared each other to cross the threshold as an initiation into the gang of the moment. But nobody had dared spend a whole night in a long, long time.

Until now.

Kirsty shoved her backpack against the larder door. She couldn't hear telltale squeaks or scratches over the storm, which was something. Frankly, it would have been rude if mice hadn't taken up residence, but ignorance was bliss. Spiderwebs, thick and matted with age, draped over every shelf like macabre Christmas decorations. Ivy had broken in through a crack in one of the windows and covered the ceiling.

She set about lighting the stove. Kirsty reached for some kindling stacked against the side of the stove, then had to stop to swallow the lump in her throat.

Did her mum pile it there that last morning?

She shook off the thought and searched the old kitchen drawer for matches. The stove was ancient enough to be heated by actual fire. If this pile of bricks and grime were in an English country house with a Range Rover in the drive and a tennis court in the back garden, the stove would probably be called an *Aga*. Kirsty's family only ever called it the cooker.

The fire took, and relief snaked through Kirsty as a touch of warmth softened the bite in the air. Her sleeping bag was good quality, at least. She had gotten it in Vancouver a few years back when she taught yoga at a fancy studio in Yaletown and, consequently, was dizzy with disposable cash. Designed for Arctic camping, it had a hood she could pull tight until only her nose was exposed to the elements. She had woken up feeling like a human boil-in-the-bag in the snow-covered Himalayas, so it should see her through a Glasgow night in April. It was only for a couple of nights, anyway.

It wasn't as though she would hang around after the funeral.

After a moment's consideration, Kirsty spread the sleeping bag on the faded pine kitchen table. It might be fractionally warmer off the ground and would hopefully keep her out of reach of the army of creepy crawlies who must have taken up occupation of the kitchen. She had a bottle of fizzy water, an apple and a granola bar she picked up at Heathrow. It was practically the Ritz.

A night or two, she reminded herself. *That's it.*

She perched on the table facing the fire as a deep yawn just about engulfed her whole. Exhaustion clawed at her bones. She was at that spacey, surreal level of tiredness, so far beyond sleep that the idea of closing her eyes seemed absurd. She kept jerking as though they'd re-routed a marathon over her grave. She watched flames crackle in the heart of the cooker and tried not to think about what she was doing here.

There were no lights. It stood to reason the utilities had

been cut off yonks ago. Kirsty had nicked a few fat candles from her hostel in Brisbane twenty-four hours earlier. They glowed in the darkness, casting dancing shadows over ivy and the spider webs. It was oddly cosy.

Or at least it'll do till cosy gets here.

She could almost hear her gran cackle, shaking her head at Kirsty's idea of a bed for the night. *You're a wan-aff Kirsty, hen. I'll tell you that for nothing.*

There had been an Australian woman coming for Kirsty with a kayak paddle when she got the text.

That's Morag away. Funeral Thursday 10 a.m., St Theresa's.

She'd frowned. *Who's Morag?* Then realisation clicked. Ice slid through her veins, and the kayak paddle had whacked her in the face. It served her right.

Kirsty took a few surfing lessons each time she'd come through Oz. She quite fancied the idea of herself effortlessly catching waves, at one with the ocean. However, it very much appeared that the combination of Kristy and the Pacific Ocean defied the laws of physics. One instructor, years ago, a Mauri dude with a thick Kiwi accent and incredible tattoos she later used as a road map to kiss her way all over his body, kept going up to randoms along the beach after her lesson, yelling *she fell forwards! How can you even do that?*

She mostly seduced him just to shut him up, but it turned out to be more than worth her while.

Her latest instructor seemed different. Which was such a cringey cliché that she was disgusted by herself for even thinking it. Ben was more cute than hot, with dimpled cheeks, a cheeky smile, and freckles sprinkled over his nose and shoulders. Not to mention the dangerous twinkle in his eye that would have any sensible woman scarpering in the opposite direction.

Kirsty was not, however, any sensible woman.

By the end of her first lesson, they could have powered a small city with the sparks from their banter. They seemed to have the exact same daft sense of humour. There was a moment when they were outdoing each other with impressions of sharks hanging out by the reef, just waiting for tourists to doggy paddle by—there was a whole joke leading up to it. You had to be there. Kirsty looked at him and thought, *isn't this how it's supposed to be?*

She'd known him for about an hour, and she wasn't bonkers. She wasn't saying *this was it* or anything. Giggling like idiots after knowing one another for barely an hour felt like...

A good start.

The kind of start you looked back on years later, chuckling as you mock-argued over which one of you had fallen first.

The lesson led to drinks, followed by the inevitable moonlit walk on the beach. Waves crashed on the sand as Ben wrapped his arms around her from behind. He grazed the underside of her bra with his thumb, and a delicious shiver ran through her. She leaned back against him and thought, *I could get used to this.*

Three seconds later, he was kneading her boobs like dough and grinding himself against her thigh like an eager collie while she tried to seductively murmur, *maybe just a little bit more gently, if you could.* Then he licked her ear and growled that he was *as hard as a cliff and would make her as wet as the ocean.* She burst out laughing, thinking, thank goodness the daft banter was back. *Then* she realised that was actually his idea of *sexy* banter. Which had made her getting the giggles all a bit socially awkward.

Afterwards, she told herself that first times were always a bit rubbish. It just takes a while to find that rhythm together. Practice makes perfect and all that. He walked her back to the hostel, all dorky and funny again. They ran into each other at the beach café the following day, and that was that. For a few weeks, anyway. Sun, surf, and sex that did improve a bit but never entirely lost that collie-going-at-your-leg vibe. Kirsty persuaded herself it just meant he was adorably keen.

Obviously, she didn't imagine it was any great love affair or anything. She wasn't stupid. She was just enjoying having that sparkle in her life for a minute. That was all.

Until one day, Kirsty's hostel roommate told Kirsty that she'd seen Ben with another woman. Kirsty marched right round to confront him. Battered on his front door and yelled every dirty name she could think of.

And *she* answered the door.

The other woman.

Because she lived there too.

On account of being his wife.

Yes, ladies and gentlemen, there is no way to lose your feminist high horse quite as quickly as discovering that *you* are the random slapper he's been knobbing on the beach. And that even with a significant baby bump, she's still capable of giving you a doing with a kayak paddle.

Which was when Kirsty got the text that her gran had passed. Kayak Woman noticed she wasn't running anymore and asked what the matter was. Kirsty told her, and the woman's face fell.

'Oh, chook, you've got to get going. Your mum'll need you.'

'My mum died years ago. Both my parents did. I'm an orphan.'

Kirsty still had no idea what had made her blurt that out. She hadn't told anyone about her parents in years. Couldn't stand the awkward horror that emanated from folk like a cloud of midges.

'You poor bastard. No wonder you've been putting up with old shit-for-brains. I'm gonna get shot of him the second

I drop the sprog, just can't fucking reach anything at the moment.'

She'd given Kirsty a hug and driven her to the airport.

The candles danced in the icy draught, and Kirsty yawned deeply. She just needed to get through the next few days, then she would go somewhere with sunshine and good food and start looking after herself properly. Take up yoga and meditate her way into becoming somebody mildly less of a walking disaster.

The cooker made the air almost bearably mild, and Kirsty yawned again. First thing in the morning, she would treat herself to a full Scottish breakfast in some nearby café. She would charge her mobile and book the first flight to anywhere-but-here on the café's WiFi.

Except now that Kirsty had thought about food, a supper of an apple and a granola bar seemed less than satisfying. Without her phone, she had no idea what time it was and even less idea of whether or not anything would be open. Had 24-hour café culture reached the Southside of Glasgow? Once upon a time, Kirsty would know all the late-night lock-ins around here and would be welcome at approximately half, but that was a long time ago. She reckoned now that her best bet was a late-night garage.

Ooh, British sweeties. She hopped off the table and rummaged in her backpack for a dry jumper. *Fruit pastilles and salt and vinegar crisps.* She smiled. The prospect of some fruit pastilles was more than worth venturing back out into Armageddon.

The storm had blown itself out and the night was eerily silent. Kirsty clambered back through the mint-and-rhododendron jungle and onto the road where she once learned to ride a bike. It was a quiet crescent looping off Nithsdale Road.

Imposing sandstone mansions nestled behind electric gates. It was the sort of road folk, who have only ever seen misery-porn films about schemes teeming with heroin, would never believe exist in Glasgow. *Maybe that suits us*, Kirsty thought cynically. *Better the world sees us as pathetic victims of our English overlords than admit that half the city sits quietly on fortunes built on the slave trade.*

Both versions of Glasgow were accurate, to be fair. In high school, Kirsty had plenty of pals who lived in tower blocks made more or less of cardboard. Their homes were riddled with damp and asbestos which culled pensioners before the council bothered to send anyone around to inspect.

Belatedly, Kirsty noticed that she'd wandered farther than she meant and was now at the edge of the Gorbals. Or at least, what was once the notorious Gorbals was now a desultory collection of half-empty buildings and eternal roadworks. She was only a couple of blocks from the flat she grew up in.

She would be awake. Whatever time it was. She never rested. She was like a Great White Shark.

It was just her and Kirsty left now.

A flicker of fear sprang to life in Kirsty's guts at the thought of coming face to face with her great-grandmother after all this time, but she was being daft. Agnes must be in her mid-nineties by now. What would she do at her daughter's funeral, for goodness sake?

Kirsty scanned herself for a shred of compassion for her great-grandmother. She smiled in relief when she found none. Grief or not, Agnes McIvar could go hang.

THREE

A pale, watery dawn peeked through the clouds. Kirsty sat by the side of the Clyde river in front of the science museum, eating a packet of stale crisps she got at a late-night supermarket on Paisley Road West. She'd wandered all night, endless loops up and down sleepy streets, shadowy buildings and empty roads. She hadn't walked all night in a long time.

This was what being back here did to her.

She shouldn't have come. What was she thinking? Wasn't there some saying about how you can never go home?

The air was still bitterly cold, but the dawn freshness woke her up a bit. The river glistened in the pale morning sun as it meandered through the heart of the city. Kirsty saw the hazy purple outline of distant hills. She tossed the empty crisp packet in the bin, hopped down from the concrete slab, and a movement caught the corner of her eye.

She froze, ice snaking down her spine.

It was nothing.

Of course it was nothing. It was a city. Things move.

It would be a train rumbling along the raised tracks across

the river. A car or an ambulance zipping along the Expressway. Or a seagull scanning the riverside for half-eaten sandwiches. Nothing more than that.

The unsettling feeling stayed with her as she brushed gravel off her bum and headed for the main road. It was just one more reason to bounce the second that horrible curtain closed in front of the coffin.

Kirsty had always been fascinated by the old shipyards. They lay empty and abandoned along the banks of the Clyde, huge football fields of space, stark monuments to an industry that once powered a city. She stared at the man-made inlets at the edge of the river, long rectangles bordered by Victorian cobble-stones, where shiny new ships were launched into the world once upon a time.

'They're like nurseries for ships,' she had said to her gran once. They were out for a walk, just the two of them. Gran had spotted a gap in the fence just around the corner from where Kirsty was standing and beckoned Kirsty over. 'Let's go on an adventure,' she grinned, clambering through.

Kirsty's gran never quite seemed like a proper grown-up. Long after she was grey and wrinkly, in knitted cardigans and sensible shoes, she was always up for an adventure or a midnight snack. Trespass was one of her favourite pastimes. Luckily, Glasgow was absolutely hoaching with abandoned buildings and boarded-up waste grounds, begging for a wee girl and her gran to break in for a spot of make-believe.

The cobblestones were covered in a thick thatch of weeds that grabbed Kirsty's ankle twice and flipped her on her arse as she scrambled to follow Gran's quick steps. Gran was never one for dramatics and ouchies that needed to be kissed better, so each time, Kirsty got up and picked the bits of stone and sand out of her knee herself. Gran strolled ahead, apparently intent on a mission.

'Are you looking for something?' Kirsty asked, watching her frown as she looked around the vast emptiness.

'Ooh, pirates and ghosties, darlin,' she smiled, but there was something a bit distracted about her expression. 'Just the usual.'

'Are there pirates here?' Kirsty looked around as though Captain Bluebeard might pop out from behind a bush and shout *boo*.

'There's been everything here,' Gran said thoughtfully. 'Once upon a time, the Clyde was the gateway to the whole world. Pirates and adventurers and prisoners sailed from these waters to every place you can think of.'

'Even India?' Kirsty was learning about India at school at the time. 'Do you know how Christopher Columbus thought he got to India, but it was South America because nobody knew that South America was in the way?'

'Christopher Columbus wisnae a good man,' Gran muttered.

Kirsty was about to object because that wasn't what her teacher said, but Gran had wandered off. Kirsty flicked the last bit of gravel out her knee and scuttled after her.

Kirsty smiled now as she was drawn to a hole in the same fence all these years later. This was how Gran would want respects paid to her, she thought as she squeezed herself through and emerged in the shipbuilding graveyard. Forget sitting in a church listening to a priest who never even met Gran drone on about how she was a good person. Aside from anything else, being a *good person* was a low bar amongst the McIvars.

The rain was a fine mist now, that peculiar Glasgow weather where it's less that it's actually raining and more just that the air is wet. The weeds were every bit as intent on flinging her at gravel as she wandered across the cobblestones. Her stomach grumbled mournfully. A single packet of stale crisps didn't keep a person going as long as one might hope. A yawn overtook her, a huge one that just about swallowed her whole. Her kitchen table was calling her.

The moment of weakness was down to hunger as much as anything. An image of her wee gran marching over these cobblestones, searching for ghosties and pirates, flickered to life in her mind. The wave of grief that crashed over her was so strong it took her breath away. She clamped her hand over her mouth, choking back the hard, aching sobs. It wasn't time yet.

She was going to cry at the funeral. That was the plan. That's what funerals were bloody well for. But she missed her. She was sorry for everything, and it was too late to tell her.

That was when she heard it.

She wiped her face with the back of her hand and frowned, trying to place the noise. It was metallic and sort of echoey. Construction going on beyond the high redbrick wall that surrounded the vast yard? Roadworks, probably. But the weird thing was, it sounded nearer than that.

Kirsty stood still and listened. Goosebumps prickled over her as the air filled with clangs of hammers on metal, bangs and thuds and the whine of welders' torches. Songs and laughter, shouts that were commanding and amused, joyful and frustrated. A shadow fell over her, and she could sense the gigantic ship behind her, five, six storeys high. Its vastness blocked the sun as men swarmed over her like ants.

Kirsty didn't want to turn around. She didn't want to see—

She thought she was done with all this nonsense. It had been years.

Exactly, she told herself firmly.

It had been years. She was a child then, and she was an adult now. She *was* done with all this nonsense. It had been a

long time since she had imaginary friends or saw pirates or
ghosties.

She gritted her teeth and turned around, and there was—

Nothing.

No ghostie shipyard workers or mammoth hulk blocking
the sun. The clouds were low and nearly black, casting a heavy
shadow almost as dark as night. Kirsty shivered. It was time
to go.

There would be cafes open by now. A cooked Scottish
breakfast would set her world to rights. Square sausages,
potato scones, and baked beans never taste quite the same
anywhere else in the world. Fried tomato and black pudding.
Thick toast and a chunky mug of builders' tea so strong the
spoon would stand up in it.

Mouth watering, Kirsty turned to leave and spotted a
group of people crowded around by the water's edge. The sun
must have gone behind a cloud because she could barely make
them out in the gloom. *Teenagers mucking about.* Early on a
Wednesday morning was an odd time for it, but unless
teenagers had changed a lot since Kirsty was one, there was no
end to the weird shit they would do.

Except they weren't teenagers. They were men. Tall,
broad-shouldered men. *Wee Glasgow guys have developed,* she
thought. *They must be putting steroids in the lager.*

The men stood around in a circle wearing cloaks. Not
raincoats, but proper long, heavy cloaks, like monks or high-
waymen. Or vampires. Were they in fancy dress? Steroids or
not, there was no excuse for a Wednesday Morning Cloak-
Wearing Club.

Out of nowhere, a strange, woozy sensation hit her like she
was in a lift that stopped too fast. She had come closer than
she'd meant, creeping through the jungle of weeds, wildflowers, and discarded cans. She should turn around, she thought.
Whatever nonsense they were up to, she doubted she wanted

to know. She could smell fire now, crackling and spitting, sharp and acrid in the cool air.

Then one of the men stepped aside, and ice-cold horror swept over Kirsty. A long bed of burning coals glowed red and black in the shadowy gloom, snapping and sizzling with heat.

And a man lay across it.

He was naked, his body a mass of scars and crudely drawn tattoos. He was alive, just. He writhed and jerked in agony, sweat pouring down his brow as his skin blistered and burnt. Kirsty's breath caught in her throat as her brain struggled to process what she was seeing.

The man was going to die. A human being, right in front of her. That fire was going to kill him. He shouted, a twisted, half-strangled howl of torment that vibrated in Kirsty's bones.

Another man stood over him, dark beard and hair tumbling to his shoulders. Kirsty wanted to yell, to shout that she was phoning the police, but she couldn't move. Her voice was trapped in her throat. The dark-haired man raised his arms above his head. An axe glinted in the fire's light, and Kirsty finally screamed.

The men turned as she came howling from the undergrowth like a manic banshee. Everything she had ever learned about using an opponent's superior size against them in Thai boxing classes flashed through her head and back out again. She lunged for Axey Man and kicked him in the balls.

FOUR

He staggered with a grunt of pain, but in seconds he was back up, and the axe flew past Kirsty's nose with millimetres to spare. She ducked, drew back, grabbed the collar of his cloak and nutted him with all her might. His nose shattered beneath her forehead, and he swung for her. She aimed a sharp kick directly at his hip bone which threw him off balance, then drove her shoulder into his guts, sending him flying across cobblestones.

He was down but far from out. Kirsty grabbed his axe, so much adrenaline coursing through her body she could barely see straight. She had no idea what she'd do with an axe, but its weight and the smooth, worn wood of the handle felt ever so slightly comforting in her hand. She whirled around in a kind of half squat, waving the axe above her head like a demented sumo wrestler.

She tried to make herself seem as big as possible, then remembered that was more for actual bears than men who resembled them. She vaguely recalled the advice of some women's self-defence class that acting bonkers can make you seem more trouble than you're worth. She did a few goblin-type leaps and screeched like a monkey.

Sure enough, they backed away. Terror etched on their faces, a couple fell to their knees and stared at her with unadulterated horror. *The bonkers thing was working.* She did an evil-plan laugh, a seagull impression, and a bit of the Macarena. One of the men retreated so far that he toppled into the river. She found the splash more satisfying than was strictly dignified.

Naked Man had managed to roll off the fire. He was on his hands and knees, his face twisted with pain as he clearly tried to gather the strength to get to his feet. The wall and the fence were half a football pitch away, Kirsty thought in dismay. How on earth were they supposed to escape? She was no dainty wee thing, but Naked Man was as broad-shouldered and steroided-up as the rest. A coal carry was out of the question.

But there was no way he would make it on his own, and Kirsty's seagull impression would only keep his murdery pals at bay for so long. She shimmied under his armpit, hugged his giant forearm to her chest like a lever, and staggered to her feet. She couldn't quite wrap her other arm around his waist on account of the painful-looking welts and blisters, so she kind of hoiked him over her shoulders like a huge human cloak. They managed forward a few steps.

Pressure built in her chest, presumably the after-affects of adrenaline, but it was hard to breathe. A fierce wind whipped up around them, which really didn't help matters. They managed a few more steps, somehow getting into a rhythm. Finally, miraculously, the wall was inching closer.

Naked Man managed to find his feet, and though he still leaned heavily on Kirsty, he helped with a bit of momentum. Her lungs burned and every muscle trembled. For a couple of seconds, she thought she was going to puke, which would slightly undermine the whole *feminist in shining armour* thing she had going on. After what felt like an age, they made it to the fence and through the hole. They collapsed in a sweating, shivering heap on the pavement beyond.

For a few seconds, Kirsty couldn't do anything. She trembled on her hands and knees, taking slow breaths to pull herself together. She was frozen by the realisation that she had absolutely no idea what to do now.

It wasn't often she had no idea what to do. She had been mugged in a snowstorm in Toronto, run out of petrol in the outback of Central Queensland, and arrested in Athens. She always managed to figure it out step by step. But she had never been collapsed on Govan Road with a naked, half-barbecued man before.

'What's your name?' Her throat was raw, and her voice croaky from all the monkey screeches. She coughed.

The man stared at her, terror swimming in his deep blue eyes. *What was his problem?* Oh, wait. The monkey screeches.

'The monkey screeches were just to freak them out.' She gave him her most reassuring grin. 'It's the first thing I thought of. Seems to have kept them from following us, so that's something.'

He stared blankly, his eyes intently following her lips. He was worryingly pale under his maze of tattoos. Though the closest Kirsty had come to medical training was multiple seasons of *Grey's Anatomy*, she had a horrible feeling that didn't bode well.

A bus rumbled by, and the poor guy jumped a mile. His nerves must be shot to shit. He needed a hospital. Kirsty yanked off her long-sleeved T-shirt—she had a vest top underneath, so she'd be chilly but decent—and handed it to him. It wouldn't keep anyone his size warm, but maybe he could use it as a loin cloth.

It was then that she noticed the world glowed orange under street lamps. It was dark.

Kirsty blinked, confused at the twinkling stars scattered across a midnight-blue sky. It had been morning. She had been just about to get breakfast.

How could it be nighttime again? She couldn't have been doing seagull impressions for ten hours straight. Was there... had there been an eclipse?

She spied a taxi pulling out of the BBC car park down the road and staggered to her feet, waving wildly. It drew to a stop, and Kirsty turned to help Naked Man to his feet. The driver took one look at her well-done companion, shook his head and pulled away again.

'Selfish bastard!' she roared at its brake lights. 'Where's your human compassion?'

Naked Man shrank back, clutching Kirsty's T-shirt to his chest as though it would protect his pecs from the taxi. For a big guy, he was awfully skittish. Though so would Kirsty be if her pals had just tried to roast her alive. He was probably in shock and couldn't even think straight.

Kirsty wracked her brains for the nearest hospital. It would be that big new super duper one where the Southern General used to be. It was at the other end of Govan, but she thought she could walk there. Whether or not she could walk wearing a giant naked dude as a cloak was another matter, but she didn't appear to have a choice.

They couldn't sit there on the pavement all day. Or all night, or whatever it was. He needed medical attention, and she needed to inhale a toastie or seventeen. A wee nap wouldn't go amiss either. The hospital suddenly seemed very, very far away.

She mimed that they needed to make tracks, and he seemed to get the message. He nodded and hauled himself painfully to his feet. He was still grasping her T-shirt to his chest, but she supposed if he was okay with his willy waving to the world, then so was she. It was, to be fair, the least of his problems right now.

Their standing coal-carry-cloak-dance felt strangely well practised, and they shuffled a few steps forward. They were almost at the traffic lights when Kirsty spied her least favourite sight. The blue light flashed as the car pulled up next to them.

The fucking polis was all she needed.

Every instinct, bred in her for generations, screamed at her to scarper. She may not be a *professional* McIvar, as it were, but hatred of these truncheon-wielding arseholes was in her DNA. However, due to the giant naked man draped about her person, running away while merrily giving double fingers over her shoulder was not currently an option.

Two officers, a man and a woman, got out of the car. Kirsty could hear their radio buzzing static and polis chat. Her every cell was weighed down with loathing as she plastered on a *helpful citizen* smile.

Naked Man was rigid with fear. She could hear his breath taut in her ear and flashed him a grin of companionship. They could be pals if he was averse to the authorities as she. Assuming the whole *rescuing him from becoming a human hot dog* thing hadn't already bonded them sufficiently.

'Kirsty?' said a voice.

Kirsty froze, utter confusion curdling in her guts at a friendly face rising from a luminous waistjacket. The voice was horribly familiar, but her brain was mince, and she couldn't place it.

The male polis grinned and shook his head. 'Where the hell have you been?'

Harry *fucking* Finnegan. As if her night couldn't get any better.

FIVE

Six

The Finnegans were one of those families that everybody knew. There were seemingly dozens of them in a two-bedroom flat one close along from Agnes's. Kirsty remembered them fondly as always filthy and full of fun. Harry's four sisters had hair down to their bums, scraggly locks that flew out behind them as they chased each other with shrieks and giggles until they were yelled in for tea.

In those days, Agnes insisted that Kirsty wear her hair in neat plaits. One of the many downsides of being raised by one's gran and great-gran. Plaits might have been fine in their days, but Kirsty looked like a tube in the eighties, cutting about like an Enid Blyton character while all her pals wore crimped hair in luminous scrunchies. But there was no arguing with Agnes.

The Finnegans' dad, Martin, was a wee quiet man, forever vaguely bemused by his rowdy progeny. He told funny stories and was often found wandering about playing an unexpected instrument, like a ukulele or a mouth organ, for no apparent reason. Anyone who made inadvertent eye contact with him would be treated to a wee serenade. His children had perfected

the art of scampering to their rooms with their eyes firmly on
the floor, but Kirsty was regularly caught. Though she'd
pretend to complain, she secretly enjoyed clapping along to
whatever seventies folk tune he had just learned.

Kirsty had never been able to bring herself to blame him
for any of what happened.

She and Harry had been best pals since she knocked his
front tooth out in the playground on their last day of primary
school. Neither of them could remember how the fight
started, but they both agreed Harry deserved it, which served
as a solid basis for friendship. In high school, everyone
assumed they were at it. Kirsty had even—*briefly*—had a
minor, low-level wee *thing* for him. When it came down to it,
though, she loved him too much to ever allow him to go out
with someone like her.

They did get off with each other once. In a playground,
late one summer's night when we were about twelve or thir-
teen. Harry asked out of the blue if she wanted to French kiss.
She thought he meant on both cheeks like the French do,
which seemed odd, but then she never understood boys. He
came in for a winch, and Kirsty turned her head to go for his
cheek. Long story short, he licked her ear. That was the end of
any romance between them.

Over the years, she and Harry had seen each other through
breaks ups and exams, disastrous haircuts, and failed driving
tests. Then his dad's coma. His dad's funeral.

Harry shook his head, taking in the sight of Kirsty and her
giant naked companion.

'You're never boring, Kirsty. I'll gie you that for nothing.'
He turned to his police pal and nodded towards me. 'This is
Kirsty MacIvar.'

Icy daggers slithered through Kirsty, and she wasn't sure if
she wanted to burst into tears or gouge his eyes out.
Kirsty *MacIvar*. Harry Finnegan couldn't have gone more

over to the dark side than if he was breathing heavily through a shiny helmet. *One of those MacIvars,* his eyes said. *So no sudden movements, eh?*

The woman nodded. It might have been Kirsty's imagination, but she was almost sure she spotted the woman's fingers twitching in the direction of her polis battering stick. Kirsty felt like growling at her just to see if she cried. Harry, of all people, knew that she was not one of *those* MacIvars. Or at least, he had once.

'Who's your pal?' he asked. His easy grin suggested he couldn't feel even one of the fatal daggers Kirsty was shooting him with her eyes.

'Don't know.'

'Yous seem well acquainted.'

Harry's eyes flicked down the man's naked body, and Kirsty shifted protectively in front of him. Not that it was her willy to protect, but the poor bastard was shaking like a leaf. Human decency was clearly too much to expect from the aptly-named Filth.

'He needs a hospital. Can yous take him?'

'Can he not talk for himself?'

'No, he can't.'

'Have you taken a drink this evening?' the woman asked.

'None of your business,' Kirsty snapped.

The woman flinched, and Kirsty smiled.

Harry rolled his eyes. 'I think you'd better come along too,' he said.

'I'm not hurt.'

'You're covered in blood.'

'It's not mine.'

'Then you know we need a wee chat with you, don't you?'

'I know you farted the first time you got a blow job, and no lassie would go near you for years.'

The woman smothered a giggle, and Harry reddened. '*Sake*, Kirsty.'

Naked Man slumped over, leaning heavily on Kirsty. Harry, to his credit, caught the guy just before he squashed Kirsty flat.

'How about we get your pal to a hospital, and then we can decide who's got the more embarrassing sexual history?'

Kirsty didn't want to get in his manky polis car, but suddenly, the need to sit down overrode everything else. She clambered in, and Harry dragged Naked Man, yanking him across Kirsty's lap so she was cradling his head and shoulders. His warmth brought a bit of feeling back to her legs, and she felt strangely grateful. They were an odd wee team, Naked Man and her, but a team all the same.

Kirsty glanced at the man's poor back as the woman started the polis car. She noticed that the burns weren't his only injuries. His body was covered in cuts, bruises, and grazes, and there was a deep gouge in the fleshy part of his lower back. Kirsty had seen her fair share of stab wounds, and this one hadn't been done by a knife but something much blunter. She thought of Axey Man's axe with a shudder. The edges around the wound had started to scab. It must have happened at least a few days earlier.

Kirsty absentmindedly stroked Naked Guy's hair as he dozed on her knee. It was long. Reddish-gold waves reached his shoulders, woven in a series of intricate plaits.

She smelled smoke, for obvious reasons, and something she reluctantly suspected was charred flesh, but there was another scent too. Something peaty and rich, as though he'd bathed in an Islay malt. And a herb, one you'd have with a roast. Bay or sage or sandalwood.

He was dozing, slipping in and out of consciousness, but he held on to Kirsty's knee as though he was scared to let go.

She felt a rush of something unfamiliar. As if she'd saved a puppy from the rain.

She sighed to shake it off and looked out the window. They passed a sign for the Clyde Tunnel. They would be at the hospital any minute. She would discharge this giant human puppy into the hands of medical professionals and say whatever was necessary to get Harry and his pal off her back.

Then she would return to her sleeping bag on a kitchen table and sleep for a week.

Just as Kirsty was contemplating the rammed A&E waiting room with a sinking heart, Naked Man rather helpfully collapsed again, which solved the queue issue. He was helped onto a stretcher by an efficient team of cheerful angels in blue and wheeled through a set of double doors.

Kirsty firmly pushed away the odd pang she felt when the doors swung shut behind him. Naked Man half sat up and stared in panic when he realised she wasn't coming, but Kirsty wasn't family. They probably wouldn't let her stay with him even if she wanted to. Which she didn't.

A drunk guy slumped in one of the chairs roused himself enough to shout merry abuse at Harry. An arrogant man in a suit cradled his sore finger as he loudly announced the waiting time *just wasn't good enough*, and another wailing ambulance approached. Kirsty was being ridiculous. She just felt a bit wobbly because she was—hungry.

'Sure you don't know him?' Harry asked.

Kirsty jumped a mile. 'The guy's had a helluva morning,' she shrugged. 'I've got a heart, you know.'

'You do not,' he grinned, sounding for just a second so much like old Harry that Kirsty got a lump in her throat. *I hate him*, she reminded herself, though, in truth, she wasn't sure she had the energy to hate anyone right now.

'What do you know?' she muttered.

'What's going on, Kirsty? You know I can help. Are you okay?'

'Nothing a roll and sausage won't fix.'

'We need to have a wee word first.'

'No, we don't.'

One thing about being one of *those* MacIvars is that Kirsty had her rights drilled into her before her ABCs. 'Am I under arrest?'

'What would you be under arrest for?'

'It doesn't work like that, sunshine. I'm away home.'

'Where are you staying?'

'None of your business.'

'I could drive you.' Harry sighed impatiently. He followed her as she made her way outside. 'Where have you been, Kirsty? You just took off without a word ten year ago—'

'Are we pretending you don't know why?'

'I was on your side. You could have trusted me.'

Kirsty flashed a pointed look at his uniform and scoffed as the automatic doors opened. The packed ambulance bay was flooded with bright sunshine, and the air was warm. *Hold on a minute. It was—*

Morning. It was daytime again. It had been Wednesday, then it was nighttime, and now it was morning again. That made it, almost undeniably, Thursday.

That's Morag away. Funeral Thursday 10am, St Theresa's.

'Shit—shit. Can you take me to St Theresa's?'

'You're wantin' to go to mass?'

'Please, Harry. I can't be late—'

'Late for what?'

'Can you just shut up and take me?'

The sun hit the emergency department doors, and Kirsty caught a glimpse of her reflection. The running gear she put on three days ago in Brisbane was filthy and probably stinking to high heaven. Her hair was sticking in every which direction. Agnes would be appalled at the state of her, which took the edge off the horror.

Harry opened the boot of his police car and rummaged in what looked like a sports kit. 'Here,' he said, handing her a black hoodie. 'It's a bit manky, but it's probably cleaner than any of your stuff.'

Kirsty put it on. It smelled like Harry. More specifically, it smelled like endless nights in Harry's room. They'd watch cult horror films while a selection of his wee brothers snored, companionably munching every variety of crisp known to man. Suddenly, everything was too much. Grief smashed over her. For an instant, Kirsty felt as though she couldn't breathe, and then Harry grabbed her in a fierce bear hug.

'There, doll,' Harry murmured into her hair. He held her against his chest as she gasped and choked, struggling to catch her breath over dry, painful sobs. 'You can tell me what's going on, Kirsty. Whatever—'

'I need to go.' She pulled away, wiping her nose with the sleeve of his sweatshirt. 'Can you take me to St Theresa's?'

'You want to go to chapel now?' He frowned and rubbed her shoulder. 'You should maybe—'

'I'll slip in the back. They'll never know. Are you taking me or am I walking?'

Kirsty must have nodded off in the car because the next thing she knew, Harry was pulling up outside the ornate chapel where she had spent every Sunday morning of childhood from the age of seven onwards.

She once overheard a conversation between her mum and gran when she was too young to understand. It hinted that part of the reason her dad's family cut him off when he married her mum was related to the papal tendencies of the

MacIvars. Kirsty would have thought that Agnes's penchant for razoring her enemies would have counted more against her than she doesn't take fish on a Friday, but who was she to judge.

Kirsty was an atheist who couldn't give less of a crap about football if she sat down for a week and tried. She thought the whole business was a load of absolute nonsense and further considered any grown adult who started fights over whether Virgin Israelis or Dutch Kings are better in severe need of a word with themselves. But nobody asked her.

All the same, *deja vu* hit her like a train. She scrabbled out of the car in a dazed mess and belted in late for mass. This was, after all, how she spent most of her teenage Sunday mornings. She could tell you that the Communion wafer did precisely nothing for an alcopop hangover.

Harry shouted as she clattered up the steps, but she waved him away—the last thing her reputation needed was a bloody polis escort—and shoved open the heavy chapel doors. The scent of incense and beeswax hit her.

She slipped into the back row, hoping she'd get a moment or two to catch her breath before the next round of kneeling and standing. Given that the median age of any given congregation these days was about a hundred and five, you'd think they'd cut down on the cardio portion of mass. The air was alive with the sound of knees creaking as they got up and down, in and out, shook it all about.

Finally, it was time to sit again. The priest launched into a rousing speech about Hell or something. She couldn't really hear him from the back, and she'd heard it all before anyway, so she tuned him out and looked around.

She didn't see anyone she recognised. To be fair, most folk here at the back would be here just for the mass. Any old friends or errant McIvars would be crowded down in front with Agnes. Kirsty sat up to peer through the gloomy candlelight, bracing herself for her first sight of great-grand-mommie dearest. All she could see was row after row of carefully set white hair. Any one of them could be her.

The door screeched as it was opened again, and someone slipped into the back pew across the aisle. Kirsty wasn't the last to arrive, after all. The newcomer was a young guy in his early twenties or so. He wore a neddy tracksuit, his hair a shock of thick, jet-black curls that reminded her of that noncy comedian from those old movies Agnes liked.

The kid turned, and icy recognition prickled over Kirsty. His eyes were so startlingly familiar she had goosebumps under Harry's jumper. He was clearly a distant cousin, some genetic quirk making him look like—

Who did he look like?

Who cares. The MacIvars could all go hang, remember? The *Little Tramp* guy and his tracksuit included. Kirsty turned her attention back to the altar, where the priest carried on about lost souls or something. Her eyelids grew heavy.

She woke with a start to find everyone queueing up for Communion. Her last Confession was in the previous century, but some treacherous muscle memory propelled her into the queue. She decided she'd get a blessing to be polite and hoped she wouldn't burst into flames.

The coffin was propped open on the altar, gleaming walnut and rich white satin, decked with flowers of every colour. Too late, it hit Kirsty that she would be able to see into it in just a couple more steps. Icy chills raced down her spine, and hot tears prickled behind her eyes.

This wasn't how Kirsty wanted to see her gran again.

She wanted to give her a cuddle. She wanted to say sorry for everything. She wanted to split a rich, sticky ginger pudding cake and a pot of tea with her. Gossip and bitch and set the world to rights and hear her promise, for the millionth time, that Agnes's bark is worse than her bite.

She really wanted to give her a cuddle.

Tears half-blinded her, and the lump in her throat was so sore she felt as though she'd never be able to swallow again. She had promised herself she could cry at the funeral, but now she was here, she couldn't. It was as though the pressure was too great, like a vast river thundering against a dam.

The second Kirsty saw her gran's face, she would shatter into a million pieces. Her wee gran. An aching void of loneliness reared up and threatened to swallow Kirsty whole.

She took a deep breath and tried to pull herself together, but she didn't want to be there. She didn't want this to be happening. The permanence of Gran being gone clawed at her, tore at her guts.

Pretend it's not.

Kirsty almost laughed. When she was a kid and upset about a bad mark at school or not being invited to a party, Gran would cuddle her and whisper, *pretend it's not.* It was her wee game.

Kirsty would wail that she was gonnae get in trouble or that she had no friends, and Gran would grin and shrug, *aye maybe, but pretend it's not.* The daft thing was, it worked.

She was one step away from seeing in the coffin.

Pretend it's not.

She couldn't

She wanted to turn and run away, but she was hemmed in by a swarm of pensioners clamouring for their body of Christ.

She had to do it. This was why she came. She would not chicken out.

She took one more step, steeled herself and looked.

It wasn't her.

SEVEN

Kirsty blinked and stared into the coffin. Black spots danced at the edge of her vision.

It wasn't her.

Mother of Christ, it wasn't her.

It wasn't her gran in the coffin.

Some other wee old lady lay in the coffin, all angelic and dead. Holy fucking buggery shite Kirsty was at the wrong funeral.

'Sorry, sorry,' she muttered, trying to push her way through the sea of elderly folk. There seemed to be hundreds of them all of a sudden. For a desperate moment, Kirsty considered crowd surfing *Crocodile Dundee* style until she remembered all the brittle bones.

She had to get out of there. She'd never been one for perfect etiquette, but she was reasonably sure you're not supposed to just rock up at a stranger's funeral.

'You're alright, darlin'.' A warm, dry hand clasped Kirsty's. 'Just you let it all out. Did you know Marjorie well?'

'I've never even met her,' Kirsty blurted.

Then she turned and ran.

· · ·

'You said it was at St Theresa's!'

Kirsty slammed the door behind her. The thud reverberated around the tiny flat where she grew up.

Agnes looked up as Kirsty burst into the living room. An uncomfortable feeling Kirsty didn't have time for unfurled in her stomach. *Was Agnes always this wee?*

She was perched in her armchair by the fire. It was bright green wool, and she'd had it longer than Kirsty had been alive. The fire was the same glowing electric bar monstrosity it always was. Orange and brown swirled merrily on the carpet, and every shelf was crammed with spectacularly ugly knickknacks. Between the fire and the heating on full blast, Agnes could make a fortune renting the place out for hot yoga.

You would never know that once upon a time, this was the headquarters of the most feared gang in Glasgow. *The MacIvar Boys.* The moniker made them sound like an unruly table of cheerful adventurers who solved mysteries and helped old people cross the street. Even today, the very name could make folk of a certain age shudder.

Some of the scarred, hatchet-faced men with dead eyes and yellow teeth would be nice to Kirsty. If she didn't scuttle out the way fast enough, they'd pinch her cheeks with nicotine-stained fingers and press a few pennies into her hands for the ice cream van. But most of them slunk in tense silence towards the living room for orders or punishment, then back into the night to do terrible things.

Agnes used to take great pride in the fact that long after the Gorbals were cleared, her men would commute back from the schemes they had been exiled to.

'It's the journey that's doing him in,' a quivering-voiced wifey once begged.

Kirsty had been doing her homework at the kitchen

counter, and she could feel the woman trembling from across the room.

'It's three busses back tae Drumchapel. He falls asleep and ends up in Helensburgh twice a week. The kids hauvnae seen him in a month. Could he not maybe manage things for you up at our bit? Get a wee satellite operation going?'

'I don't have any business in Drumchapel,' Agnes said coldly. She bit into a caramel log, which was the wifey's cue she was dismissed. The wifey didn't know that, so Agnes nodded to her henchman of the moment, who hauled the terrified woman to her feet and flung her halfway down the close steps.

Agnes sat in the same chair, practically swinging her legs as though she were under a spell in some trippy eighties kids' movie. Then she gave Kirsty a stare that both curdled Kirsty's insides and confirmed that she was still Agnes, frail old lady or not.

'You've got a nerve showing your face around here.'

'I came for my gran's sake,' Kirsty snapped.

'Whit funeral?' Agnes demanded. 'Morag's funeral? Of course it was at St Theresa's. Where else would it be?'

'When then? Have I missed it? I got on the first flight could when I got your text.'

'You think I was gonnae wait for you to show your face? Ma wee girl's half turned to dust while you've taken your sweet time to pay your respects.'

'I told you I came right away. You said it was Thursday. You just didn't want somebody who actually loved her there. You were always jealous of us.'

Agnes's henchman of the moment, a gargoyle of a man with a broken nose and no teeth, stepped forward as Kirsty raised her voice. Agnes waved at him to stand down. *Shame.* Kirsty was itching to punch somebody, and evil witch or not, it was probably frowned upon to belt a 97-year-old.

'You always did think the world revolved around you, Kirsty,' Agnes sneered. 'You think I gave a monkey's about the pair of you, with your wee whispers and games? I was glad she had the company. I was too busy supporting this family.'

'Oh yeah, working your fingers to the bone doling out your orders from your bloody throne.' Kirsty laughed. 'You wouldn't know a day's work if it bit you on the bum.'

Agnes cackled. 'At least I made it to Morag's funeral.'

Kirsty refused to flinch. She wouldn't give her the satisfaction. 'I'm here. You said Thursday.'

Was today definitely Thursday?

That weird *morning-then-night-then-morning-again* thing. Did Kirsty pass out at some point and lose track of more days than she realised? A wave of dizziness hit her, and she clutched the back of the couch. *She wouldn't sit down.* She couldn't. *Agnes would smell weakness.*

'Ten years I've not heard fae you,' Agnes said. There was a gleam in her eye. 'How would I have told you Thursday?' Agnes clearly didn't know how Kirsty had managed to miss the funeral, but sure enough, she'd smelt weakness, and she loved it. 'Folk asked where you were. They never thought you'd stoop so low as to let Morag down. After all she did for you as well, taking you in like you were her own.'

'I *was* her own,' Kirsty snapped. The familiar hot flash of guilt stabbed at her.

'Folk thought better of you,' Agnes grinned.

'Well, they should have known better, seeing as I'm related to you.' The fight had gone out of Kirsty. She needed to get out of here and soon. As soon as Agnes was certain she'd got the upper hand, she would eat Kirsty alive.

'Aye, right enough,' Agnes grinned. 'That's what I said.'

'Where are her ashes?'

Sadness draped over Kirsty like a heavy cloak. The ashes might still be at the funeral home. Maybe she could take them and have a private ceremony for Gran, just the two of them. Just like it had always been.

'Me and Derek here scattered them on the Campsies,' Agnes sneered. Derek was presumably the gargoyle. 'She always liked it up there. He drove me up, and we let Morag float away over the waterfall.'

'Shame he never shoved you in after her.'

'It was awfa windy, probably brought half of her home in my good jaiket,' Agnes added cheerfully. 'It's hanging up by the door if you want to check.'

'You didn't hang about.' *How many days had she lost track of?* 'Were you feart you might catch a feeling or something?'

Agnes cocked her head to one side, and the glint in her eye shifted as she considered Kirsty's words. There was something not right, and Agnes was intrigued. Dread settled in Kirsty's stomach. Whatever she was about to say next, Kirsty didn't want to hear it.

'We scattered her weeks after the funeral, Kirsty,' Agnes said softly, going in for the kill. 'I don't know what calendar you're on these days, hen, but Morag died over a year ago.'

EIGHT

Kirsty swiped a tenner off Agnes's hallway dresser as she stormed out. If Agnes was going to play these kinds of sick jokes, then she could pay for Kirsty's taxi home. Not *home*, the house. Her parents' house. The place she was going to get on the market today, then immediately get on the next plane heading bloody anywhere.

She clattered down the last steps from Agnes's top-floor flat and shoved open the front door. There used to be an old lady in the ground floor flat. She'd sit at her living room window all day long, shouting at kids who played too loudly and telling Agnes's goons to scram. *Mrs McCafferty.*

Despite her rage, Kirsty smiled at the memory. Mrs McCafferty wore high-necked, fussy blouses like a prim and proper character in a seventies sitcom. Her snowy white hair was always in an elaborate updo that looked like it could withstand nuclear warfare.

She was terribly well-spoken. If anyone talked slang on the front step, Mrs McCafferty would fling up her front window and take a strip off them. Once, Kirsty even heard her sternly lecture Agnes that the plural of the second person pronoun remains *you. She lectured that it should be clear from context whether it is singular or plural.* Kirsty had held her breath, waiting for Agnes to take Mrs McCafferty's head off, but Agnes nodded meekly like a wee girl getting into trouble.

All the neighbourhood kids were convinced Mrs McCafferty was a witch and therefore hated her. Until the day Kirsty left home. She slammed the tenement door shut behind her and then stood on this very step, stunned at suddenly finding herself a homeless fifteen-year-old.

Mrs McCafferty rapped on her window. Kirsty whirled around, ready to snarl that she'd not even said a word. Mrs McCafferty beckoned her inside. Kirsty must have been dazed because she obeyed.

Mrs McCafferty's flat stank of stale smoke. It was stuffed with chintz, like a Victorian doll's house come to life. Kirsty sat on the flowery couch, sipping a glass of Irn Bru and nibbling a packet of salt and vinegar crisps. Mrs McCafferty announced that the problem was that Agnes was afraid of Kirsty. Kirsty burst out laughing, a shrill, shaky laugh.

'You've no idea what you are, do you?' the old lady rasped in her posh voice.

'I know I'm buggered,' Kirsty sighed.

'You'll work it out,' Mrs McCafferty chuckled, lighting a cigarette with hands that trembled with age. 'Whenever you don't know what to do, just think to yourself, *what's the next step?* Don't worry about the one after that or the tenth step down the line. That's when you get yourself mixed up. Just work out the next one, and you'll be fine.'

Kirsty had followed that advice ever since. She stepped out into the blinding sunshine and noticed for the first time that it was warm. Hot, even, which was unusual for Glasgow at the best of times, never mind April. Eglington Street would be her best bet for a taxi, she reckoned. Her next step, therefore, was to walk there.

· · ·

The taxi driver was mercifully the strong silent type, and Kirsty dozed in the back as the Southside rumbled by. The fare was £6, but she gave him all of Agnes's tenner, which earned her a grunt of thanks. Getting out, she was hit by another wall of heat.

This was the kind of heatwave that made Glasgow lose its mind. Kirsty made her way up the formerly gravel path and prepared to battle the rhododendron bush. The kind of heatwave where it would take the police a week to pacify Kelvingrove Park.

They'd had a summer like this the year she moved in with Gran and Agnes. There was an ice cream shortage, so acute, a black market sprung up, with furtive Cornettos and Nobbly Bobblies being exchanged on shady street corners. One enterprising unfortunate took his life in his hands by sticking yoghurt in the freezer and passing it off as the real thing. Agnes had to intervene before his enraged customers tore him limb from limb.

Kirsty could have sworn the rhododendron bush was wilder and jaggier than the first time she battered through the other night. She kicked at the thick, dark leaves, trampling twigs and wishing they were Agnes's head. Her joggers snagged and ripped as she finally cleared the worst of it.

The kitchen door was open.

Prickles danced over Kirsty as she took in the gaping doorway. She remembered kicking the lock off the other night and rolled her eyes at her ridiculousness. She had thought she shut the door behind her, but with a busted lock, it was no wonder the wind blew it open again. She couldn't imagine many robbers were willing to take on the rhododendron bush for the sake of her manky backpack, so probably no harm done.

She shoved a few mint vines out of the way, then stopped,

unease dancing over her. The mint trailed over the threshold of the door and into the kitchen. Mint grew like a wildfire—but it hardly quadrupled overnight. She must have...she must have kicked it in when she thought she was shutting the door. Or something.

Pins and needles prickled as she hacked her way through the mutant herb. Clambering into the kitchen, a cloud of dust made her sneeze. Her backpack leaned against the larder door, and her sleeping bag was spread on the kitchen table. Just as she left them.

Except that they were both covered in dust.

Kirsty's heart hammered as she took in the mint vines spreading over shelves and ceiling beams. The dust must have been blown around in the night. It had covered her footprints and seemingly spread over her things.

She grabbed her sleeping bag to shake it out, then screamed like a banshee as about a billion tiny mice came scampering out in every direction. Kirsty flung the sleeping bag away. She stood stock still in utter horror as about thirty-five generations of mice disappeared into nooks and crannies. Her heart thudded, revulsion trickled over her, and *she just wanted none of this to be happening. Thank you very much.*

All those mice weren't born overnight.

Kirsty rolled her eyes at the thought. She was going daft in her old age. She was exhausted and scunnered, and everything would make sense if she could just get a few hours' sleep.

However, no level of tiredness would induce her to climb into a sleeping bag where hunners of mice had been shagging with abandon. She shoved the heavy kitchen door reluctantly and ventured deeper into the house.

A couple of shallow steps led to the entrance hall, which glowed a pinkish colour through the stained glass window above the grand front door. The fancy furniture in the good room was covered in dust sheets, and there was what looked like an old nest in the grand oak fireplace. Kirsty had once loved to stand on the window seat of the deep bay window while her mum dusted and polished antique knick-knacks. She'd watch the road and report any goings-on.

'The big boy from the house on the corner got a new bike,' she would announce. 'It's got a scratch on it already. I bet he'll get a skelp.'

The velvet covering the window set was coated in dust but seemed surprisingly intact otherwise. Crucially, there was no sign of the presence of mice. Kirsty curled up into a ball, pulled Harry's jumper over her and fell into a deep sleep.

NINE

Kirsty had no idea how much time had passed when she finally woke, but it was daylight.

Still? Again? Who knew.

Even through the cracked and filthy glass, she saw that the street was flooded with sunshine. The deep blue sky was dotted with nothing but a couple of fluffy *Simpsons* clouds. She struggled to pull herself into a sitting position, feeling dozy but indescribably more human. She wrapped herself in Harry's jumper and leaned against the walnut panelling with a yawn.

Food. She needed food. Specifically, a cooked breakfast. Square sausage, potato scone, fried tomatoes and beans, and an absolute mountain of toast. Her stomach grumbled at the thought. She had no idea what time it was, but there must be a café that served an all-day breakfast somewhere nearby.

She stretched again. Something caught the corner of her eye, and chills darted through her. A man stood on the road, staring at the house. Kirsty froze. The man had his hands in his pockets and was just standing there, frowning as though trying to figure something out.

Kirsty slipped behind the heavy brocade curtains and peered out. *It was the kid from the funeral.* With the curly hair and neddy tracksuit and startlingly familiar eyes. The kid she figured was a distant cousin—except why would a distant cousin have been at the funeral of a random lady called Marjorie?

And more importantly, what the hell was he doing standing outside her house now?

Looking for me, a voice whispered.

Did Agnes send him?

A spot of psychological warfare was precisely her style.

Agnes, standing on the steps of the courtroom that long ago day, screeching that she would make Kirsty pay. Kirsty shivered. Agnes would indeed make Kirsty pay. She had been surprisingly docile yesterday, but Kirsty had had the element of surprise on her side. Agnes was not the forgive-and-forget type.

But she hadn't sent the kid to the funeral yesterday. Agnes had been genuinely shocked to see her, and she couldn't have known that Kirsty would go to the funeral of a lady called Marjorie. So it was a coincidence. The kid was just a random ned who went to mass this morning and was now casing an empty house to potentially rob it.

Or he was part of the Wednesday Morning Murder Club.

Kirsty had almost forgotten all that was actually real. If there was one thing Kirsty knew about murderers—and she knew more than she'd ever wanted to—it was that they're not fond of being interrupted. And even less fond of leaving witnesses alive. It had all been such a blur. Kirsty couldn't identify them if she wanted to, but they wouldn't know that.

All she needed was a murdery culty man on her back, but if he thought he could scare her away from her breakfast, he could run and jump. Because if there was another thing she knew about murderers, it was that they tend not to do it in broad daylight in all-day-breakfast cafés.

So he could stare at her all he liked. She was going for a square sausage.

The long-delayed square sausage hit the spot. As did the potato scones, the fried tomatoes and beans and the mountain of toast. A mug of strong tea and Kirsty almost felt as though all was right in her world.

For a few minutes, anyway.

Kirsty managed to plug her phone in under the table, and as she scooped the last of the tomato sauce up with her toast, it finally came to life. She wanted to look at the text she got about Gran's funeral. It had been from an unknown number. Kirsty had assumed that either Agnes got a new phone in the past decade or she'd got one of her goons to send the message. Kirsty wasn't convinced that Gargoyle Man from Agnes's flat yesterday had opposable thumbs equal to texting, but someone had sent it.

There would be a date on the text confirming when it was sent. Kirsty couldn't for the life of her think what Agnes would have to gain by claiming Gran died a year ago or by having someone text Kirsty to invite her to the funeral a year late. That said, if Kirsty were ever to understand the working of Agnes's mind, she would immediately go and lie down in traffic.

It could have been some kind of bizarre technical issue. Hadn't Kirsty heard stories of messages lost in cyberspace for no apparent reason? Kirsty's money was still on a sick prank by Agnes, but anything was possible.

There must have been an obituary. Maybe even news articles. It had been a good few decades since Agnes was at the height of her gangland power, but her daughter's death would have rated a mention.

Once upon a time, Agnes was one of Glasgow's most notorious gang leaders. There was even a film about her, one of those Scottish-made, *Life is Hard*, where they put a greyish-sepia filter on it, so the audience knows that *Life is Hard* in Glasgow. It was better than some of them, to be fair, even if it did depict Agnes as altogether more charming and interesting than the reality.

Kirsty would never understand films that depict organised crime leaders as debonair and charismatic, romantic anti-heroes that take care of their own. A life of crime was inherently narcissistic. It was a deliberate decision not to bother with the rules everyone else abided by.

Her phone was doing its whirl ball thing connecting. She jabbed at the screen. She had no idea why she imagined that would speed matters up, and sure enough, the whirring continued unabated.

Her gaze rested on the date on the calendar app and—

Chills washed over her. A sore feeling formed in her chest. Because—*because it couldn't be.*

It didn't make sense.

'Scuse me.' She turned to the young guy drying mugs behind the counter. Her voice sounded shrill and panicked in her head, but he didn't seem to notice. 'What's the date today?'

'Fourteenth.'

'Of July?' Kirsty tried to affect a grin as though she were joking because what kind of nutcase doesn't know what month it is?

Never mind what year.

'Aye, July. It's Bastille Day in France.' The guy grabbed another tray from the glass washer with a clatter. 'It's like their Bonfire Night. I went to Paris when I was wee, and aw' these nutters at the Eiffel Tower were pure throwing fireworks at people's feet. Fucking French, man. They're mental. Love them.'

Kirsty left him reminiscing about childhood holidays and stared at her phone. Her hands were shaking so much she had to put it on the table, but the date didn't change. It was the 14th of July.

A year and three months later than it should be.

The text. Kirsty opened her messenger app.

That's Morag away. Funeral Thursday, 11am, St Theresa's. Sent on the 5th of April.

Last year, according to the calendar.

Her boarding pass. Her phone had refused to scan at the airport in Hong Kong, so the check-in desk had printed off a paper pass for her. She rummaged in her bag, and there it was, folded into her well-worn passport.

Dated the 6th of April. With the time difference, it would still have been the 6th when she arrived in Scotland. The following day would have been Wednesday, 7th of April, of Wednesday Morning Murder Club fame. So today should have been Thursday the 8th. Maybe Friday the 9th, at a stretch.

Except it was Wednesday, 14th of July.

Kirsty had misplaced a year and three months of her life.

She grabbed a pen from her backpack and copied the text onto the boarding pass. She couldn't trust her phone not to evaporate or something, and she felt the need for the words to be on something tangible. *That's Morag away. Funeral Thursday, 11am, St Theresa's.*

A gaggle of teenagers passed the window, heading toward Queens Park. They wore matching joggers snipped off at the knee, their bare tummies soft and glowing so red that Kirsty felt itchy on their behalf. A female runner slowed to a walk and squirted herself in the face with her water bottle, looking as though she might evaporate on the spot. She nodded at the elderly man pushing a walker. An ice pack designed for sprained ankles was tied to the back of his neck by a kerchief. The people of Glasgow had never handled the heat well.

Kirsty glanced up, and he was standing across the road.

The kid with the eyes. The Little Tramp. Tracksuit Man. Murdery Culty Boy.

He had followed her.

And she had had enough.

Whoever this wee prick was, he was giving her answers.

She yelled to the guy behind the counter that she'd stuck a tenner under her plate, and he waved her off. She raced out of the coffee shop and across Pollokshaws Road. The driver of a sleek car honked in indignation at having to touch his brakes.

Tracksuit Man's eyes went wide, and he turned and sprinted, swerving to dart through the gates of Queen's Park and past the duck pond. He was fast, but so was she. They wove around dog walkers and buggies, and cyclists tinkled their bells, affronted at their eternal right of way being questioned.

Kirsty hated running with the passion of a thousand suns, as all sound-minded people should. But she got hit by energy surges now and then, as though she'd been plugged into the grid. It was like drowning in a tidal wave of pins and needles. She'd learned over the years that the only way to quell it was to chase it away over twenty or thirty kilometres. As a result, she was a level of fit that made her judge herself. Even at a full-on sprint, she was barely puffed when they got to the flagpole at the top of the steep hill.

Tracksuit Man was starting to tire, she noted with satisfaction. Kirsty was still a few metres behind, but she was gaining on him. It belatedly occurred to her that she didn't know what to do when she caught him. She supposed she'd take a flying leap and rugby tackle him if it were a film. They'd roll down the hill in a cloud of dust and maybe a hail of bullets, but she wasn't entirely convinced people did that in real life.

Grabbing his jumper would be her best bet. Then the whole thing became moot because he stopped dead, and she crashed right into him. They were in a quiet, wooded area behind the flagpole. Nobody else was around, which was a good thing because they had run into a bloody great pig.

Tracksuit Man put an arm out to steady Kirsty, and she blinked like a cartoon character because *what the hell*. It wasn't just any pig, either—though any pig in Queens Park would have given her pause. It was a huge, angry, hairy bastard with yellow tusks. And it was growling at them as though it knew about every bacon roll Kirsty had ever had in her life.

She desperately tried to remember anything she knew about pigs. They ate the bad guy at the end of some film. That didn't help. She thought they were supposed to be clever, but she wasn't sure that challenging this guy to a Sudoku would be particularly constructive at this juncture.

'Stay really still,' Tracksuit Man muttered. He was American. That threw her, but she didn't have time to process it. 'They don't have good eyesight.'

Ahh, a third pig fact. Kirsty obediently froze, staring at the pig, who was now snuffling along the path. Just as she was thinking it wouldn't have a lot of luck finding truffles around here, it came up with a Double Decker wrapper and started chewing it in confusion. Its hair was dark, muddy brown, thick as steel wire, and it was enormous. To be fair, Kirsty wasn't sure what size pigs typically were, but this guy was like a wee horse.

Suddenly noticing that they were more appetising than the chocolate wrapper, the pig abruptly spat it out and charged, its beady eyes practically glowing red. Kirsty raced for the nearest tree and flung herself at it.

Her wild leap was no dignified or graceful affair, but she

managed to haul herself out of reach with an unladylike grunt. The pig crashed into the tree with such force that the whole thing wobbled and nearly dropped Kirsty from her perch. She hoped that nutting itself on a venerable oak might slow the pig down, but apparently, a mutant-pig skull can take a good deal of punishment.

By the time Kirsty righted herself, her quads howling that she'd not done *nearly* enough squats in her life for all this nonsense, the pig had Tracksuit Man backed against the fence. Tracksuit Man was feeling his way up the mesh, obviously thinking about climbing it. The pig licked its lips. Tracksuit man wasn't going to have time.

Which presented Kirsty with a dilemma. If this wee arsehole had been one of the boys setting Naked Man on fire the other morning, then maybe this served him right. It was an extreme *fuck around and find out*, but karma worked in mysterious ways. On the other hand, call her a big softie, but Kirsty didn't think she could just sit in a tree and watch a human be eaten by a pig.

Her dilemma was solved by a kid, about five or six, who came tearing around the corner on an orange bike shouting *nee no nee no* like a police siren. The pig hurled itself around, its beady eyes glowing. The wee guy screamed for his Daddy, and Kirsty leapt from the branch, flailing wildly with absolutely no idea of what she was going to do next—

Something flashed. A light brighter than anything Kirsty had ever seen. Like Magnesium but times ten. It was gone in seconds, and they were all left blinking red dots, dazed and stunned. And the pig—

Where did the pig go?

Kirsty turned around slowly, her legs wobbly as though she'd been on a ship for days. There were trees everywhere, but none were thick enough to hide a pig the size of a tank. No way could that snuffly bastard run fast enough to be out of sight already.

So where the hell was it?

A guy with a neatly clipped beard came jogging around the corner.

'Harris,' he called. 'C'mon, son, mummy wants us to bring milk home.'

'Daddy, the lady magicked a pig away.' Harris pointed at Kirsty accusingly.

'Oh really, that sounds like fun.'

Kirsty was about to query precisely what about a mutant pig on the rampage sounded *fun* when Harris flung his bike on the ground and started to wail.

'Make it come back!' Harris screeched. 'I want to see the pig again!'

'Come on, Harris, we don't want to keep mummy waiting.'

Father and son disappeared down the path, leaving Kirsty and Tracksuit Man alone. With a pile of dust on the ground that wasn't there a minute ago.

'What are you?' asked Tracksuit Man.

'Pissed off and hungry,' Kirsty replied.

'No, mean, like, a witch? Or a fairy?'

The mad wee Yank was actually cracked. *Fan-dabby-dozy.*

'Why didn't you zap him before?'

'I didn't zap anything,' she snapped.

'Perhaps I'm not using the correct terminology,' he said with a shrug. 'But it sure looked like a zap to me.'

'Why are you following me?'

'I was hoping you could tell me how I ended up here.'

'Ehh, you're the one that ran here. I followed you.'

'Not here, *here.*'

'I beg your pardon?'

Kirsty's head ached, and she couldn't be bothered with a

mad wee Yank who talked in riddles. He grinned, and she was struck by those eyes again. He shook his head, staring at Kirsty in wonder.

'You look just like her.'

'Who?'

'Agnes,' he smiled. His face lit up with an affection that Kirsty had never known to be associated with her great-grandmother.

'*Agnes*,' she repeated, dumbfounded. 'Agnes *MacIvar*? How do you know Agnes?'

The mad wee Yank hesitated a moment, then shrugged.

'My name is Private Nathan Williams of the 129th Infantry Division of the United States Army, Illinois National Guard,' he said formally. 'I think I might be your great-grandfather.'

TEN

'I —need an ice cream,' Kirsty said.

'Sure, but—'

She held up a hand. 'You will explain when I've got ice cream.'

He nodded, and they walked in silence until they reached the ice cream van next to the duck pond. The queue was long, but eventually, Kirsty bought two 99 cones with chocolate flakes and raspberry sauce. Harry once told her that when he worked in an ice cream van during his Highers, wasps would go mad for the raspberry sauce. If he ever squashed a wasp, it would explode with raspberry sauce.

Kirsty remembered thinking that sounded bonkers. She missed the days when exploding-raspberry-wasps were her measure of bonkers. She led the young man to a bench by the duck pond and bit into the chocolate flake. A swan tried to stare them out, then wisely swam away when Kirsty gave him the evil eye.

'Start talking.'

'I was born in Harrisburg, Illinois on January 12th, 1923.'

A toddler in a giant blue helmet rattled by on a scooter, a

beleaguered parent in hot pursuit. A police car screeched along Pollokshaws Road, siren blaring. The young man sitting next to her, with jet-black hair and wrinkle-free skin, was telling her he was one hundred years old. Kirsty considered whether he'd created an elaborate ruse to get his royal telegram seventy-odd years early.

Except Morag died over a year ago. Somebody sent Kirsty a text to come to her funeral over a year ago. Mice had been having a giant incestuous orgy in her sleeping bag for over a year. A horrible sense of inevitability prickled over Kirsty.

'I enlisted Christmas Day in '41,' Nathan continued. 'Before the draft came. Did my basic training in Texas. Fought in Greece and Italy, then landed in Normandy in '44. US Division Omaha Beach. An hour in, I got shot in the chest. Doc said it was a miracle the bastard missed my heart, excuse my language.'

He unzipped his baggy tracksuit top, and Kirsty saw the mass of angry scars crisscrossing his chest. Fresh scars, red and sore. From the Battle of Normandy.

'They sent me to Glasgow, to the Royal Infirmary, for surgery and convalescence. Seemed like the whole city was just one big pile of rubble after years of air raids, but damn, it was beautiful. Never saw buildings so grand in my whole life. First walk I took, a few weeks after I arrived, I came across a tenement that had been chopped clean in half by a bomb. One side was a pile of bricks, the other pretty much untouched but open, like a doll house my kid sister had.'

'What does any of this have to do with Agnes?'

Nathan smiled, his eyes filled with warmth. Even if his WWII story wasn't pish, Kirsty was far from convinced they were talking about the same Agnes.

'When I recovered enough, they sent me to the base in Dunoon and put me to work clearing bomb sites and making walls safe again. My pa was a builder, so I grew up doing that kind of thing and liked it. After a while, my buddy and I started going dancing. The Locarno, the Dennistoun Palais, we hit them all—but the best was the Barrowland Ballroom. It's towards the east of the city, think—'

'I know where the Barrowlands is.'

She and Harry saw Blondie there after their final exams.

'Well, that's where I met her.' Nathan grinned, lost in memories for a second. 'Spotted her the moment I walked in, although it took me just about half the night to work up the courage to ask her to dance. I thought I was the best Lindy Hopper around until I met Agnes. That gal flies through the air like nothing you ever saw.'

Kirsty tried to imagine the crabbit old bat she'd known all her life flying through the air like *nothing you ever saw.*

'We were thick as thieves from that night on. I walked her home that very night. Took us 'til morning because we kept stopping to talk and to kiss.'

That was a mental image Kirsty didn't need.

'By the time we got to her neighbourhood, Sunday Services were just starting, so I took her straight to church.'

'That—was that why you went there the other morning?'

He nodded. 'I figured maybe somebody might know what happened to her. And I saw you, and you look so like her—'

Well, he was havering there. Kirsty didn't look *anything* like Agnes. But Morag looked like him. His eyes. That's what she kept seeing. *Morag's* eyes. Goosebumps prickled over Kirsty, and she shivered.

This man was Morag's father.

'Agnes always said she got pregnant at a VE Day cele-bration.'

Nathan stared in horror, the tips of his ears turning a distinct, guilty pink. 'It was a crazy day. The freedom we felt, after so many years—Agnes and I snuck away to a quiet little lane behind George Square. Agnes had confetti in her hair.'

'How romantic.'

'We were engaged,' he added defensively. 'I asked her to marry me that very first night, and she accepted. After I was discharged back home, I brought my mom's ring back to Scotland. I was on my way to get the marriage license when—this happened.'

'Wait, what? Agnes always said she didn't know who you were. That you were a handsome stranger who melted back into the crowd, leaving her with a crushed skirt and a baby.'

Nathan hesitated a second, hurt flickering in his eyes. Then he shook his head and chuckled. 'You know Agnes. Do you think she would tell if she thought I abandoned her?'

Kirsty had to admit he was right. Agnes and the truth were rarely bedfellows at the best of times. She would never admit she had been ghosted.

It was almost as though this kid actually did know her.

Nathan fished in his pocket and brought out a little pack of papers. He handed over his military ID. Private Nathan Williams, born January 12th, 1923, enlisted on September 1st, 1942, just like he said. Kirsty automatically held the old paper carefully, then realised with a shiver that it wasn't old.

He then handed Kirsty a photograph, sepia-tinged but not faded. It was of a lady in a high-necked blouse who sat stiffly on a high-backed chair, her hands crossed on her lap.

'This is my mother,' he said, 'Millicent Williams, of Evanston, Illinois. She ran a grocery store, raised seven kids, and baked the best apple pies you ever tasted in your whole life. You recognise her ring?'

Kirsty peered at the photo, a chill slithering down her spine. The ring, with its thick band and dark, oval ruby, was distinctive. Agnes wore it on her right hand. She stopped wearing so many rings years ago when arthritis set in, but when Kirsty first went to live with them, Agnes had a ring for every finger and a story to go with each one.

The story often consisted of how she'd stolen said ring or confiscated it in lieu of a loan repayment. She told those stories with glee, cackling her head off as she described the pleading and the sobbing. Kirsty had never heard the story of the ruby ring.

'She was wearing it when I saw her the other day,' she said quietly, handing Nathan the photo. His cheeks turned pink. 'Your mum looks like my gran.'

Nathan's face lit up, and too late, Kirsty realised that she had to tell him his baby daughter died of old age a year ago.

'Gran?' he breathed in awe. 'Like Grandma? It was a little girl?'

Kirsty nodded. She couldn't do it. Not yet.

'Her name is Morag,' she said.

ELEVEN

Kirsty brought Nathan home with her. The house wasn't exactly salubrious, but it was a roof over his head. She could hardly have her great-granda sleeping rough, even if he was over a decade younger than her. They walked to the house via the camp he made for himself deep in the woods in Pollok Park, and it turned out he had an army-issue sleeping bag, tent and cooking utensils.

When they got to the house, Nathan wasted no time digging out Kirsty's dad's toolbox from the garden shed. He set to work, fixing the lock Kirsty had kicked off the kitchen door and then hacking the rhododendron bush into submission. It was such a Granda thing that it made Kirsty's head spin a bit. Not that she'd had much experience with Grandas, but she'd read about them in books.

Her first instinct was to sit around and freak out, but instead, she filled a bucket with water and half a crusty bottle of vinegar she found in the pantry and rolled her sleeves up. To start with, she made more of a mess than she cleaned, but then she came across some proper dusters and a mop and started to make some headway. They worked in companionable silence until the sun lay low in the sky, casting a deep orange glow over the garden.

Kirsty couldn't bring herself to think consciously about this reality she had found herself in. It was too much to take in, but somehow mindless physical work made it all seem... handleable. If it was real, if Nathan was who he said he was, then it just *was*. There was nothing to believe.

Nathan polished the stove, and Kirsty dragged some mattresses down from the bedrooms. They had been covered in plastic and were in surprisingly good nick. The thought of a decent night's sleep on an actual mattress in her sleeping bag brought a lump of relief to her throat. She could handle anything with a good night's sleep. Nathan had found an old laundry tub and a drying mangle and thoroughly washed the sleeping bag with bleach a few hours earlier. Kirsty had to admit that a housemate who knew how to work this ancient house with no electricity or hot water would come in handy.

Two alcoves were tucked off either end of the kitchen. They were likely a maid's quarter and a scullery once upon a time. Kirsty vaguely recalled a kitchen table in one, and the other had been used as a den for her. She would colour or dress up dolls while her mum cooked. She and Nathan decided to use them as a sleeping nook, thus turning the vast kitchen into a studio apartment.

It wasn't though they would be staying long, Kirsty reminded herself as she scrubbed caked-in dirt off the old stove. She would still sell up and get the hell out of Dodge just as soon as possible, but a decent sleep or two in habitable living quarters in the meantime wasn't a bad idea. Plus, she couldn't just take off and abandon Nathan. Even if she had no idea what to do with him.

Just figure out the next step. The next step was sorting out a space to eat and sleep. The step after that would become apparent when they arrived.

The sun lounged on the horizon, casting a soft orange glow across the overgrown garden. Bees buzzed industriously as they zoomed from wildflower to wildflower. Kirsty and Nathan sat on the patio, the large slabs baked warm from the heat of the day. Tin mugs of strong tea and a supper of baked beans and sausages were doing wonders to revive Kirsty.

'We must have been sent to the future for a mission,' Nathan announced. 'I read every comic book ever made about time travel, and when folks get sent to another time, it's for a reason. Like something they have to fix, somebody they have to save.'

Sadness closed over Kirsty. She put her tea down. If they were supposed to save Morag, they were too late. He would want to meet her. She had to tell him.

'It's gotta be Agnes, right?' Nathan continued. 'She has to need our help somehow.'

'I hate to break it to you, but Agnes isn't exactly a damsel in distress.'

Nathan chuckled. 'Oh, I know. We were out dancing one night when a young man danced a little too close, and I thought we would have to take him to the hospital. I didn't even get a chance to defend her honour before she broke his nose.'

'Now that sounds more like the Agnes I know.'

'But you and I both time-travelled, and she's our link.'

'There's nothing wrong with Agnes. I saw her yesterday, remember? She was right as rain.'

'What's Morag like?' he asked suddenly.

Kirsty flinched. His eyes sparkled, and Kirsty tried to

reconcile this proud young dad with her seventy-something-year-old gran. At least, that was one question she could answer without feeling as though she was staring into an abyss of insanity.

'Morag's the best,' she said simply. 'She always looks on the bright side of whatever happens and she loves an adventure. She took me in when my mum and dad—' A hard lump formed in Kirsty's throat, and she needed to take a few deep breaths before she could talk again. 'They went away for their anniversary. A weekend in Skye where they had taken their honeymoon, and I stayed with Gran and Agnes. Gran and I were making fairy cakes when the police knocked on the door.'

Kirsty paused as the familiar rage seeped through her like acid. The pair of polis guys had been more starstruck at meeting Agnes than interested in the news they were there to break. Morag had to ask twice for more details before they bothered to remember why they were there.

'What happened?'

Kirsty shrugged. Her jaw ached with the effort of holding herself together. What was the matter with her? It was thirty years ago, for goodness sake. 'Car crash,' she said shortly.

'Oh, honey—'

'Morag is the worst cook in the world,' she blurted, cutting him off. 'Her speciality is burned frozen peas with raw potato waffle. Potato waffle is kind of like American *tater tots*. And I literally mean burned-yet-still-frozen peas.

'The only thing Agnes and I ever saw eye-to-eye on is how to get out of being poisoned by Morag. She made me blue fairy cakes for my birthday one year. Forgot the sugar and the baking powder, so they were like tasteless rocks, and to this day, no one knows how they ended up blue. My pal chipped a tooth on one of them, but you can never get mad at Morag. She's too lovely.

'I miss her,' Kirsty whispered, her eyes shining.

'When did she die?' Nathan asked quietly.

Those dark eyes of his missed nothing.

'It was less than a week ago for me. That's why I came back to Glasgow. I've been living abroad these past ten years, but something happened—'

'The elevator-stopping-too-fast-feeling?'

Kirsty stared at him. 'Yeah. Is that—what this is?'

He shrugged. 'All's know is I was on my way to pick up Agnes for our wedding. I took a shortcut over a bombed-out tenement at the end of her street—'

Kirsty knew the bit he was talking about. It was still a wasteground when she was a child. She and Harry and their pals used to play there, even though they were forbidden. They spent entire summers inventing great civilisations amongst the rubble and rusty shopping trolleys.

'I climbed over the fence at the far end,' Nathan continued. 'There's a kind of grate there. I guess the sewer runs beneath. I felt the elevator-stopping-too-fast feeling, and the next thing I knew, everyone was dressed crazy. And the cars—' He shook his head in wonder. 'I need to get me a ride in one of those cars. You think they could do a hundred miles an hour?'

'Some of them can go much faster than that, but you're only supposed to go seventy.'

'Have you ever ridden that fast?'

'Over a hundred? Once or twice, I think. I've not been in that many fancy cars.'

'I was a mechanic. I had an auto shop back home, and I was going to open one here after the wedding. Ain't nothing I don't know about cars that's worth knowing.'

'Hold on a minute—' Memories rushed over Kirsty. 'This happened to you at the grate at the far corner of that waste ground? And you were wearing your army uniform?'

Nathan nodded.

Kirsty laughed and shook her head. 'Nobody ever goes near that corner. We were all scared.'

'Scared?'

'Of you.'

He stared. 'Of me?'

'You're the Ghostie Solider.'

TWELVE

The following day, Kirsty and Nathan awoke early. They made tea and porridge and took turns having what Gran called a whore's wash at the kitchen sink. It was still boiling out, so Kirsty pulled jean shorts from her backpack and one of her favourite tie-dyed vest tops.

It had transpired that when Nathan realised he stood out like a sore thumb in ins 1940s US Army get-up, he nicked the neddy tracksuit off a washing line. Kirsty promised they'd go shopping for some summer clothes just as soon as they'd examined the Ghostie Soldier's Grate.

She had first heard the story from one of Harry's big brothers, who'd heard it from one of their older cousins. He lived in the sewer below the wasteground. Kirsty and Harry were solemnly warned not to venture too close to his grate lest the Ghostie Soldier grabbed their ankles and eat them.

Only true locals know about the Ghostie Soldier, but plenty of folks have heard of the Gorbals Vampire, also known as *Jenny wi' the Iron Teeth*. In the mid-fifties, a couple of kids claimed to have seen a seven-foot vampire with teeth of iron prowling around the Southern Necropolis. Stories spread that she had kidnapped and eaten two local children. One gloomy evening, an army of local kids headed out to patrol the cemetery after school. They were armed with sticks and stones, ready to fight her to the death to avenge their fallen comrades, until they were caught by a local copper and sent home to their beds.

Kirsty often wondered if this obsession with being eaten by local ghouls was typical or if Gorbals kids were especially concerned with becoming snacks. As she watched Nathan tuck into seconds, part of her was tempted to track her childhood pals down to let them know the Ghostie Soldier was more of a porridge man.

Somebody must have seen him disappear in the autumn of 1945. He said it happened around 11 a.m., so it would have been broad daylight. Neighbourhood kids heard about the man disappearing, added their own spin, and another local myth was born.

'Do you want to visit Agnes while we're nearby?'

Nathan was washing their breakfast dishes. He was surprisingly well housetrained for a man of his generation. She had to admit that she was more than a bit curious about how Agnes would react to her long-lost love rocking up after all these years. In his twenties.

'Not until I get me some threads and a haircut,' Nathan said firmly. 'Agnes likes me to look fresh.'

Later, as they hauled themselves over the crumbly old wall into the wasteground, it occurred to Kirsty that Glasgow had a lot of holes. Empty lots, boarded-up buildings, and wastegrounds slowly submerged by weeds and rubbish. Entire blocks that had burned to the ground once upon a time and left to rot. Many of them are in the centre of town, in what would be prime real estate in any other city.

The Gorbals wasteground was much as Kirsty remembered. Great piles of rubble looked like they'd been there since the Blitz. Sundry broken furniture, odd prams, and the ubiquitous shopping trolley. The lonely apple tree Kirsty recalled was still there.

Fuelled by dreams of hammocks and tents, she and the Finnegans had planted many an apple core a couple of metres from the single tree. None of theirs grew, but they never stopped trying. Kirsty and Harry must have been at least nineteen or twenty the last time they clambered over here, optimistically armed with cores.

Approximately a billion nettles did, however, flourish. Kirsty steered Nathan carefully around a particularly nasty patch. They balanced over a narrow wooden plank bridging two piles of rubbish and crested another to find a single can of Irn Bru perched on the top like a flag on Everest.

'I never knew such a mean country,' Nathan muttered, wiping his forehead. Even though it was still early, the sun was already blazing overhead.

'I beg your pardon?'

'Scotland,' he grinned. 'It's sharp and spiky, with brambles and nettles and holly. Every second plant will sting or bite you. We have poison ivy back home, but your national flower could make you bleed.'

'Aye, that's right enough,' Kirsty chuckled, feeling oddly proud.

There was something untamed about Scotland. She and Nathan were standing on a pile of demolished buildings, surrounded by pavements, roads, and motorway overpasses, yet greenery was everywhere. It poked through cracks, smothered concrete, and twisted over tarmac.

As they approached the corner where Nathan disappeared, they instinctively slowed down. Kirsty wasn't sure if it was her imagination, but she was almost sure she felt—something.

Wooden boards fortified the fence behind the grate, and rubbish was piled high around it, almost as though it barricaded the Ghostie Soldier inside. A bird squawked overhead, and Kirsty jumped.

Nathan stopped. Kirsty shot him a questioning look, and he gave a tiny nod. At first, it was too faint to fully discern over the city noise. Gradually the traffic and sirens faded, and the sound became clearer. It was a bell. A dull, clanking peal, almost like a hand-held school bell, but heavier.

There was a thrum in the air, a vibration Kirsty felt deep in her bones. It reminded her of being in a club, bass pounding through her until her blood juddered with the beat. Goosebumps prickled over her and the lift-stopping-too-fast feeling grew. It was oddly familiar: a palpable sense of *déjà vu* crept over her.

One day, not long after Kirsty came to live with Morag and Agnes, Morag took her out of school in the middle of the afternoon. It was a dull October afternoon, the kind where it felt as though the sky was right on top of your head. They had been doing art, glueing tin foil onto card for some reason that escaped Kirsty now. The lights were on, and rain pitter-pattered against the windows.

Kirsty had been contentedly picking glue off her fingers when the door flew open and Morag burst in. She announced that Kirsty was going home sick immediately. Kirsty's teacher, Mrs Rogers, who Kirsty loved because she had hair like Princess Diana and never shouted, blinked in terror at the sudden appearance of a notorious MacIver. She didn't say a word as Morag gathered up all Kirsty's things from her cubbyhole, took her by the hand, and propelled her out into the rain.

Kirsty learned later that the headmistress had called Morag in to discuss her concerns that Kirsty didn't seem to have cried enough about her parents' deaths. Morag informed her, in no uncertain terms, that Kirsty could grieve however she pleased.

Then she collected Kirsty from her classroom and took her for ice cream on Duke Street.

Kirsty had no idea why Morag chose ice cream on a chilly autumn day, nor why they went to Dennistoun for it. But she did remember sitting in the café, happily swinging her legs. She licked the cream from a waffle oyster and thought about her pals doing maths.

'Do you ever see Shadows, darlin'?' Morag asked her suddenly.

'What, when it's sunny? Aye, of course.'

'No, not those sorts of shadows.' Morag watched her for a long time, an expression in her eyes that made Kirsty feel a bit funny. 'I mean people that are there but not really?'

Kirsty felt cold. She put her oyster down, her appetite gone. Her fingers were sticky, but she couldn't bring herself to even lick them.

'Are they ghosties?' she asked finally.

'No.' Morag shook her head firmly. 'You don't need to be scared of them. They can't hurt you.'

Kirsty stared at the cracked Formica table for a very long time. 'Not really,' she lied. 'Maybe, sometimes. I suppose.'

'Do you see that lady now?'

Kirsty didn't want to look, but she did. Outside the café, traffic inched up Duke Street, red brick lights distorted in the drizzle streaking the window. It was late afternoon and nearly dark, so Kirsty could see the fire clearly.

It was a huge bonfire, burning ferociously, seemingly right in the middle of the road. The old lady was tied to a post in the fire, her hands trapped behind her back. She wore a raggedy dress that was already smoking, and her face was filthy. Her hair was pure white and was whipped up by a furious wind as huge flames licked at her. She was flinging herself back and forth, yelling and howling and cursing. Kirsty couldn't see her face, but she could feel her pain.

She knew it was sore being burned like that, sorer than anything Kirsty could even imagine. Even worse than when she remembered that she would never see her mummy and daddy again.

'She wants help,' Kirsty whispered.

'You can't help her,' Morag said fiercely. She reached over and took Kirsty's cold hand in her warm one. 'I know you want to help, pet, but it's already happened. There's nothing you can do. I want you to close your eyes tight and imagine a big explosion, like *kaboom*.'

Kirsty did as she was told. When she opened her eyes, the fire and the lady were gone. She took a shaky breath and was glad the lady was gone.

Morag squeezed her hand. She smiled, though her eyes were still sad. 'Just do that whenever you see a shadow,' she said softly. 'Promise me you'll never go closer to them. Promise me you'll never try to help them. Never ever, not even when you're a grown-up lady.'

Kirsty nodded solemnly. 'I promise.'

And she kept her promise. Every time she saw something out of the corner of her eye that wasn't supposed to be there, she would close her eyes and think kaboom, and it would be gone. Eventually, she forgot, leaving the Shadows behind, along with imaginary friends and monsters under her bed. Or at least, that was what she told herself.

But now, she could see a shadow.

He stood over the grate, looking at her and Nathan as though he could see them. He wore a rough tunic of a heavy, dark green fabric. It was knotted at the waist with a rope belt, and he was barefoot. His feet were swollen and misshapen, with two toes missing on one foot and three on the other. It looked painful, but when Kirsty met the man's eye, he gave her a proud, challenging grin as if to say that he managed *just fine, thank you very much*. His face was also deformed. A significant growth covered from ear to chin on one side, and part of his nose was missing.

Kirsty knew him. She'd seen him before. Goosebumps prickled over her as the memory came drifting back. She used to see him all the time. He would stand right where he was now, watching Kirsty and her friends playing.

The first time was one of those endless summer evenings when you're allowed back out to play after tea. She burst out the door, ready to pick up the game they had been playing all day, but there was no sign of the Finnegans. They hadn't been allowed out again.

Kirsty hated it when that happened. During the day, when they were all playing in the street together, they were one big messy gang. But when the Finnegans mum kept them in after tea, it was a stark reminder that they were actual brothers and sisters, and Kirsty was just her.

It was fine. She was used to it. It just meant that she was forced to cut about her wee none self.

When she saw the man, Kirsty was chucking clods of crumpled brick at the wall to watch them shatter into dust. Curious, she'd crept closer, half-scared and half-excited, as that dull ring reverberated in her ears. When she got close enough, he smiled. Then he waved. They ended up playing a game, a bit like *Simon Says*, copying one another's gestures back and forth.

After that, he often popped up on those summer evenings when the Finnegans stayed home. Kirsty never told anyone about him. She knew they would all think she was nuts, playing *Simon Says* with her imaginary friend.

The man grinned. He waved his free hand, just like he had that first night. Then he cocked his head from one side to the other, making a funny face. *Simon Says.* Kirsty copied him, and he smiled.

'There was a hospital over there on Adelphi Street,' she

said to Nathan. 'We learned about it at school. It was established by Lady Marjorie Stewart in the 1300s, to care for the city's lepers. They had to ring the bell when they crossed the stone bridge into the city centre to warn people to stay inside and away from them.'

The man maintained eye contact as he rang his bell, almost as if daring Kirsty to be repulsed, to look away. The ringing reverberated through her, and she winced. The lift-stopping-too-fast feeling washed over her, and she was drawn forwards.

'No!' Nathan shouted, yanking her back.

His voice had the *kaboom* effect. When Kirsty looked back at the grate, it was empty.

'Did you see him?' she asked urgently.

'Sorta. He wasn't exactly clear. It was more like—'

'A shadow,' she finished.

THIRTEEN

'Do you think she knew?' Nathan asked.

The sun was high in the sky and beating down ferociously. They were sitting on the wall in front of McDonald's Pollokshaws, and Kirsty had just introduced Nathan to his first Big Mac. He kept calling it a hamburger sandwich, but other than that, he seemed to be handling it well. Kirsty would have thought McDonald's had been around for longer, but she searched on their Wi-Fi, and it turned out they opened in the fifties. Who knew?

'Morag,' he added. 'Do you think she understood about all this?'

'I don't know,' Kirsty replied, wiping the salt from her fingers with a napkin. 'It could be that she saw Shadows as a wee girl and that was how Agnes explained it to her, so she passed that on to me.' The thought of Agnes as a mummy, comforting Morag when she woke up with bad dreams, wiping gravel from scraped knees and kissing bumps and bruises, seemed absurd to Kirsty. 'If she knew anything more, she didn't tell me.'

'Do you think she was scared?'

Worry furrowed Nathan's brow.

'I don't know,' Kirsty said. 'I was eight. Adults never seemed scared to me.'

'Did she ever ask about me? Wonder where I was?'

Kirsty hesitated. She had never heard Morag mention her erstwhile mysterious father in her life. When Agnes told the story of him melting back into the crowd with a cheery wink, Morag would laugh along with everyone else.

'Oh aye, we used to make up stories about you all the time,' Kirsty lied. 'Every time we watched an old film with an American, we'd pretend it was you. We decided you were Clark Gable or Gary Cooper a hundred times. We were stuck on Cary Grant for a long time.'

'The young fellow from *Bringing Up Baby*?' Nathan frowned. 'He comes from Wales.'

'Did he?' Dammit, Kirsty figured all those black-and-white movie stars were American. 'Like Anthony Hopkins.'

'Who?'

Right. Anthony Hopkins was in nursery school the last time Nathan went to the cinema.

'*What evil lurks in the hearts of men? The Shadow knows,*' Nathan murmured, and Kirsty wondered if he'd lost it. He caught her look and grinned. 'Mr Orson Welles? You never listen to stories on the radio?'

'Not often.'

'The Detective Story Hour is on every Sunday night. I never miss a single episode, not ever.'

Kirsty noticed that Nathan still talked in the present tense about his life as it was. She supposed it was a lot to process all at once. She probably still referred to Morag in the present tense.

'When I was a kid,' Nathan continued, 'I really wanted to

be a reporter, a regular scoop on the crime beat. I listened to detective stories every chance I got, so I could learn. The Detective Story Hour is about a mysterious guy called The Shadow, who solves mysteries. The real mystery is who he really is. At the end of every episode, that's what he says. *The Shadow knows...* And then he laughs.' Nathan chuckled and shook his head as he neatly folded his burger wrapper. 'It sure terrified me. I thought The Shadow knew every bad thing ever did.'

'Did you do many bad things?'

Nathan's smile faltered, and he shrugged. 'Just your regular putting slugs in brothers' beds and stuff.'

'Charming. You wanted to be a journalist?' Kirsty asked. 'Thought you said you were a mechanic?'

'There was a fellow who came on the radio this time.' Nathan ignored Kirsty's question. 'I was in the fifth grade, maybe ten years old. He said he was a time traveller and told us what it would be like in 200 years. He said that World War II would break out, and it did. And he said that we would be able to listen to the radio and devices much smaller than the ones we had then and that we'd be able to watch pictures in our own homes.'

'Those both happened,' said Kirsty. She held up her phone. 'I could listen to radio on this, and look—' She opened YouTube—thank you McDonald's Wi-Fi—and played a video, a clip for a Scottish sketch comedy show. Nathan's eyes widened.

'You can make the picture play just by touching it?'

'I do have that power,' grinned Kirsty. 'What else did the man on the radio say?'

'That vehicles would drive themselves, and we would simply ride in them.'

'That exists,' Kirsty nodded. 'More or less, at least. I met somebody with a fancy car that could change lanes and park itself. It's not common yet. Most of us still drive like normal people, but maybe it will be soon.'

'And he said we would meet a species from a distant galaxy and live together.'

'Ah, he was doing well till the aliens,' Kirsty laughed. 'Though if this guy was making predictions about the next 200 years not even a hundred years ago, then there's plenty of time. It's impressive he got four out of five already.'

'Do elevators talk to people?' Nathan asked, gesturing at the YouTube clip, which Kirsty had paused.

'Some of them,' she laughed. 'And yes, they are the enemy of Scottish accents. Not all progress is positive.'

Harry showed up that evening with several bags of Indian takeaway. The smell emanating from the white plastic bag made Kirsty's mouth water so much that she nearly tackled Harry to the ground when he hugged her hello. Despite hating him forever for going over to the dark side, Kirsty admitted that Harry was the most logical person she knew. Whenever they got into scrapes as kids, Harry would be the one to sit down and think up a solution. If anyone could help them make sense of their predicament, it was Harry.

Kirsty would have torn right into the foil packets, but Nathan set out the plates and cutlery he had washed earlier like a grown-up.

'You look tired.' Kirsty watched Harry open endless cartons. She stuffed half a popadom in her mouth with one hand and rooted in a drawer for a bottle opener with the other.

'Have you not got electricity in here?'

Nathan was lighting the stack of candles they'd found in

the pantry. As it was July, it would be light out for a good while yet, but the kitchen faced north. It was shadowy and chilly even on the hottest day.

'Nobody lives here,' Kirsty shrugged.

'You do.'

'No, I don't.'

'Better drink these fast, then.' Harry handed Kirsty ice-cold bottles of beer from the bag. She opened them, and Nathan blinked in horror as they clinked and gulped straight from the bottle.

'Work has been full on,' Harry said as they tucked in, companionably handing cartons back and forth around the big table.

'That's what you get for turning filth,' Kirsty grinned.

Harry gave her the finger, and she laughed, relief spreading through her that maybe she hadn't completely lost her pal after all. Now that the moment was here, Kirsty wasn't entirely sure how to bring up the subject of time travel. Turned out it wasn't the sort of topic that naturally comes up in conversation.

Harry hadn't reacted much to Nathan's presence, greeting him with the same easy *awright pal* he'd given all the random men that Kirsty had shown up with over the years. And he hadn't been concerned about Kirsty disappearing for over a year. He hadn't even known she was missing.

Nobody, in fact, had noticed Kirsty missing for a year and three months. She hadn't told anyone that she was coming to the funeral, so nobody had expected her. Nobody had missed her anywhere.

It wasn't as though Kirsty didn't have pals. She had hunners all over the world. She was rarely short of company when she wanted it. It was just that everybody, over the years, had learned to expect Kirsty when they saw her.

A handful of texts, messages, and emails came through when she finally got her phone on. They'd asked how she was, reported bits of gossip, and checked if there was any chance she could swing by a party in Rio in September. One or two commented that it had been a while since they'd heard from her, but nobody was worried.

Kirsty disappeared for a year and three months, and nobody noticed.

Which was fine.

It was how she had chosen to live her life. She was a free spirit, as Morag used to say. It was handy. It saved her the hassle of explaining to anyone what she didn't yet understand herself.

'I'm working on the murders,' Harry said around a mouthful of popadom. Something was hesitant about his voice, as though he had dreaded bringing the subject up. He watched Kirsty, waiting for her reaction. But she didn't have a reaction. She had no idea what he was talking about.

'What murders?'

Something flickered in Harry's eye, and Kirsty was sure she didn't want to know *what murders*. Harry glanced at Nathan, wondering how much he could say in front of him.

'Nathan's family,' Kirsty said quickly. 'He can hear whatever you have to say.'

Harry nodded. He stared at his chicken makhani for a few moments. 'We don't know for certain that Morag was one of the victims,' he said finally.

Cold, hard lead trickled through Kirsty. Her Gran was murdered. Her chest felt tight as horror spread through her. It was such a harsh, horrible word. *Murdered.*

There's been a murder, she thought, stupidly. She should have bloody known. As a family, they were no strangers to murder. Agnes may have retired in the last millennium, but her enemies had long memories. Morag deserved better than the life she got. *Fucking Agnes.*

'There's DNA evidence linking Morag to the other victims,' Harry said.'But the circumstances make it—'

'Morag was murdered?' Nathan snapped, his voice tight. He shoved his chair back, staring at Harry as though he wanted to punch him. 'Somebody hurt my Morag?'

'Here, pal, let's take it easy, eh?' Harry got slowly to his feet, his tone soothing.

'Nathan,' Kirsty said gently.

'Somebody *killed* her?'

'Let's hear what Harry has to say.'

'What's he talking about, *his* Morag?' Harry asked. 'What's going on, Kirsty? Why weren't you at her funeral?

'I was so sure you would show—I made them hold up the ceremony. All of us pallbearers stood outside in the pissing down rain like tubes waiting for you to show your face. What was so important that it kept you from Morag's funeral?'

'I did come.'

'No, you didnae—'

'Listen. The other morning, at the hospital—I told you I was going to a funeral. You drove me to St Theresa's.'

'Aye, that was a bloody year—'

'Harry, I said listen. I thought I was going to Morag's funeral. I thought it was on that day.'

'I don't—'

'You need to shut it and listen a minute. I need to tell you something weird.'

'Won't be the first time.' Harry tried to smile, but he glanced warily from Kirsty to Nathan.

'Are you okay?' Kirsty asked Nathan.

He nodded but stayed standing, a fierce current of emotions ravaging his face. Kirsty turned back to Harry.

'Don't interrupt with questions until I've said it all.'

'Gonnae just start talking, Kirsty?'

So she did. To his credit, Harry did indeed listen, quietly processing all in his trusting Harry way. Nathan interjected a couple of times, explaining his injury at the Battle of Normandy and how he was brought to the Royal.

'You were there, man?' Harry said in awe. 'I've seen *Saving Private Ryan*.'

'I didn't know a Private Ryan, Sir.'

Finally, it was all out. Harry sat silently for a moment. Then he turned to Nathan. 'Sorry, pal. I'd never have telt you that like that if I'd known you were her da.'

Nathan nodded. His jaw was tight, his eyes wretched. Kirsty's heart went out to him. It had to be a helluva thing to learn that you have a baby daughter and that she was murdered in her seventies in the space of seventy-two hours.

'You never knew she was murdered, Kirsty?'

Kirsty shook her head. 'I got a text telling me she'd passed away. I figured it was a heart attack or something. Let's face it, the closest she got to her five-a-day was the odd Jaffa Cake. I got on the first flight could. I arrived in Glasgow on the Tuesday night before her funeral.'

'But then—'

'But then I lost a year and three months.'

Harry sat back in his chair and exhaled. He rubbed his forehead as though he could massage sense into his brain. 'Kirsty, you've come up with some excuses in your time for not being where you are meant to be, but time travel—ten out of ten.' He chuckled suddenly. 'Mind when you learned to forge Morag and my Ma's signatures? You wrote notes into the school that our whole street had been quarantined for rabies.'

'I got detention for a whole term for that. Agnes thought it was hilarious.'

Harry shook his head. 'Funny how there's loads of stuff you were scared off as a kid that never turned out to be a thing? As a wee guy, I gave a lot of thought to the possibility of catching rabies. Never even met anybody that had it in my whole life.'

Kirsty smiled. This was Harry's way of giving them a breather, of letting Nathan have a moment to gather himself after the news of his daughter's murder. Harry was a kind man.

'Primary school also gave me the impression that catching on fire would be a bigger day-to-day concern,' she added.

'So it did,' Harry nodded. 'All those times practising Stop, Drop and Roll in the gym. Never once even needed tae Stop.'

Kirsty grinned as another memory came back to her. 'Remember we rolled your wee sister down the stairs in a bit of carpet your ma was throwing away? Why did we do that?'

Harry burst out laughing. 'To see if we could. I've still got a red bum from the smacking I got for that.'

'You must have been about fourteen.'

'As if that would stop my ma.'

'We rolled my youngest sister off the barn roof on a sled my brother fitted with wheels,' Nathan piped up with a ghost of a smile. 'Why do we do that to little sisters?'

'Ach, they always survive,' Kirsty grinned. 'Toughens them up.'

'So this, losing time thing,' Harry began, returning to the matter at hand. 'It happened sometime between you landing at Glasgow Airport that night and the morning I found you with that naked boy?'

'Did you ever find out who he is?' Kirsty asked. 'Or did the hospital?'

'He turned out not to be as badly injured as he first looked so they let him go.'

'He was lying on fire.'

Harry shrugged. 'I only know what they told us.'

Nathan cleared his throat. 'Tell me everything you know about Morag's murder.'

Harry glanced at Kirsty. 'I don't know if that's a good—'

'Please,' Nathan said with quiet firmness. 'I need—I wasn't there when she was alive. Let me know her death.'

Harry nodded and took a moment to gather his words. 'She was strangled.'

That was unusual. Despite what the movies suggest, gangland murders were generally quick and efficient. They didn't bother with protracted torture nearly as much as middle-class film directors imagine. Generally speaking, they got rid of who needed to be got rid of without any fancy business.

To be fair, Agnes did have a flair for the dramatic. She once hanged a group of her enemies upside down by their ankles from a bus stop on Cumberland Street. The poor buggers twisted in the wind for a full day, complaining it was raining up their noses. A handful of local folk got into the mediaeval spirit of things by flinging mushy peas at them. After two days, Agnes had them cut down with explicit instructions to let them land on their heads. As far as Kirsty knew, they all survived, but none of them pissed Agnes off again.

Strangling was a messy, drawn-out, largely ineffective process. Quite frankly, it was a terrible way to kill somebody. Only amateurs would attempt it. *Some halfwit newcomer who'd seen too many shoot-em-up films*, Kirsty thought with disgust.

'Morag had dinner with a pal in the city centre,' Harry said. 'They said goodbye at the bus station behind St Enochs Square and she was found the next morning in a lane near the Clutha pub. She had been strangled with her own tights,'

Kirsty took a shaky breath, hating the bastard that did it with every fibre of her being.

'The method, and the DNA evidence, are what links her to the other victims,' Harry continued. 'The other two were young women who met the killer in clubs. That's why there's a question mark over whether Morag is one of them, but—'

'Hold on,' Kirsty interrupted. 'Other victims?' Harry had said something about that but she hadn't registered. 'This isn't —business-related?'

Harry shook his head. 'I'm so sorry, Kirsty. We believe Morag was the victim of a serial killer.'

FOURTEEN

'We have to save her,' Nathan said.

The takeaway had long been demolished, but Kirsty wiped the last of the curry sauce out of a carton with a corner of naan bread.

'Nathan, she's already—'

'I know,' he cut in impatiently. 'But we're time travellers.' His eyes shone. 'This must be our mission. We solve Morag's murder—we prevent it from ever happening, and we'll be sent back to our own times.'

'Nathan, I don't know if—'

'This is what I'm supposed to do for her,' Nathan said firmly.

'If the police haven't solved it, how are we going to?' Kirsty glanced at Harry for support, but maddeningly, he was nodding.

'I'll take all the help we can get,' Harry said. 'You know that there is—information that the likes of Agnes have access to. Stuff civilians can do—corners you can cut that I can't. If you can do anything, knock yourselves out. It's been over a year, and we've got nothing.

'Victims were hoaching with DNA, but without a match, that's about as much use as an inflatable dartboard.' Harry's voice was tight with anger, a muscle in his jaw working overtime. 'Both the younger victims' friends were sure she left with a guy, but CCTV images show them both alone. This bastard is—something else. You find him and stop him murdering lassies who're just out for a good night, and I'll be right behind you.'

Kirsty smiled. Even if Harry wore a stupid luminous waistcoat and called folk Sarge, he was the same old Harry after all. He was still one of them.

'Just gies one wee shot at him, and I'll get right out your way,' he added, licking sauce off his fingers.

'Who were the other two victims?' Kirsty asked.

'The first was Katy Davidson, a nurse at Queen Elizabeth's. She'd been on a pal's hen do. They did a pub crawl through the city centre, then ended up at SWG3. Most of them were single, so by the time they got to the club, there were various boys optimistically tagging along. All her friends have given statements, but none of them is sure exactly when or where Katy picked up the man she left with.

'They describe him as above average height, fair or redhaired, and one or two mentioned his front teeth stuck out or were wonky in some way. They all agree he was quiet, never joining in any of the taxi banter, and he talked a bit posh. Some thought he was from Edinburgh, but others reckoned it was just a Glasgow University accent. They all described him as a bit buttoned up and disapproving, as though somebody had brought their aul' da along. No offence Nathan.'

'And they said she left with this boy?'

'Two of them were sure they saw him waiting for her at the door when she said goodbye to them.'

'Isn't SWG3 massive?' Kirsty said. 'How could they be certain?'

'They're not,' Harry said tightly, his eyes exhausted. 'Katy was found the following morning in the lane behind her tenement in Scotstoun by the binmen. She had been strangled with her own tights. This was about six months after Morag's death. It was when I was brought onto the case because I made the connection. My Sarge didn't want me to work Morag's death, but I had to.

'The next victim was found about three months later, in February of this year. Eileen Roberts. She was a bit older, in her thirties, and she stayed in Battlefield. Eileen's husband had got their kids' nursery teacher pregnant, so Eileen was out celebrating her divorce, and they ended up at the Shed.'

'Poor woman,' Kirsty muttered.

'Eileen's pals all remembered her winching this guy on the dancefloor. They'd given her a cheer for getting back on the horse.' Harry smiled sadly. 'The description matched the guy following Katy about. Six-foot, smartly dressed as though he'd come fae court. Ginger, wonky front teeth, posh voice. One of them said he sounded like a judge.'

'And Gran was also seen with this guy?' Kirsty asked.

Harry shook his head. 'That's the bit that doesn't fit. Someone of his description was drinking at Babbity's earlier that evening and possibly walking at the Trongate towards where Morag was last seen, but not actually talking to her.'

'A lanky ginger with bad teeth, but,' Kirsty couldn't help pointing out, 'not exactly a precious rarity.'

'Tell me about it,' Harry replied dryly. 'We've had to put out statements exonerating every second guy in the city who was getting hassled.'

Harry rubbed his face and yawned deeply. 'I need to get to my bed. I'm on in about five hours.'

Kirsty should get up to see him out, but she couldn't quite move. In her defence, the door was only about a metre away from the table. He wasn't much of a detective if he couldn't find it.

Harry paused by the door. 'Listen. This is the deal. I'll tell you what I know, but if you find anything I need to know, then you tell me, okay? I mean it, Kirsty.'

'Shitebag if dinnae?' she grumbled. The thought of sharing information with the police gave Kirsty the boak. She nodded reluctantly, and Harry left.

She got up and cleared dishes to avoid Nathan's eye. He stood by the window, staring out at the darkness. Kirsty gulped the last of her lukewarm beer and shook out a new bin bag liner.

'I'll be a good dad to her when I get back.'

Kirsty shoved takeaway cartons into the bin bag.

'It must be that I need to do this first,' Nathan said. 'To prove that I can protect her like a father should.'

'I'm going for a run,' Kirsty announced abruptly, abandoning the bin bag by the door. 'I won't be long.'

FIFTEEN

The night air was cool on Kirsty's flushed face as she made her way down the driveway and broke into a jog. She had to get out. She couldn't face Nathan's hopeful eyes.

She would find out what happened, for Morag's sake. Kirsty wouldn't have Morag's murderer walking the streets if she could help it. But she knew it wouldn't save Morag. Morag was already dead before Kirsty ever felt the lift-stopping-too-fast feeling. Even if they solved her murder and got sent back to their own times, it would be too late for Morag.

The streets were quiet as Kirsty pounded along the pavement, feeling energy surge and settle as she got into a rhythm. She heard a stramash in the distance and the inevitable sirens wailing towards it. A yappy dog expressed its displeasure at a squirrel. Clinking glasses and classical music piped through expensive speakers wafted over her as she passed the big house on the corner.

She didn't plan it, yet it was inevitable that she wound her way towards the river and the shipyards. She ran down a steep hill, over the railway bridge, under the motorway, and zigzagged through a maze of warehouses. A crowd of teenagers had a carry-on outside a centuries-old pub decked in Union Jacks, and a wee drunk couple in cowboy gear line-danced their way to the bus stop.

What Nathan said about them having a mission kept rattling around in her head. It couldn't be saving Morag. But what if there was another mission?

What if they succeeded and got zapped back? Kirsty in time to make it for Morag's funeral. And Nathan to 1946 to sweep Agnes into his arms and—*What would happen if he did?*

Would Agnes take over her father's business dealings if she married Nathan as planned? Agnes's father, who founded The MacIver Boys after breaking away from the Norman Conks in the early twenties, had died in the autumn of 1945. Ironically, for one of the city's leading hard men, of a heart attack.

Agnes would have been pregnant then. She could have let operations die a death alongside their original godfather and allowed henchmen to scatter into other gangs and lives of disorganised crime. She could have consigned The McIver Boys to the history of the no mean city along with the Penny Mobs, the Billy Boys and the Govan Team.

But in those days, girls in trouble were either marched into marriage or sent away to convents to have babies under clouds of shame and fear. Agnes would never have put up with that. She certainly had her faults, but Kirsty had to admit that Agnes did nothing under a cloud of shame and fear. Kirsty could picture her, evil and defiant as ever, but also young and frightened, determined that nobody would tell her how to live her life.

A strange and uncomfortable feeling slithered through Kirsty. Just a sliver of sympathy, but that was enough. It couldn't have been easy for Agnes, left alone with a broken heart and a baby, when Nathan disappeared. Kirsty had been ghosted many times, but at least her tragic love life was launched long after contraception became dependable.

Not that she was letting Agnes off the hook altogether. Even in those days, most single mums made it through life without kneecapping a soul. But somehow, the appearance of Nathan had slid Agnes into a new and unfamiliar context. One in which she seemed almost human.

Kirsty slowed to a walk as she hit Govan Road. The moon was bright and full, glistening on the water that glides through the heart of the city. She stopped, watching the moonlight dance in the inky black river. The darkness was deep, almost as though it had taken form and wrapped itself physically around her.

There were street lights nearby, and if Kirsty looked directly, she could see them, yet somehow their light didn't reach her. She frowned. Something was off, something that danced just out of reach. The river. The river didn't usually come right up to the road. Had there been a flood?

Nathan was a mechanic. If Kirsty's mum had known her granda, would she have driven on treacherous Highland roads in the clapped-out heap of junk that resulted in Kirsty being orphaned? The thought slammed into Kirsty with breath-taking force.

Her knees went wobbly, and she held onto the railing for support. Nathan would have given the car a once-over before her parents left. He would have checked the brakes, fixed them or maybe lent his granddaughter his car. He might have been sitting by the fire with a pipe and a newspaper as Kirsty and Morag made fairy cakes when her mummy and daddy got home from their weekend away.

There was a nip in the air, which was a relief after days of oppressive heat. A breeze ruffled Kirsty's hair, and she shivered. *She was supposed to be here right now.*

She looked up. The black sky was now a mass of twinkling

stars, brighter than she had ever seen. They weren't your standard silvery-white but every colour of the rainbow, sparkling and dancing across the blackness. Kirsty stared in awe, her whole body tingling at the sight. It was as though the sky itself was alive, celestial winds and galaxies sweeping and swirling, promising infinity. Promising magic.

A vibration settled over Kirsty, thrumming in her bones. It was old and organic, natural at a profound level, almost as though it were an element so fundamental that humanity was afraid to remember it. It connected to oceans forming and Teutonic plates shifting and mountains emerging. It was more potent than Kirsty could grasp, and for a moment, she was overwhelmed. She wanted to step back, to shake her head and break the spell, but somehow she knew she couldn't. She closed her eyes and let the feeling fill her.

Voices drifted through the darkness. A deep rhythmic chanting rumbled back and forth as though riding a wave. Wood creaked, and heavy fabric flapped in a wind she could not feel.

Kirsty opened her eyes, and the Clyde was packed with ships. Hundreds and hundreds of them, stretching back until the river bent out of sight to the west. Wooden ships. Some with a single sail, some without. All with proud, high boat bows carved and painted with intricate dragons and serpents.

Each boat was filled with people. Dark cloaks over leather tunics. Scars and pleated hair and crudely drawn tattoos.

A man stood at the head of the largest ship as it approached the Govan Parish Church, more than a hundred metres from the twenty-first-century bank of the river. His ship was a little in front of the others, and Kirsty could see its gilded side shimmering in the soft moonlight. The man's cloak fluttered behind him in the wind, and dark hair tumbled to his shoulders.

Kirsty had kicked him in the balls. Her breath caught in

her throat as recognition slammed her like a train. It was him. Axey Man. The head of the Wednesday Morning Murder Club.

He was leading an army to invade Govan. Kirsty had felt his nose shatter beneath her forehead.

You can't help them, pet. Morag's voice echoed through her mind. *Promise me you'll never try to help them. Close your eyes and think kaboom.*

Kirsty reached for the fence, clambered through the hole and stepped onto the weed-covered cobblestones of the old shipyards. The shadows were deep but the moon was bright. After a few moments, her eyes adjusted to the darkness, and she saw him.

Sixteen

The deep darkness faded into a twenty-first-century, streetlight-orange glow. Kirsty could hear traffic again. Her heart thudded as she approached slowly, not wanting to startle him. He sat on a large stone slab next to one of the ship nurseries, knees pulled up to his chest as he stared at the inky water.

He was no longer naked. In fact, judging by the tightness and the neddiness of his tracksuit, he might well have robbed it from the same washing line Nathan did. Some poor bugger put out a wee washing only to lose all his tracksuits to historical characters.

Kirsty cleared her throat and took a small step closer. He looked up, watching her warily. The scent of smoke, sage, and peat hit her, and she felt a tiny spark.

A *spark*-spark.

A spark she hadn't felt in a good wee while without the aid of some heavy-duty battery-operated device. *Jeez-o Kirsty.* There was a time and a place for all that carry-on, and this wasn't it. Several key bits of her, however, pointedly disagreed.

'Are you a Viking?'

Her voice seemed to echo in the moonlight as he stared at her with mesmerising, deep blue eyes. His hair fell in ruddy waves to his shoulders, the maze of plaits pulled back from his face by a rough strip of leather. There was a jagged, white scar at his collar bone, which looked worryingly as though somebody had tried to decapitate him once upon a time. Between that and the small matter of him almost becoming a human barbecue when they first met, Kirsty couldn't help thinking that this boy was a menace himself.

Belatedly, she remembered that the chances of him understanding modern English were about zero. Sure enough, he fixed her with an intense stare, watching her lips, almost as though he were trying to read a translation on them.

'*Viking*,' he repeated slowly. It sounded more like *vee-king-uur*. His voice was soft and deep and sent dizzying tingles cascading through her. *Christ, he would make a fortune doing a podcast.*

Once upon a time, Kirsty spent a summer teaching paddleboard yoga in Stockholm. She picked up a smattering of the lingo from a series of soft-spoken lanky blonds she tossed out her hostel room the minute they'd got their breath back. She suspected modern Swedish would be about as comprehensible to him as Chaucer was to her, but it was worth a try.

'*Mitt namn är Kirsty*,' she said in an accent that would make ABBA faint with horror.

He smiled, revealing surprisingly straight, white teeth. Kirsty had a vague recollection of reading something about that. He may have lived long before toothpaste, but very little in his diet would have rotted teeth the way modern food does. *This poor man wouldn't know a Tunnock's teacake if it bit him on the bum.*

'*Namn*. Kirsty,' she repeated, tapping her chest for good measure.

He nodded. 'Frej,' he said, his hand on his distractingly powerful chest.

Kirsty couldn't help but feel sorry for the tracksuit. It wasn't built to contain muscles like that.

'There's a band called The Fray. They had one quite good song. They're no ABBA, though.'

She was rabbiting like a budgie that hadn't seen a human in a decade. It was good to know her usual level of sexy seductiveness was firmly in place. Frej chuckled, his rumbling laughter hitting her right in the fanny.

Then, because she was a menace to herself, Kirsty burst into tears. And not cute girly tears. Not romantically tragic, *heroine-in-a-Victorian-novel-who-dies-of-a-cough* weeping. Huge, gulping, burping, gasping sobs.

It was as though a tidal wave of grief, weirdness and general *world-being-knocked-off-its-axis-ness* crashed all over Kirsty at once. She was a blotchy, snotty mess when Frej gathered her in his arms. Kirsty didn't have a complex, but the word *strapping* had been used to describe her more than once. She usually cringed when a guy lifted her, steeling herself for the inevitable grunt when he realised he'd bitten off more than he could chew. Frej sat with his back against the iron ring slab, holding her against his chest as though she were an injured bird.

This was usually Kirsty's cue to make a daft comment, to pack her feelings back in and laugh that she was fine, she was joking, but she didn't. She couldn't. She felt the warmth of his chest, the steady rhythm of his heart, and she felt safe.

She cried and cried until she was empty. It wasn't until the storm was over and she was racked by those horrible empty sobs that were like sore hiccups that she noticed he wasn't smothering her. She was on his lap, but one huge hand stroked her hair and the other bridged over her to rest on his knee. She could get to her feet, and he wouldn't have to move.

'Shhh,' he murmured into her hair, and as if by magic, she did.

SEVENTEEN

I t was dawn when she awoke. The sun glowed on the
horizon, silhouetting the Armadillo and the Finnieston
crane across the water, streaking the sky with deep pinks
and oranges. There was a morning chill in the air, but Frej
seemed to have unlimited body heat, and Kirsty was toasty-
warm, curled in his arms.

He snored softly over her head. His arm had fallen over her
lap sometime in the night, but it was okay. She could shove it
out the way if she wanted to, but she was too comfortable.

She blinked, slowly coming to, feeling rested and—solid.

Moving carefully to avoid disturbing Frej, Kirsty got to her
feet and looked around. The shipyard lay empty and abandoned, cracked cobblestones strewn with weeds and decades of
rubbish. Kirsty stared into nothing, willing the past to spring
to life before her eyes. She had seen Shadows all her life, but
she had never looked for them before.

Did she need to be in a particular spot? The Bell Man
from the Gorbals appeared over the same grate where Nathan
disappeared. That suggested there are holes or windows in
specific places.

Kirsty wandered around a little, trying to retrace her steps from the other morning. She tripped on a dark green, gnarly weed that looked vaguely familiar—had she been standing there when she saw the Vikings? She took a few more steps back and forth, and then she felt it. The vibration. The lift-stopping-too-fast feeling. The tips of her fingers tingled, and her bones shivered. A gigantic skeletal hulk of a ship took form in front of her.

It must have been five or six storeys high, the sheer vastness humbling. Hundreds of men swarmed over her like ants. A sharp smell of tar mingled with sweat and tobacco and the tang of burning metal. She heard thuds, clangs, and shouts as the shipyard came back to life before her eyes. *When?* While the industry was in decline from the Second World War, Kirsty knew ships were built here until the late 1990s, but she wasn't looking at the 20th century. She could hear no whines of welders' torches, no screeches of machinery or rumbles of heavy-duty vehicles. An ornate sign on wrought iron gates read *Victoria Regina et Imperatrix.*

Queen Victoria was on the throne. She died in 1901, which narrowed this period to the mid-late 1800s. Thrill fluttered over Kirsty. She was looking at people who might be reading Dickens' serial stories as they were released.

An enormous woman marched determinedly across the yard towards a scuffle. Yells and shouts filled the air as some wee guy got a doing with the crowd's encouragement. The woman was well over six foot, with a stunningly hacket face and a glorious bust that could brain a man at ten paces. Her ankle-length dress was a dark blue, made of rough fabric. Her shawl was a grubby grey, tucked into a wide, surprisingly masculine-looking leather belt.

The men, flat caps and shapeless trousers held up by rough leather braces, stood about, smoking and cheering the fighters on. The woman strode into the thick of them, grabbed the bigger guy by the scruff of the neck and, without hesitation, flung him headfirst into the nearby river. He gave a wee yelp which was followed by a hefty splash. The woman carried on her way, followed by a chorus of boos and calls of *spoilsport*.

The shouts rang in Kirsty's ears as she blinked and saw that Frej was awake. The yard was abandoned again. An ambulance wailed along the Expressway, and the wind scuttled an empty Irn-Bru can around the cobblestones. Frej smiled, then pointed to his cheeks with a questioning look as though to ask if Kirsty was happy enough to smile now.

She gave him a shaky grin and nodded. Then, for some reason, she gave him a *thumbs up* for good measure, which completely baffled him. He copied the gesture, leaning forward to softly touch the pad of his thumb to Kirsty's.

'Breakfast,' she blurted, trying to ignore the shivers that ran through her at his touch.

She mimed eating, and he nodded eagerly. He obediently followed her through the gap in the fence, and they made their way towards Paisley Road West and breakfast rolls.

Eighteen

'I thought the killer got you,' Nathan yelled. 'I didn't know you're the kind of hussy who stayed out all night.'

'Well, I am,' Kirsty snapped.

'Where have you been?'

'None of your business.'

'I thought the killer got you!'

Kirsty flinched. She brushed past Nathan into the kitchen and started busying herself with making tea to avoid Nathan's accusing stare. Frej stood in the doorway, considering the kitchen with an uncertain expression.

'Why would you think that?'

'Because we were told a serial killer was on the loose, and then you disappeared all night.'

'I told you I was going for a run,' she muttered.

'Seven hours ago.'

'I like to run.'

'Kirsty—'

'Fine. I could have phoned, I suppose.'

Nathan's eyebrows furrowed quizzically. 'Called me on the

telephone?' he repeated in surprise. 'How would I have known to go wait at a box?'

Kirsty tried not to snigger at the image of Nathan waiting patiently all night outside an old red phone box that had been turned into a flower stall or a coffee stand.

'Look, I am sorry,' she said. 'I'm not exactly used to telling people what I'm doing. It's a long time since I've lived with a great-grandparent.'

Nathan acknowledged her apology with a nod, then turned to Frej, still blocking the sun in the doorway. 'Who is your young man?'

'Not *my* young man,' Kirsty said a bit too quickly. 'I just —found him.'

'Pleased to meet you, Sir, 'Nathan said. 'Nathan Williams, at your service.' He approached Frej with an outstretched hand. Frej stared at it with mild alarm.

'He doesn't speak English.'

'He doesn't? What gives? Where did you find him?'

'The Dark Ages, I reckon. Or thereabouts.'

'There's more of us?'

Kirsty nodded. 'There's more of us.'

She brought three mugs of tea to the table. Frej accepted the one she handed to him and sniffed it dubiously. He watched as she took a healthy gulp of hers.

'*Skål*,' she said, hoping that how Scandinavian say cheers hadn't changed much in a millennium. He smiled in recognition and raised his mug to hers.

'His name is Frej. He's the guy I saved from the fire. I'm pretty sure he is a Viking.' If she said it fast enough, it almost sounded normal.

Nathan watched Frej gingerly sipping tea as he took this in. 'They were burning him, you say? Like some kind of ritual?'

Kirsty thought about the long bed of coals that Frej had

been lying on, the way the Vikings stood solemnly around, waiting for Axey Man to finish the job. 'I suppose so.'

'Like maybe a magic ritual that made this happen?'

'Vikings aren't magic,' Kirsty said. 'They're just —historical.'

Over breakfast, Kirsty had tried to remember everything she knew about Vikings. She remembered from school that they invaded the west coast of Scotland in the 800s, plundered Iona, and ruled Dumbarton for a long while. There were Runes in the Govan parish church. She had gone to see them on a school trip and had been fascinated with the huge hog-shaped stones carved with intricate, mysterious-looking symbols. Harry forgot his packed lunch. Kirsty had given him half her sandwich and then was mad because she was hungry.

'They were pagan,' Nathan muttered, looking warily at Frej.

Frej slipped his tea, seemingly entirely unbothered as to exactly how many gods it's okay to believe in.

'I've read about them too,' Nathan continued. 'They did rituals. Human sacrifices.'

The realisation hit Kirsty and turned her stomach. She put her tea down. 'That was—I think that was what they were doing to him. They were burning him, and they were going to slit his throat. He was being sacrificed. I'm sure I've read it's a myth that it was common, but it did happen, especially in wartime.'

'You think he volunteered?' Nathan asked doubtfully.

'He seemed pretty happy when I appeared screeching like a seagull.'

'I'm glad you saved him.'

'Even if saving him is what brought us all through time? I've wondered if I—I don't know, broke some kind of seal. I've seen Shadows all my life, but I've never gone into one, never touched one. Morag warned me not to.'

Nathan was quiet for a moment, emotion churning in his dark eyes. 'What's done is done,' he said finally. He picked up a spiral-bound notebook from the kitchen table and leafed through the pages. Frej stared in awed fascination as Nathan clicked open a pen. 'I never tried to catch a murderer before, but I read a lot of stories about detectives.'

Kirsty leaned over his shoulder. Nathan had jotted down all the information Harry had given them last night in his neat, old-person script. 'A particular book I read once was written by a detective who studied many famous cases like Jack the Ripper and HH Holmes. This fellow believed that killers work their way up, so to speak. They often start by hurting animals, then family members, maybe children.' He took a shaky breath. 'Harry said that the main reason they weren't sure they were searching for just one killer was the fact that Morag was older than the other two victims—'

'You think she might have been like—practice?'

Nathan nodded, his eyes flashing with loathing. 'The fact that the killer used their own stockings—it feels too specific to me to be a coincidence. Plus, while she wasn't out dancing like the younger women, she was out with a friend in the city centre.'

'Okay, so we start on the basis that all three were murdered by the same man.'

'A man who is hunting in clubs and bars,' Nathan said.

'Then it looks like we're going clubbing.'

NINETEEN

Kirsty took the boys shopping. However bizarre her life got, she would not show her face and Sauchiehall Street on a Saturday night accompanied by two men in tracksuits.

Nathan chose khaki trousers and a button-down shirt that made him look like a nerdy scientist in an American film. Kirsty tried to persuade him to go for jeans at least, but he insisted that "blue jeans" were for working on farms.

Frej went for skinny black jeans and a plain white T-shirt, thus proving beyond a shadow of a doubt that he was Scandinavian and that understated style was in their DNA. He hadn't been keen on shoes, but given that most of the places they were going that night would have STDs ground into the carpet, barefoot was not an option.

Kirsty eventually talked him into some flip-flops. She hoped any bouncers they encountered would be so dazzled by him that they'd turn a blind eye to the footwear situation.

Kirsty and Frej seem to communicate impressively well through gestures and charades. Whenever she clicked what he was trying to convey, she would cheer, and his deep blue eyes crinkled with laughter. She hadn't succeeded in breaking his fondness for the *thumbs up*, which even he wasn't quite dreamy enough to pull off. Whenever Kirsty tried to dissuade him, he would chuckle and do it again.

Viking banter, eh?

They had found some retro Brylcreem in a hipster barber-shop in Finnieston. Nathan tamed his curls into submission, then came across a trilby hat stuffed at the back of the hall cupboard. Kirsty informed him several times that it made him look like a fanny, but he was insistent. Between Nathan cutting about like a Men's Rights Activist and Frej giving a cheesy *thumbs up* every two seconds, if Kirsty had ever had any street cred, tonight would shred it.

Luckily, she'd never had any anyway.

It was early for dancing, so she led them to the Griffin, which seemed as good a place to start as any. The horseshoe-shaped bar was utterly rammed. Screeches of laughter and shouty chat filled the air. A couple of guys were shoving each other for no apparent reason while a band tuned guitars in the corner.

Frej looked around the raucous crowd with an easy grin as though feeling at home for the first time. Nerves prickled over Kirsty as she scanned the crowd. She was both dying and terri-fied to spot the lanky ginger from Harry's description.

Heading into his hunting ground to talk to women seemed like the obvious course of action a few hours ago, but now that they were here, Kirsty felt daft. What exactly was she playing, thinking she could catch a murderer? She could barely catch a beach ball.

'What about those ladies there?'

Nathan nodded towards a group of women crowded around one of the standing tables. They were dolled up to the nines with ironed-straight hair, eyelashes half a mile long and boobs spilling out their tops in that celebratory way Kirsty was in awe of.

One of them was in full flow, telling a funny story. Her friends laughed in between tasting one another's cocktails. Kirsty shrugged, not quite sure how one went about approaching groups of strangers in the wild. She had fallen into conversation with random lassies a billion times, but she had never... targeted them before.

Just as she thought maybe they should give up and go home, one of the lassies burst out laughing, and Kirsty saw it was Nathan. The wee chancer had just wired right in there. He was charming the pants off them, even in his stupid hat.

Kirsty caught Frej's eye, and he chuckled. She had no idea how much he had gathered of their plans for the evening, but he seemed to have gotten the measure of Nathan. He watched happily as a group at the bar necked a round of Flaming Sambucas with a loud cheer.

Nathan's instant harem all burst out laughing, and Kirsty couldn't help trying to picture him making Agnes giggle like that. She shuddered, instantly regretting the mental picture the moment it formed.

'You lookin' at ma burd?'

A voice broke through the babble, and Kirsty's heart sank. She knew exactly what kind of roaster it was before she turned around. Sure enough, his jeans were tight enough that she could count his bawhairs. He wore a designer shirt with the top button done up, and with light brown hair and fake tan, he was all one colour. Not only was he a head and shoulders shorter than Frej, but his steroid-inflated muscles looked like a kid's He-Man costume next to Frej's sinewy bulk.

This was going to end an absolute disaster.

'No, he's no',' Kirsty said in what she hoped was a conciliatory tone. 'He's with me. He's no' looking any other burds.'

Unfortunately, other men were now watching, so there was no backing down for He-Man. Frej grinned as he looked the wee orange guy up and down. His eyes sparkled, and he said something in his language.

'Fuck's he saying?' demanded He-Man. 'Tell him to talk right.'

According to Kirsty's research that morning, the Scots language and the Weegie dialect were heavily influenced by Old Norse. Strictly speaking, they were speaking a bastardised version of Frej's language, but now didn't seem an opportune time to point that out.

'He's just on holiday,' she murmured, in the kind of soothing tone she would use for a spooked horse. 'He's no' wanting any trouble. Listen, we'll just get out your way—'

He-Man leaned back. In a split-second, Kirsty registered that he was going on for a *Glasgow Kiss*, which was actually impressively ambitious given his height. He-Man lunged forward to head-butt Frej. Frej casually raised a forearm, just about braining He-Man on a rock-hard tricep.

He-Man grunted, his right eye already turning purple as he registered how effortlessly Frej had stopped him. Fear flickered behind his aqua contact lenses before toxic masculinity took over. He gritted his teeth and swung wildly. Kirsty bundled Frej right out the door before things turned regrettable.

They emerged onto Bath Street. Frej was laughing his big booming laugh, clearly keen on heading back in to flatten He-Man. *Christ almighty, did men not grow up in a thousand years?* There was a queue of wee mammies across the road, waiting outside the Kings Theatre to see some reality star sing hits of Broadway or something. They gave Kirsty and Frej a chorus of whoops as Kirsty skelped her giant Viking sex god and yelled at Nathan to shake a leg. It was dawning on Kirsty that Frej was a red rag to a bam. And that it would be a very long night.

'They know him,' Nathan announced breathlessly as he joined them on the pavement. They headed up the hill towards town.

'Know him?' Kirsty repeated. 'Like, know who he is?'

'No, but they've met him. They met him in church, they said.' Disapproval dripped in Nathan's voice. 'I never heard of courting in church, but—'

'What church?' Kirsty asked.

'St Lukes.'

Kirsty chuckled. 'Saint Lukes and the Winged Ox. That's a pub. It was an actual church once upon a time.'

Nathan blinked. 'They turned a house of worship into a drinking establishment?'

'I happen to think that people gathering socially inside a church is more true to its original intention than sitting empty gathering dust,' Kirsty shrugged.

Nathan didn't look convinced. 'Well, anyway, the tall one with the long hair said she met our guy about a month ago. She said she had a gut feeling that he was a creep right away, but she had just—something about the ghost and tinder? Maybe her sweetheart had died in a fire?'

'She had been ghosted by somebody off Tindr,' Kirsty translated into twenty-first century.

'Maybe that was it. She was feeling vulnerable. The guy told her that he never talked to strange women, but he would never forgive himself if he didn't introduce himself to the most beautiful woman he had ever seen. She was going to let him walk home, but her friends said she had drunk too much, so they intervened.'

'Probably saving her life,' Kirsty said grimly. 'I suppose he didn't tell her anything that could help identify him. His job or where he lived or anything?'

Nathan shook his head. 'She said he was very prim and

proper. They called him Prince Charming, like in the Cinderella story. But we already knew that.'

'Still, though, it's not a bad start.'

TWENTY

By 3 a.m., they had made good headway through the social establishments of the city centre. Nathan had met three more groups of women with stories of the lanky ginger. Kirsty overheard a conversation about him in the loo at Firewater. Frustratingly, they hadn't discovered any new information—other than the sobering fact that he had been busy.

Something bitter curdled in Kirsty's stomach as she realised that the murders the police knew about were likely to be the tip of the iceberg. His hit rate couldn't be that low. Some of his prospective victims may have escaped with their lives, but his trail of destruction ran deep. No woman in the city was safe until he was stopped.

'That's the whole 'hing about him,' a lassie with huge eyes that made her look like a doe slurred to Kirsty on the stairs at Broadcast a few minutes earlier. 'He never talks about hisself. Know the way most guys, you go on a date an' you can barely get a word in edgeways while he jist does a Ted talk at you about how brilliant he is? This guy asks you loads an' loads of questions as if you're dead important or famous or something.'

She shook her head in wonder. 'I was pure raging at my pals for no' letting me go with him. See how he looks right your eyes —and he touched my arm like this—' She demonstrated, trailing her fingers lightly down Kirsty's forearm. Kirsty had to admit it was a good move. 'No' that many guys are worth the effort of waxing yer fanny like a snooker ball these days, but he would be. He'd have a whole routine. It's a pure shame if he's a bad yin.'

Kirsty Bluetoothed her a link to a really good vibrator and made her promise to always check with her pals before going home with anybody.

Kirsty threaded through the crowd on Sauchiehall Street, ducking under armpits and winding around fights and winches. Some chancer put his hands on the small of her back to move her out his way. She stamped on his toes. Nothing changes.

Nathan and Frej were waiting for her. Frej, she was amused to learn, was an adorkably giggly drunk. He had given several women and a handful of men piggyback rides at various points in the night. It was dawning on Kirsty that it may have been irresponsible to give him his first taste of cane sugar in the form of alcopops.

'Where to next, boss?' asked Nathan.

Kirsty shook her head. 'There's nowhere that will be letting folk in at this time. We need to call it a night.'

'But we didn't find him.'

'We found some stuff worth passing on to Harry,' Kirsty said. 'That's not bad going for our first try.'

Nathan nodded, trying and failing to cover his dejection. 'I guess.'

The thought that the lanky ginger could be whispering in the ear of some unsuspecting lassie right this very minute gnawed at Kirsty. She felt as hopeless as Nathan looked. It was all very well and good setting out to catch a killer, but it probably would have been helpful to have gone to detective school first. Or at least done an online course.

'We were never going to catch him in one night,' she added, trying to convince herself as much as Nathan.

The street filled with general mayhem as the pubs and clubs shut and revellers swarmed into the night. Kirsty, Nathan and Frej swerved past a guy flinging a woman around by the waist. Kirsty was just about to send Frej to set him straight when she realised the woman was laughing her head off. A bald guy with chunky gold earrings and no teeth proclaimed Frej a *total smasher* and instructed him to *have a good one* before carrying on his way.

The crowd spilling out a chip shop caterwauled something vaguely resembling a nineties rock anthem. Kirsty bought them all chips, and Frej accepted the existence of potatoes and grease with aplomb. They sat on a bench in front of the Royal Concert Hall and wired in. Despite the salty sustenance, exhaustion seeped into Kirsty's bones. She wondered about the chances of Frej carrying her on his shoulders back to Pollokshields.

A passing crowd of women wolf-whistled Frej and demanded he show them his pecs. He gave them a *thumbs up*, which resulted in spilling his chips, and one of the lassies shouted at her pals to leave the poor boy alone. Nathan attempted to instruct Frej on being cool in the face of female attention, but icy shivers scuttled over Kirsty.

Because she could see them.

Frej's gang. Frej's warband. The Wednesday Morning Human Sacrifice Club. The dark-haired psycho and his merry band of men in cloaks were marching up Sauchiehall Street. Or marching through the forest of willow trees that once stood there.

They were nowhere near Govan. Kirsty's history wasn't good enough to guess what they might be doing this far from the river, but there was no mistaking them. They strolled across the pedestrian paving, presumably busy hunting an unfortunate Celtic monk or woolly mammoth or something.

But just as Kirsty noticed that she wasn't feeling any vibration or lift-stopping-too-fast feeling, Frej stiffened beside her. Then he was on his feet, and Kirsty wasn't seeing Shadows. The Vikings were there.

They were *now*.

And so was the axe that glinted in the street lights.

Axey Man was focused on Frej, who squared up to him with a satisfied chuckle. Nathan leapt off the bench and nimbly kicked the axe out of Axey Man's hand.

'Fuck's this?' demanded one of the wolf-whistling women. The axe had scuttled to stop by her glittery platform shoes, and she held it aloft like a triumphant warrior.

One of the Vikings lunged for it, but she blocked him with the handle and aimed a sharp kick with her heels at his hip bone. Kirsty swung her handbag into Axey Man's nose, which she conveniently knew was broken a few days ago, and they were off. It was carnage within seconds.

The drunk people of Glasgow were no slouches regarding hand-to-hand combat. Kirsty spotted a woman battering a Viking with a sequinned stiletto while a group of guys lifted another ancient warrior over their heads. He floundered helplessly like a giant hairy beetle. But it was all a bit like the tartan army playing some slick and gigantic South American side. The Glaswegians had the heart, but the Viking warband definitely had the edge.

A couple of uniformed coppers were pale with terror as they tasered wildly to no avail. Frej was going hand-to-hand with Axey Man. He kicked him square in the chest, then stumbled as Axey Man nimbly spun and delivered a punch to the side of Frej's neck. They were evenly matched. Frej's expression was a mask of focus as he slowly but consistently drove Axey Man ever backwards with a series of sharp jabs.

Nathan balanced precariously on the metal rail leading up the steps to the concert hall, wildly whacking Vikings with a street cleaner's broom. A busker smashed his guitar over a Viking's head, then yelped as the Viking lifted him high and smashed him down on the pavement. The warrior then raised a foot, ready to crush the busker's skull, but a woman in a sparkly dress pepper-sprayed him in the face, and he screamed.

Blood sprayed Kirsty's face, and she heard the horrifying crack of bone. One of the coppers yelped, and Kirsty flew at the Viking who held the copper by his severely broken arm. She clung to his back like a monkey and bit his ear until he let the wee guy fall to the ground. The Viking whirled, trying to whack Kirsty off as though she were a wasp—she yanked his hair and steeled herself against serious heebie-jeebies to stick her fingers in his eye.

Then the white light came.

It seared through the darkness with a deafening crack. Kirsty was dumped unceremoniously onto the pavement. The Viking had crumpled to dust beneath her.

Screams of terror filled the air. The brawl scattered, revellers and Vikings scarpering wildly in every direction. One guy tried to scale a drainpipe to escape Kirsty and her magic fingers, and his pal yanked his trousers down while pulling him to the ground. He collapsed in a heap and scampered after the others, wee white bum glowing in the moonlight as deafening sirens approached.

Kirsty turned to the police guy with the broken arm. He was deathly pale but conscious. Kirsty tried to remember bits of first aid she'd picked up over the years, but he took one look at her and scrabbled backwards, muttering *no no no*. He scaled the steps to the concert hall like a three-legged upside-down crab, and Kirsty tried not to take it personally. A few other injured people were crawling away or being dragged or carried by others.

Then it was just Kirsty, Frej and Nathan.

And the pile of dust that was once a pal of Frej's

Kirsty's chest tightened, and she struggled to breathe. She had just turned a man to dust. She had been on his back, had felt him beneath her, warm and vital and living, and now he was nothing. *What if she turned everything to dust?* Frej? Nathan? The Buchanan Centre, the subway or the busker who was currently getting off with the pepper-spraying woman who saved him?

'You zapped him like you zapped the pig,' Nathan observed helpfully.

'We need to go before the police get here.'

Kirsty's voice sounded echoey and distant in her ears. Her knees gave way. Frej flung her over his shoulder, and then he did indeed carry her to Pollokshields.

TWENTY-ONE

The boys were still snoring their faces off when Kirsty woke the next morning. She made a cup of tea as quietly as possible and brought it out to the garden. The morning sun streamed brightly as Kirsty sat cross-legged on the grass. Icy dew soaked into her jammies, but the hot tea warmed her.

She felt fizzy, yet strangely sort of calm. Drained and still. Exhausted and powerful.

And more than a little bit afraid of herself.

She had always been a one-off, as Morag used to say. Never entirely just one of the crowd. But the white light was a level of individuality she hadn't prepared for. She reached gingerly for her teacup. No sudden movements in case she blew up the house, she thought ruefully. The white light was part of her, and yet it frightened her.

'Ach, there's nothing the matter with you,' Morag would scoff as Kirsty wailed over some teenage disappointment or other. 'Everybody thinks that everybody else is normal except them. Truth is, everyone is as much a mess as everyone else. Some of us just hide it better.'

'What do you know?' Kirsty would demand. 'You've never had a feeling in your whole life.'

Morag laughed merrily and flicked the dishcloth at Kirsty. 'Away, you wee drama queen. If you don't like how life is, just pretend it's not.'

I don't think that's going to help now, Gran. Kirsty gulped the rest of her tea without blowing the Southside to kingdom come. So that was something.

For days now, Nathan had been dutifully hacking away at the garden using a variety of medieval-looking tools he found in the shed. Despite his best efforts, it seemed as though it wasn't quite tameable. Wildflowers sprung everywhere, scattering pinpricks of every colour of the rainbow. Ivy claimed the high red brick wall, and the lawn was a teeming mass of daisies, buttercups, and dandelions.

Kirsty absentmindedly picked some daisies as the dawn chorus filled the pale morning sky. They needed to be able to talk properly to Frej. He didn't seem perturbed by the white light, which might mean that he understood something of it. Or, it might just be that it's no weirder to him than a smartphone or pavement.

But evidently, Kirsty had brought the entire war band through. The small matter of travelling over a thousand years didn't appear to have dampened their ardour for sending him to Valhalla. Kirsty would quite like to know what their beef was before they attacked again, and Kirsty inadvertently turned them all to dust.

She was sure she had read once that Icelanders could talk to Vikings. Iceland was so geographically isolated for such a long time that its language barely changed in centuries. It ran a vague bell that Vikings might sound to them as Shakespeare does to English speakers: a bit odd and old-fashioned but basically intelligible.

There was a guy from Iceland who trained at a gym that

Kirsty went to once upon a time. Aevar. A tall, quiet boy. He didn't say much, but he had a friendly smile and always wiped his weights down when he was finished, so Kirsty had been a fan. The chances of him—or the gym, come to think of it— still being around were slim, but it was worth a go.

The guy who ran the gym was brilliant. Kenny. Big mad Kenny. He had a man bun long before it was cool, scars, and tattoos to rival Frej's. Plus a missing eye tooth that altogether too many women found inexplicably sexy.

Kirsty never did. He was more like a big daft brother to her. She would scream with horror when her pals described a particularly filthy fantasy about Kenny, but each to their own.

Kenny was one of those uniquely Glasgow characters equally likely to put your teeth out or talk to you about meditating, depending on which way the wind was blowing. He could be tricky, but he gave sage advice if he was in the right mood. Whether or not Aevar was still around, Kirsty would like to see Kenny again.

To cover all bases in the meantime, she did a quick bit of googling and discovered that there was a department for Scandinavian studies at the University of Glasgow. It was headed by a Dr Solveig Ljotrsdottir, whose bio proclaimed her an expert in Icelandic history. Kirsty sent her an email asking if she would be willing to meet.

Looking at the photograph of Dr Ljotrsdottir at an archaeological dig on her website reminded Kirsty of the Govan hogback stones. Perhaps she should take Frej to see them. Maybe the symbols would be like text messages to him. Or at least, maybe visiting the Viking centre would help her figure when in the 300-odd years of the Scottish Viking Age Frej and the war band had come from.

Kirsty had a gut feeling that the more information she could gather about any of this, the more chance it had of beginning to make sense. It was like a jigsaw, one of those huge hellish ones with eight billion identical bits of sky. Right now, she had a tiny handful of random pieces. The more pieces she could add, the more chance she had of seeing the whole picture.

There was no sign of either of the sleeping men rising, so Kirsty left a note and headed to the gym.

TWENTY-TWO

The heavens had opened by the time Kirsty reached the city centre. Gutters were overflowing, and a coffee shop sign skidded merrily across slick pavement slabs. The gym wasn't open yet, so Kirsty strolled up Buchanan Street, enjoying the bracing wind and driving rain. She got to the top of the road and paused by the concert hall steps.

Saturday morning retail workers were sprinting from the subway with hoods pulled up and umbrellas blown inside out. The pounding bass of heavy house music blasted from a nearby window. Last night, Kirsty battled Vikings and turned one of them to dust.

An ancient man who shouldn't be here and had no business breaking a wee polis guy's arm. But a person all the same. A man who had never done anything directly to Kirsty. He must have had friends and siblings, probably a wife, possibly children. Hopes. Dreams. Annoying habits. A runny nose and itchy balls. And now he was dead because of Kirsty.

Kirsty wondered about the people Frej must have killed. Monks and villagers and warriors. She wondered how Nathan felt about having shot German soldiers. Kirsty knew it was a bit rich to think of last night as a wartime battle, but it might be the only way she could live with what she did.

The Viking would have hurt her. He'd been trying to. He would have hurt more of the randoms caught in the rammy, but Kirsty had got to him first.

Not to mention he should be dead one way or another by now, in any case. Many Vikings had died young, either gruesomely in battle or of horrific diseases. Maybe being turned instantaneously to dust was a kinder end than getting a dagger to the eye and it going septic because antibiotics wouldn't be invented for hundreds of years. Call her bleeding heart, but Kirsty kind of hoped so.

A bit farther up Sauchiehall Street, a lone busker held firm against mother nature. He defiantly screeched out the Star Wars theme tune on the bagpipes as though facing down a redcoat Army. The wind was doing its best to drown him out, but he persevered.

Kirsty fished in her pocket for a few coins. If that kind of tenacity didn't deserve a pound, she didn't know what did. As the piper nodded his thanks, Kirsty stopped short. Vibration danced down her spine.

A woman stood outside the Willow tea rooms, impatiently waiting for someone. It wasn't raining where she was. *When she was.* As she looked up and down the street, she drummed her fingers on the elaborate curved handle of a silk parasol. Her satin dress was the colour of cornflowers, with a generous bustle and a ruffle down the front. Her hat was a sort of oversized top hat, made of midnight blue velvet and adorned with a large silken peacock. Its enormous feather tail reached halfway down her back.

There was a determined tilt to her jaw as she scanned the crowd on the street. A skinny guy in a drab suit and cap leered at her. She stared him down until he all but whimpered and scuttled away.

Pinpricks of thrill broke out over Kirsty. She had written an essay about Kate Cranston at school because she thought she was brilliant. The woman in the peacock hat was a female entrepreneur who invented café culture in the late 1900s, opening tearooms that were welcoming, pleasant, and an alternative to male-dominated pub culture. Kirsty always loved how, even though she was happily married, she traded under the name Miss Cranston all her working life.

The building behind Miss Cranston was blackened with soot. Kirsty could hear the clip-clop of horses' hooves on cobblestones that hadn't been there in decades and the creak of carriage wheels. Manure, smoke, and sweat assaulted Kirsty, and she understood why Miss Cranston held a beautifully embroidered hanky to her nose.

A man appeared. His tweed suit hung off his skinny frame. A jaunty teal kerchief was knotted at his neck, and his dark handlebar moustache was gelled into curly ends. Kirsty held her breath as Glasgow's most famous artist grinned and bent to kiss the hand of his patron, and she rolled her eyes in exasperation.

Charles Rennie Mackintosh was always late. She felt honoured to know that. There would be a scholar in a dusty library somewhere who would be thrilled to know that. If only Kirsty could find a way to inform them without them phoning the men in white coats.

Mackintosh opened the door for Miss Cranston, and Kirsty spotted the leather-bound portfolio tucked under his arm. *Designs for the refit of the tearoom.* The original sketch of the Art Deco rose that would become synonymous with Glasgow could be there.

'I've got your rose tattooed on my bum!' Kirsty yelled. She'd gotten the tattoo in San Francisco in a fit of homesickness. She'd once flung a promising one-night stand out when he critiqued it as *not a real rose*.

Mackintosh and Miss Cranston looked around, startled. Nerves jolted through Kirsty. *They heard her.*

'You okay, hen?' the piper asked.

Kirsty jumped a mile. The rain was bucketing down, and Kirsty was soaked to the skin. The tearoom was once again the modern, restored version. Its owner and architect faded into the ether.

'You look a bit peaky.'

'I'm on, uhh medication,' Kirsty lied. 'They make me dizzy.'

'You not going to drive, are you?' The bagpiper's eyes were full of concern. 'My old neighbour crashed into the bins on blood pressure tablets. She was okay, but we never got new bins for bloody months.'

'I don't have a car.'

'That's okay then. Cheery-bye.'

Kenny's gym was tucked away on a back lane near St Enoch's Square. The rest of the building was disused, and the gym spread over a vast open space in the cellar. This wasn't a gym of high-tech machines and stencils of inspirational quotes. The walls were unfinished cement and the equipment was battered. There was so much testosterone in the air that Kirsty had always been a bit afraid that if she breathed in too deeply, she would grow a beard.

A couple of gigantic guys, more gorilla than men, cheered on a wee lady as she trembled through lifting a couple of tins of beans. A group, including a few teenage lassies and a middle-aged man wearing an eighties sweatband, worked together to flip a huge lorry tyre. A skinny guy with horrific facial scars was doing squats with a giggling five-year-old on his shoulders.

Kirsty paused by the door as a wave of nostalgia hit her. She was in her early twenties when she had trained here. She was living in a squat Garnethill, a happy, eclectic home that advertised as an artists' colony. Most of the artisticness was reserved for rolling exquisite spliffs.

Despite two bar jobs and a cleaning job, she didn't have two pennies to rub together, yet never wanted for anything either. She would head to a club or an empty as soon as she clocked off for the night, dance until dawn and make it here by the skin of her teeth for a lethal Ashtanga class. She existed on adrenaline, weed and toast, and she loved it.

She and Agnes had formed an uneasy truce at the time, in which they pretended that the other didn't exist. This meant that Kirsty could have a cup of tea with Morag now and then without World War Three breaking out. Life was good, and Kirsty fucked it up, but what was done was done.

'Hurricane Kirsty in the flesh. How're you doing, doll?'

Kenny leaned by his office door, his lazy grin so familiar that Kirsty wanted to hug him. He had always called her Hurricane Kirsty. She must've chucked a tantrum in the gym once upon a time.

'How've been doing for ten years, you mean?'

'Ach, it's no' been that long,' he chuckled. 'I knew you couldn't stay away forever. Good to see you darlin'. You're looking well.'

Kirsty laughed. 'I am not.'

'You always were a smasher. Are you wanting a workout?'

'I want some fight training.'

'For fitness?'

Kenny's pale blue eyes met Kirsty's with a flicker of concern and something else—curiosity?

'Aye,' she said firmly. 'And because men piss me off.'

'Happy days, then. 'Mon.'

'Right now?'

'How not now?'

Kirsty considered. A session with Kenny would kill or cure her, which didn't seem like a bad deal. Kenny jogged with Kirsty around the perimeter of the gym to warm up.

'Do you believe in ghosts, Kenny?'

There had always been something about Kenny. Kirsty just had to look at him, and she would spill her darkest secrets. He was the only one to whom she had ever admitted exactly what she did to Agnes. Harry might have put two and two together, but only Kenny *knew*.

'Depends on what you mean by ghosts. Give me some big circles with your arms. Open up those shoulders.'

'Dead people,' Kirsty deadpanned. 'People who aren't there anymore.'

'That's two different things.'

'How?'

'Ten squats.'

'Away tae fuck, Kenny. What have squats got to do with fighting?'

He just grinned, so Kirsty rolled her eyes and obeyed.

'They used to believe there were women who could see beyond time.'

Chills dashed over Kirsty and she tried to concentrate on her squats. She hadn't said anything about time.

'Aye, they used to believe in dragons and curses and that the world was flat,' she muttered.

'The world isnae flat. That's true.'

'You believe in dragons and curses, Kenny? What are you smoking these days, and where can I get some?'

Kenny chuckled and, without warning, flipped on her back. Kirsty lay winded for a second. He crouched next to her.

'I just think it's awful arrogant of us to believe that we

know all there is to know about the universe, and folk for tens of thousands of years were just daft,' he said softly.

Kirsty sat up and forced herself to meet his eyes. A heavy wall ball thwacked off the concrete, followed by an encouraging cheer. Something about Kenny's stare reminded Kirsty he could kill her with his thumb.

'I never said daft.'

'They explained things with the information they had at the time.' Kenny shrugged with a grin that crinkled his eyes, and he looked like the old Kenny again. 'Loads of beliefs and myths and religion aren't against science. Worship of the natural world is human nature, whether we call it praying to Thor or gawping at the majesty of a thunderstorm.'

Kirsty nodded. She admired the way that Frej took the modern world in stride. Nathan, from less than a century ago, was alternately fascinated and appalled by modern technology. The other day he'd watched in horror as the woman in the café warmed their sausage rolls in the microwave and refused to eat anything that had radiation running through it.

But Frej's quiet curiosity was oddly calming. Kirsty supposed there was more acceptance of the unknown in his day. Perhaps it was easier to accept the notion of motorbikes, planes, and factories when you had the imagination to set sail towards the horizon with absolutely no idea what was beyond it. Modern people think we have it all figured out, but as Kirsty was learning by the minute, the universe held many more wonders than could be explained.

'See,' Kenny continued, 'Einstein's theories proved that all energy in the universe is constant.'

Kirsty blinked. 'When did you get to be such a brainbox?'

'I'm no as daft as I look, doll,' Kenny grinned. 'Studied all this once upon a time. Every energy particle that has existed since the beginning of time still exists. In that case, the energy of all the things that have ever happened must still be here in some form. You with me?'

'I need a lie down in a darkened room, but more or less.'

'So if it's all still here, who's to say that you can't see it?'

'Why can't everyone see it then?'

Kenny shrugged. 'Everyone can see stars. Every time we look at a star, we time travel. Half of them have been deid millions of years.'

'But that's because of the distance,' Kirsty frowned. 'I've been seeing these things on Sauchiehall Street.'

'Who knows what there is cutting about Sauchiehall Street that only some of us can see,' Kenny said. 'The hill between the villages of Partick and Cathurse was a sacred ground for a long time. Druids came from all over Scotland to get advice from long-dead ancestors.'

'Sauchiehall Street is a lot of things, but sacred is a new one.'

Kenny grinned that twinkly grin of his. 'Ach, don't know hen, I'm just a wee guy that owns a gym. 'Mon, I'll teach you to flip me like that.'

TWENTY-THREE

'I think we should talk to her friend,' Nathan announced Kirsty put the old copper kettle on the stove. A steady thud filled the air as Frey chopped firewood in the garden. Kenny promised to see if he could get in touch with Aevar for her. Kirsty checked her email—still no response from the Icelandic professor.

'Whose friend?'

'Morag's—the woman she met that night for fish and chips. I know the police interviewed her, but you knew Morag. Maybe this woman remembers something nobody but you would pick up on.'

Kirsty busied herself, pouring tea so Nathan didn't see the hot flash of guilt darting across her face. She hadn't seen Morag in ten years. Agnes had been in jail, and Morag was all alone in the world for the first time in her life. Kirsty could have reached out. Sent to the odd postcard. She should have.

'I don't think Harry said who the friend was.'

'I asked him her name when he came by yesterday,' Nathan replied.

'Harry came by yesterday?'

Nathan nodded. 'I told him about the women we spoke to the other night and showed him the notes I made. He said he would start following up with them.'

Kirsty nodded. 'Sounds good.' She felt a twinge of guilt. She had half-forgotten about Harry amid all the discovering holes in time and white light carry-on.

'The friend Morag met that night was Mary McCafferty. Harry gave me her address only because he said you knew it already, and—'

'Mrs McCafferty? She's still alive?'

Surely Mrs McCafferty was about a hundred when Kirsty was fifteen. It was probably that thing where she seemed ancient to Kirsty because Kirsty was a kid, while Mrs McCafferty was forty-five or something. But Kirsty was sure she remembered the thin papery skin of her hands, the snow-white hair twisted into an elaborate updo.

Maybe it was a different Mrs McCafferty. It could be her daughter or daughter-in-law. Kirsty didn't remember her having family, but she could have. Or maybe it was some random Mrs McCafferty. It was a common enough name.

Nathan showed her the address. Kirsty's childhood address, ground floor flat. Mrs McCafferty's flat.

'You go,' Nathan said.

'You're not coming?'

'She'll open up more without a stranger there.'

'Okay,' Kirsty shrugged. 'I'll report back.'

In the garden, Frej had stripped to his skinny black jeans. Kirsty couldn't help but notice how his muscles rippled as he swung the axe overhead. He didn't have as many tattoos on his back. For some strange reason, the fact that his shoulders were scattered with freckles sent a strange rush of affection through Kirsty. It was so human.

He noticed her watching and stood up with a grin, stretching his neck from side to side. Kirsty smiled, feeling ridiculously shy. He ambled across the lawn towards her, wiping his red-gold hair off his face with his forearm.

'I'm going to talk to Mrs McCafferty,' she said, entirely pointlessly, given the small matter of him not speaking English.

'It's weird,' she added with a frown, realising it was true. 'Morag was never pals with Mrs McCafferty. She was a grouchy old so-and-so, and I'm sure she's Agnes's age at the very least. And Morag didn't like the city centre. Why on earth would she go for dinner in the city centre with Mrs McCafferty?'

Frej nodded thoughtfully, humour dancing in his eyes as he pretended to understand.

'If Morag was kicking about with Mrs McCafferty, she must have been really lonely.'

'Mmph,' Frej said with another solemn nod. Despite her words, Kirsty giggled.

'I went travelling because I wanted to.' She took a shaky breath as an unpleasant feeling slithered around her guts. 'We pretended it was for my safety, but Agnes's reign was over long before she went to jail. Most of her men scattered years earlier.

'I was shagging a roaster called Ben on a beach in Brisbane, while wee Morag was lonely enough to go into town was someone she didn't like and getting murdered. Even if we catch the bastard responsible, that won't change.'

Frej pointed to the large branch he was chopping. '*Trè*', he said. *Tree-ah*. They burst out laughing.

'Yep, that's a tree,' Kirsty said. 'Good chat.'

He gave her a *thumbs up*. After a moment's hesitation, she reached out and touched the pad of his thumb with her finger.

. . .

Twenty minutes later, Kirsty turned onto Cumberland Street
—home of the notorious Cumbie gang until the MacIver Boys
saw them on their way. The streets became depressingly familiar. *Where did memories end and Shadows begin?* If she looked
in the right place, would she see herself and Harry organising
the rest of the neighbourhood kids into a game, once upon a
time? Or Morag taking her out to the ice cream van to get her
99 with raspberry sauce to stop her crying after Agnes tore
into her? Or—the thought gave her the boak—if she looked in
the *wrong* place, would she see Agnes and Nathan going furiously at it up against a wall as an air raid siren wailed?

Nathan clearly had no idea of the extent of Agnes's business proclivities. He knew that she was, in his words, *no better
than she ought to be*. In his mind, Agnes seemed to be a cheeky
urchin, somewhere between Robin Hood and the Artful
Dodger, whose scrapes would earn her an indulgent slap on
the wrist from the powers that be.

Kirsty didn't know if he would ever forgive her if he found
out she was responsible for Agnes going to prison for murder
in her eighties.

One step at a time, she reminded herself.

As she approached her childhood home, she spotted Mrs
McCafferty sitting in her front bay window. She looked fore-
boding as always in a high-necked blouse. *Well, she was alive.*

She glanced in Kirsty's direction. Kirsty raised an arm to
wave and Mrs McCafferty—

Disappeared.

Kirsty took the front steps two at a time and stepped onto
the windowsill where Mrs McCafferty had sat. She peered into
the gloom of the dimly lit living room. The back door banged
shut. Kirsty leapt off the windowsill and raced around the
corner—

The mud in the lane that ran behind the row of tenements
was dry and cracked. Kirsty skipped gingerly over rubbish and

thistles and old hypodermic needles. The same dent in the stone wall behind Agnes's tenement was still there. It had been some time since Kirsty last used it to vault over the wall, but there was no time to question that now.

She ran at it, found the dent with her toes, heaved and scrabbled to the top in the dignified manner of a baby elephant. As she reached the top, something caught the corner of her eye. Just for a fraction of a second—then it was gone.

But she had seen something. The far end of the lane met the main road, and Kirsty had spotted a flash of white. Almost as though somebody with white hair had just disappeared around the corner.

But that was absurd. It had to be the best part of the hundred metres, and seconds had passed. No matter what age Mrs McCafferty was, that kind of speed was barely—

Human.

Kirsty thought of the Gorbals Vampire and shivered. The back door of the tenement banged in the wind. Kirsty made a split-second decision to leap from the wall and slip through before it shut again.

The close, or hallway, was shadowy and smelt a bit musty. Kirsty ventured slowly along the narrow, tiled hallway. The Victorian tiles were moss green to about shoulder height, then cream above.

It said much about the city's attitude to the poor that fancy folk in the West End got a wally close, tiled with beautiful art deco patterns. The closes for the hoi polloi were tiled in plain drab colours. It couldn't take much more effort to apply tiles with patterns. It had just been decided that their likes didn't deserve patterns.

The floor was a dark grey stone, shiny and smooth with age, and it hadn't been mopped in a good long while. Faint cobwebs crept over cracked and peeling paint overhead. Kirsty paused by the foot of the stairs outside Mrs McCafferty's front door. The staircase snaked through the heart of the building, with four flats on each floor except for the top, which just had one on either side of the landing. Kirsty used to love to lean over the railing up there, letting her eyes go funny as they drifted around a dizzying spiral of polished wooden bannister to the ground. The bannister was polished in those days, Kirsty thought, noting the dull and dusty wood now.

All the ladies in the close took turns mopping the stairs and buffing the worn wood until it shone. The chore would take at least half a day, as it would be crucial to stop at each landing for a good gossip. Kirsty would tag along when it was Morag's turn. She would sit on the steps with her crayons or dollies, listening contentedly as Morag passed news of Mr Robertson from the second floor's latest dalliance from door to door.

Kirsty was putting off going inside Mrs McCafferty's flat. The front door gaped open like a challenge. Mrs McCafferty had been scary enough even before Kirsty saw her zooming down the back lane like a bat out of hell.

Kirsty took a deep breath. It had to be done. She stepped over the threshold.

Mrs McCafferty's flat was overstuffed and chintzy as it always was. Now though, her vast array of mismatched knick-knacks took on a more sinister air. Among the doilies, lace throw cushions and china ballet dancers was a set of bronze bowls, hand hammered and green with age. The night sky had been carved across their basins, intricate constellations and galaxies dancing from one ball to the next.

Next to them was a doll, roughly fashioned from some-thing similar to wicker, with a ghoulish face stitched into twine. It wore a dusky purple dress with a wee white hanky draped over its head, similar to a nun's veil. Kirsty shivered as it grinned blankly at her.

The flowery wallpaper next to the dresser was dotted with

a series of portraits painted in oil, encased in ornate oval frames. They were miniatures, each no bigger than Kirsty's hand. They were all women. Haught, strapping women who stared defiantly at the artist as though daring him to displease them.

Icy prickles danced over Kirsty as she realised they looked familiar, though she couldn't quite put her finger on it. She couldn't identify any of them, but somehow, they were not strangers to her. Leaning as close as she dared, Kirsty squinted to read the dates written in a fine script. 1344. 1563. 1589. 1736. Then her heart stopped dead.

The centre portrait was of Mrs McCafferty, dated 1871. She wore a black silk dress with a high ruffle around her neck and pearl earrings dangled below her elaborate updo. Her hair was snowy white, and she looked a hundred if she was a day, just like she always did.

A hundred and fifty years ago.

Blood rushed in Kirsty's ears. Every instinct she possessed screamed at her to get out of there now. She spun wildly, her eyes frantically scanning the fussy living room. Her heart thudded painfully, threatening to break a rib.

Come on, come on, come on—

And then she saw it.

On the mantelpiece. A black-and-white photo in a plain frame. Morag with four other girls. Judging by their minidresses and beehive hairdos, it appeared to have been taken in the 1960s, when Morag was in her late teens or early twenties.

The girls sat on a stone wall at the seaside, laughing, squinting in the sunshine without a care in the world. Morag's smile was the widest. She was at the end of the row, her other arm flung wide.

She had freckles on her legs. Kirsty had forgotten that. Morag was always moaning about them, investing in all manner of lotions and potions that claimed to magic them away. In the photo, she wore white ankle socks and white patent T-bar shoes, with a matching white hairband that pushed back her cheeky pixie haircut.

The back door banged, and Kirsty's heart leapt into her mouth. She grabbed the photo and skipped out to the landing as lightly as she could. She could hear Mrs McCafferty on the back steps. She wouldn't make it to the front door without Mrs McCafferty seeing her. After an instant of indecision, Kirsty scuttled up the stairs.

She paused on the second landing and glanced down. Mrs McCafferty's snowy-white hair disappeared into her flat. Kirsty let out a shaky breath as Mrs McCafferty's door closed firmly behind her.

The coast was clear. Kirsty could go down and out the front door now. Then she looked up the stairs and gritted her teeth. She could almost feel Agnes's presence pulsing through the shadowy close.

It's time for some answers, great-grandmother. Kirsty ran up to the top floor and opened the door.

Twenty-Four

Agnes looked like a broken bird waiting to be swallowed by that ugly armchair. She had aged, Kirsty thought as Agnes fixed her with a cold stare. *At least somebody around here bloody well had.*

'Morag is still deid,' snapped Agnes by way of greeting. 'What are you wanting?'

'You really need to learn to get a handle on your emotions, great granny dearest,' Kirsty said. 'All this sympathy and feelings. You'll get mildew from your own tears.'

'I gave you a break when you showed up here the other day, for Morag's sake. But you're still a clipe, my girl, and you will pay.'

Behind Kirsty, Gargoyle Man shifted from one foot to the other. He was just waiting for the nod from Agnes. He wouldn't shoot her inside the flat, Kirsty mused. He might fling her from the window. She'd known a few of Agnes's adversaries to befall that fate, one or two of whom had escaped with two broken legs.

'How long have you known Mrs McCafferty?'

If Agnes was surprised by the question, she didn't show it. 'Long enough.'

'You've lived in this flat since you were born. How long has she been here?'

For the first time in Kirsty's life, Agnes broke eye contact. She reached with a trembling hand for her gold-plated cigarette case and lit up.

'Those things will kill you.'

Agnes's laugh rattled in her chest. 'Chance'd be a fuckin' fine thing.' She grinned, blowing out a long stream of smoke.

'The pair of you are about the same age, aren't you? Did you go to school together?'

'I'll gie you another three minutes of stupid questions before Martin sees you out. *Loose Women* is coming on.'

'I want to get in touch with Morag's pals.'

'Why?'

'Gather memories of her from when she was younger.' Was it Kirsty's imagination, or did something flicker in Agnes's eyes? 'Make up a wee book or something.'

'Whit's the point in that?' Agnes flicked ash into a pewter ashtray. Kirsty's eyes were beginning to sting from the smoke, but she refused to flinch.

'Because it's nice. To remember her.'

'I'll aye mind ma wee girl,' Agnes growled. 'I don't need a fucking book for that.'

'I don't remember many of her pals,' Kirsty said. 'Did any of them come to the funeral?'

'Morag had hunners of pals. A'body loved her.' Only the tiniest tremble in her voice betrayed her. The old bag had feelings, after all.

'Anyone in particular? A girl gang from her teenage years?'

'What do you care?'

Kirsty hesitated, nerves churning in her stomach. 'I

thought I remembered once seeing a photo of her with a group of pals. I just wondered who they were?'

Bingo. She definitely saw it this time. Agnes was hiding something.

'Morag gave up her life to look after you.'

'No, she never. I was one kid and I was already at school when my parents died. What would she give up her life for?'

Agnes took a deep drag. Kirsty heard her breath rattling through her rib cage. 'You were a handful.'

'Away tae fuck. I was a handful to you, but me and Morag mucked along just fine. Because you were an old bitch,' Kirsty clarified. 'And you still are.'

Over by the door, Gargoyle Man cleared his throat, and Kirsty thought he might be smothering a laugh. There was a long pause, during which Agnes could well be working up the breath to tell him to shoot Kirsty in the face. Instead, she threw back her head and laughed uproariously, a huge noise for such a frail wee woman. She nodded, pointing at Kirsty with a shaky finger as though Kirsty had finally passed a test she had been failing all her life.

'Aye, right enough,' Agnes grinned. 'I am an old bitch.'

'Why did Morag go into town that night with Mrs McCafferty?'

The electric flames of the orange fire danced dark shadows over Agnes's face as her laughter died. The mantlepiece clocked ticked heavily in the silence. Kirsty waited.

'Have you never learned not to meddle in things that are bigger than you?' she said finally.

'No, I was very badly brought up. Why did Morag go into town with Mrs McCafferty? She never liked her.'

'This is not your concern, my girl.'

'Of course it fucking is. I loved Morag.'

'There are ways that things are done—'

'What does any of that pish matter when it comes to

finding out what happened to Morag? I'll give you *the way things are done*. How many lives have been ruined, families destroyed, because of you and your stupid *way things are done*?'

'You like to sit in judgement for things you don't understand, girly, but I'll tell you this for nothing. I answered for everything ever did.'

'Including Harry's dad?'

'Martin Finnegan knew what he was about taking a loan from me. He was a grown man who made a choice—'

'You didn't have to—'

'I *did*! That's what you never understood, my girl. The same consequences go for everybody. Whole thing falls apart at the seams otherwise. Folk around here knew that. Martin Finnegan knew that.'

'He was about to be a granda. Kieran's girlfriend was pregnant. You could have at least—'

'Martin Finnegan wasn't fit to look that baby in the eye. There was more to that man than you'll ever know. They are not family, hen. We are.'

'That's where you're wrong. Harry is my family.'

'*Ach*,' Agnes spat with a dismissive wave. She blew out a cloud of smoke which dissolved into a hacking, coughing fit.

'What was my great-granda like?'

'Who?' Agnes snapped too quickly.

Her eyes flicked to the ruby ring. Nathan's mother's ring. *Busted*. Agnes wore it on her pinkie finger since her fingers swelled with arthritis.

'Your pal fae George Square. The American GI. You loved him, didn't you? You shameless hypocrite. You were gonnae marry the father of your child, like the good convent school girl you were.'

'Never,' Agnes hissed. There was a warning note in her voice, but Kirsty ignored it.

'He walked you home from the Barrowlands, and you held hands and whispered sweet nothings in the moonlight, didn't you? You *loooved* him,' Kirsty crooned, like some teenage mass of hormones who just caught her pals winching in the playground. 'Granny and Grandad, in a tree, K-I-S-S—'

'If that wee fucker showed his face in this city again, I'd have him hung, drawn and quartered,' Agnes spat, her voice twisted with bitterness.

TWENTY-FIVE

'You're *married?*' Kirsty yelled, slamming the kitchen door. She grabbed the first thing that came to hand, which was a wooden spoon, and flung it at Nathan's head.

He ducked. Frej was busy tucking into a bowl of soup. He watched the exchange with amused interest.

'You've been giving it the *tragic love story*, and the whole time you've been a dirty married cheater?' Kirsty flung another few wooden spoons. Nathan backed up against the pantry door.

'I can explain—'

'Yous can always *explain*,' Kirsty spat. 'Did your wife not understand you, by any chance? Or was it just that she was all the way in America, and you needed to get your leg over because men are animals with *needs?*'

'Kirsty—'

'Bugger you, Nathan.'

She was out of wooden spoons. Fine. She would brain him with a wee pot.

'Kirsty, listen—'

'Not if you're just going to lie to me like you've been lying since the first day. This is why you've been feart to go and see her, isn't it? You know fine she'll eat you alive and you'll deserve it. If there's one thing I can't stand, Nathan, it's a liar.'

Nathan drew himself to his full height and commanded her as though he was, well, her great-grandfather. 'Do not throw that at me.'

Kirsty hesitated, holding the pot over her head.

'Put it down.'

Kirsty obeyed. Frej smothered a chuckle. She and Nathan froze in a stand-off for a moment, then she sighed and threw herself in a chair. 'On you go then.' She crossed her arms and glared at him.

'I don't owe you an explanation.'

'Do you want to keep living in my house?'

'I never asked for any of this.'

'None of us did. And coming through time doesn't change the fact you are a dirty wee—'

'I got married right after high school graduation,' Nathan snapped.

He sat at the table opposite Kirsty and stared at the scrubbed pine, his hands clasped tightly. 'Gloria and me, we were sweethearts since the seventh grade. On our prom night—'

Kirsty rolled her eyes because she knew where the story was going. 'Nobody ever told you to wrap it?'

'What?'

They probably didn't in the 1930s, to be fair.

'I did the right thing.' Nathan's eyes flashed. 'I married her.'

'You're a saint,' Kirsty muttered.

'It wasn't the life either of us wanted. I planned on becoming a newspaper reporter, and Gloria wanted to go to Harvard to study the law. She always had her nose in a book, that girl. I used to tell her she'd turn into a book one day. But after we got married and were waiting for the baby, there was no money for either of our dreams. I went to work for her pop in the auto shop, and it was tough. Then that winter, Arthur came along, and—'

Nathan broke off, lost in memories for a second. 'He was such a happy baby. Always contented. He'd lie in his bassinet and gurgle and kick his legs all day long. He would smile at anybody. Grocery boy, mailman, and all of Gloria's friends when they visited for coffee. My Artie was happy to be handed to everybody and they would just fall in love with him.'

Artie must be in his early eighties now, Kirsty thought. Morag's big brother. She wondered if she could track him down. Maybe he had kids or grandkids who would be on social media. Then something about Nathan's expression stopped that train of thought.

'The following winter, measles came to town. Took away a lot of kids. My niece who just started kindergarten—Artie was so little, he—' Nathan took a shaky breath, struggled to find his voice again. 'At least it was quick. He got a fever one night, and by morning—'

Nathan's face crumpled, and he fought for breath. Kirsty was halfway out of her seat when she saw that Frej had beaten her to it. Frej crossed the kitchen with one leap, perched on the chair next to Nathan, and cradled him against his chest as he cried.

'I'm so sorry,' Kirsty whispered.

'That's how come I can cook, Nathan said quietly. 'Gloria, she just couldn't—it was like she was sleepwalking for months and months. She sat in bed and stared out the window. If you tried to talk to her, she would just look at you like you weren't there. All the ladies in our parish brought stews and meatloaf for the first few weeks, but they had their own families to care for. After a while, I told them we would be okay. I got me a

Good Housekeeping magazine. Figured if I learned how to fix a car from a book, I could learn how to fix dinner too.

'By summer, Gloria started to wake up a little bit, but it was like this great wall of pain grew between us, and we couldn't get across it towards each other. I couldn't even look at her without remembering the doctor telling us they would take away as much pain as possible for his last hours. Every time we tried to talk or just be together—it felt like a whole box of daggers falling on me.

'We took all the money we had saved for our own place and put her on a summer course at Harvard. We decided that a little bit of distance might ease things for us both, and that we could discuss our future when she returned. But that August, Army recruiters came. I figured we could put the conversation off a bit longer.

'We all thought that when the US entered the war, we would finish it right away. I thought I'd go to Europe, then by Thanksgiving, me and Gloria—we never knew it would be another four years.'

Frej rubbed Nathan's back as his sobs slowly subsided.

'It sounds like such a cruel disease,' Kirsty said finally.

Nathan's eyes widened in alarm. 'You never had measles?'

'I was vaccinated,' she said hastily. She couldn't decide if it would be a comfort or needlessly cruel to tell him she had never even met anyone who'd had measles.

'You mean like for Smallpox?'

'I suppose. You get loads of them when you're a baby. Mumps, Polio, I don't even know what else.'

'And then nobody gets sick?' His eyes were shining.

Kirsty decided this wasn't the time to break it to him about anti-vaxxers. She shook her head firmly. 'No.'

Nathan nodded, taking this in. Kirsty reached over and squeezed his hand. Frej covered both of their hands with his.

'You think Gloria may still be alive?' Nathan broke the silence.

'What would she be, ninety-eight or nine? I suppose it's possible.'

'Can we find out? I'd like to write her a letter. I owe her that. Maybe you could mail it, say you found it in an old book or something? I could date it '43 or '44.'

'That's a nice idea,' said Kirsty. 'I bet there will be some old-fashioned writing paper in the house somewhere.'

'And an ink pen, Nathan added firmly. I would never write her with one of those Biros the British use in aeroplanes.'

TWENTY-SIX

I t turned out that Gloria was still alive. She lived alone in a suburb of Chicago, having been widowed—for the second time, as far as she was concerned—in the mid-eighties. Her five daughters rotated visiting her daily.

'You won't get rid of an old coot like me easily,' she growled to a local journalist reporting on her hundredth birthday party a few months earlier. 'I ain't done living yet. I'll let you know when I am.'

'Gin,' she had replied when asked the secret of her great age. 'I have me a lil' gin and ginger ale every day at sundown. And ain't never bothered with men since my Donnie passed in 1986. Had to go out to work to put my girls through college. I was scared any man married wouldn't want to educate my girls, so I didn't marry another man.'

The article mentioned in passing that Gloria had lost her first husband in the Normandy landings. Her first husband frowned when he read that.

'She knew I survived the battle. I wrote her from the hospital.'

'Maybe the letter got lost something,' Kirsty shrugged. 'I

can't imagine the post-service was amazing in the middle of a war.'

Gloria worked as a legal PA for a Chicago law firm until she retired well into her seventies. It wasn't quite the same as being the Harvard lawyer she had once dreamed of, but Kirsty hoped Gloria had been happy. She was grinning away in her birthday photo, raising a gin to the camera, surrounded by her daughters, their children, and grandchildren. Her birthday tiara sat squint on a thick white pixie cut.

Kirsty found some writing paper in her dad's heavy oak desk. It probably dated from the seventies or eighties, but Nathan reckoned it looked familiar. They decided an old lady getting a letter from the husband she thought was long dead probably wouldn't conduct a forensic exam on it.

The sun brooded behind a large white cloud, but there was enough warmth in the air that the garden was pleasant. Kirsty sat on the steps, enjoying the scent of yellow roses. Frej settled by her feet and closed his eyes with a deep, contented sign.

If Kirsty didn't know better, she would have said he was meditating. Something about his solid calmness was infectious. Kirsty smiled at him. As though he sensed it from behind his head, he patted her foot.

A shiver ran through her that she really didn't have time to think about right now. She pulled out the photo she stole from Mrs McCafferty's flat and peered at it closely. The five carefree, laughing girls seemed to stare at her accusingly from another time.

Kirsty frowned. At the bottom left corner was that— sand? It was. And the hazy horizon behind them—where the sea met the sky. They were at a beach.

Kirsty sighed and drummed her fingers on her phone. Then she connected to a careless neighbour's Wi-Fi and started googling. A few hours later, her eyes were crossing from staring at her phone screen. If the four woman in the photo with Morag had an identity, nobody had told the Internet.

Kirsty stretched and smiled at Frej, who appeared to still be lost in his meditation. She had gone over every media mention of Agnes she could think of, trawling through reports on endless bank raids, money laundering, and embezzlement. Agnes hanging those boys from the bus stop got a lot of press attention. Kirsty remembered it well because she'd had to hear about it at playtime every day for weeks.

She looked up the website of Morag's old school. There was a section on former pupils but no mention of Morag. She took a picture of the photo with her phone and reverse image searched. Nothing.

Nathan shouted through the kitchen window that he would post the letter and go for a walk. Kirsty steeled herself and searched for news of her parents' deaths. A friend or two might have shown up at Morag's daughter's funeral and been helpfully identified in print.

The top hit was a front-page article Kirsty remembered all too well. Her stomach clenched as she clicked on it. The photo had been splashed across the front page. In it, she stood in front of the chapel between Agnes and Morag, clutching Morag's hand. She wore a black dress with a black ribbon in her hair, like some kind of goth Alice in Wonderland. Her parents' coffins were being carried down the steps, and Kirsty was frowning.

She recalled the moment distinctly. A gust of wind had blown icy rain in her face, and she had flinched. In the instant the photographer captured, she looked furious. Some journalists had seen fit to speculate that she might be another Agnes in the making. Kirsty was eight years old.

Frej tapped her foot gently. She glared, her chest tight and painful, decades of rage turning through her like acid. Concern swam in his deep blue eyes.

He reached up and stroked the side of her face with a touch so gentle that hot tears sprang to her eyes. She let herself rest against his warm hand. He cradled her face, his thumb lightly stroking her cheekbone. His eyes never left hers until slowly, gradually, Kirsty could breathe again.

When Nathan returned from posting his letter, Frej was chopping firewood, and Kirsty was trying to fire up their homemade barbecue. The breeze kept blowing the flame out before it got a chance to get going. Kirsty was about to give up and kick the whole thing to bits when Nathan crouched next to her and shielded the tiny flame long enough for it to take.

'Stupid bloody thing,' Kirsty muttered.

Nathan gave a ghost of a smile.

'Are you okay?'

Nathan shrugged. 'I missed a full lifetime.' His eyes were haunted and heavy. 'My parents were in their fifties when I shipped out. They must have had decades of Thanksgivings, Christmases and Fourth of Julys and I missed them all. My brothers and sisters must have had kids and grandkids, jobs and parties.

'I went to the library. The lady showed me some books about the 20th century. I kept imagining my family sitting around watching the moon landing on TV. My brother Buddy must have lost his damn mind. He always loved stories about aliens and stuff. And the music—'

Nathan shook his head. 'I wrote my sister Lois from France when I heard the news that Glenn Miller died. She was only sixteen, and she was crazy about him. Whatever she was doing when the hit parade came on the wireless, she would just stop and dance. Drove Momma crazy if it was chores she was supposed to be doing.

'But today, I read about a fellow named Elvis Presley who created a new kind of dance music. Lois must have been so happy.'

Kirsty grabbed her phone and scrolled until she found an Elvis Presley playlist on Spotify. Nathan's eyes widened as the opening bars of *Jailhouse Rock* played. Then he started bobbing his head and clicking his fingers in a way that really reminded Kirsty he was from another time.

'Lois musta wore a hole in the rug dancing to this.'

Glenn Miller died in 1944, according to Kirsty's phone. If Lois was sixteen then, she might well still be alive. 'Do you want me to find out?'

Nathan thought a moment, then nodded. 'We'd need to get some real forties writing paper to write to her,' he grinned. 'She'll check.'

The fire was pleasantly roaring away when Frej brought out the tray of chicken drumsticks Nathan had marinated earlier.

'Did you find anything out about Morag's friends?' Nathan asked as he started to cook.

Kirsty contributed by opening bottles of beer. 'Not a thing,' she sighed. 'It's tricky to research somebody when you don't even know the names.'

'Aren't their names written on the back of the photograph?'

Kirsty stared at him. 'People used to do that, didn't they?'

She grabbed the frame, carefully pried open the clips, slid the back away and—

Me, Jetta, Nan, Lizzie and Rita. Glasgow Fair, 1967.

Kirsty smiled to see Morag's neat handwriting. A million birthday cards and notes to get her out of PE, signed Broons annuals, *to Kirsty, love Gran, Christmas 1994.* Recipes for tablet and knitting patterns that Kirsty would never follow came flooding over her.

She held the photograph out to Nathan. 'Morag wrote this.'

He ran his finger lightly over the blue biro, a faraway smile tugging at him. 'She's got good cursive,' he said approvingly. 'She must have been a good student.'

The boys cooked, and Kirsty got back to Googling, armed with first names. She searched for various combinations of the names. The third hit sent chills cascading down her spine.

BARROWLANDS MURDER. DO YOU KNOW THE SHADOW?

TWENTY-SEVEN

Kirsty knew the Shadow. Or at least, she knew the story of the serial killer who had hit Glasgow in the late sixties. He murdered three women, all of whom he had met at the Barrowland Ballroom, and then he disappeared into thin air.

'He was never caught,' she said to Nathan as they sipped tea around the fire. 'There was this huge investigation. They interviewed half the young men in the city, yet never even identified a suspect.'

'But he stopped killing?'

Kirsty shrugged. 'Nobody knows. I think it's pretty much unheard of for a killer like that to just stop, but no other victims were found after the last one. Lizzie,' she added with a shiver.

Lizzie Murdoch. In the photo, she sat second from the right. She wore a short sundress, her hair in a high beehive, and her wide smile revealed a distinctive gap between her front teeth. She looked like fun.

'There was a theory that he moved away, down south

maybe. Or he had been arrested for a different crime or died of natural causes. I think there was a rumour he had been killed in a pub brawl. But nobody knows who he is, so nobody knows what happened to him.'

Kirsty tapped her phone screen. 'In this article, there is a witness statement describing him. The witness is a friend of the second victim, Nan O'Leary, who says she saw them leaving together. She's raging,' Kirsty smiled. 'She says she'd have wrung his neck if only she had caught them in time. I think it's Morag.'

Nathan looked up sharply. 'The article doesn't name her.'

'She wouldn't give her name. The late sixties was the height of Agnes's power. Even a whisper of her second-hand involvement would have been incendiary to the press. Morag knew that. But we know she was friends with the victims—' Kirsty smiled. 'And that rage sounds like her.'

'So she saw him back then, and fifty years later, she too is murdered by her own stockings.'

'What's that they say about revenge being served cold?' Kirsty said grimly. 'This wee arsehole carries a grudge.'

Rita MacLeod's terraced house sat high on a hill in Shawlands. It had a breathtaking view of the entire city and the hazy Campsies. Her tiny garden was flooded with sunshine. It was such a clear day that Kirsty could read the *People Make Glasgow* sign on the old City of Glasgow College building behind George Square. The gothic buildings of the University to the left were silhouetted against the sun, sitting high on their West End hill as though supervising the city.

'This house was an absolute wreck when I bought it in, let me see, 1983.' Rita brought a tea tray set with cups of delicate china and a plate of fancy biscuits on the table. She wore baggy dungarees over a brightly printed blouse and her silver bob was tied back with a lime green scarf.

'I had just been promoted to headmistress, and I decided that flat sharing with other girls was beneath my station,' she chuckled. 'Fifteen thousand pounds, it cost—an absolute fortune—and it was falling down around my ears. It took months of repairs to even get up the stairs. I had a cold for about a decade thanks to the damp.' She sighed contentedly. 'But never regretted it. One look at that view and I knew this was my home.'

'The house is beautiful now,' Kirsty said, eyeing the fancy biscuits.

'I got there in the end.' Rita gave the teapot a shoogle. 'Took me donkeys' years, but it was well worth it. They'll carry me out of here in a box. Now, you wanted to talk to me about the Shadow? I haven't heard that name in years, would have thought you young people had forgotten all about it. Biscuit?'

Kirsty took a biscuit, trying to figure out how to explain her interest in decades-ago murders. The biscuits were a luxury brand, with generous chunks of white, dark and milk chocolate, and something else interesting. Hazelnuts, maybe. Kirsty liked a person who didn't skimp on biscuits.

'Never mind,' Rita said, picking up on Kirsty's hesitation. 'Now, what can I tell you?' She frowned into the distance a moment, crunching a biscuit thoughtfully.

'It was a dark time,' she said. 'This city has never been a stranger to violence, as I'm sure don't have to tell you, but us lassies used to feel protected from all that. There was a certain twisted chivalry. Men who'd gouge one another's eyes out without hesitation would never raise a hand to a woman.

'I'm not saying that's a good thing,' she added, pointing half a biscuit at Kirsty. 'Being dependent on the generosity of men isn't enough in the long run. I'm simply saying that as young women at the time, we tended to think of ourselves as safe. Ironically, I worried much more about my brothers getting on the wrong side of certain unsavoury characters than about myself. Naïvely, perhaps, but still. And then they found Jetta.'

Rita fell silent a moment. Bees buzzed industriously around the well-tended flowerbeds. Kirsty waited.

'I didn't know Jetta well. We all saw one another from time to time at the various night. There were different dance halls, you see, and a different night for each was the place to be. The Barrowlands was a Thursday night.

'After a while, you started to recognise the same faces. You would have shared a lipstick or borrowed a sanitary towel in the ladies. Maybe comforted one another when a promising young man went off with someone else. Sometimes you danced with a pair of lads who were pals, and they took you out together for a late-night supper. But unless you lived near one another, that would be it. It wasn't like today, where everyone keeps up with a vast array of contacts through social media and the like. We knew each other without really knowing each other, you know.

'That photo you have. It was taken in Dunoon during the Glasgow Fair. A few of us from the dancing ran into each other and thought it funny to be together in daylight. Morag asked a young man to take our picture with her new camera. Over the years, it crossed my mind a few times to get in touch with Morag to ask her for a copy, but I never did.'

'I'll make you one now,' Kirsty said.

Rita nodded, her eyes wistful. 'I should have kept in touch with Morag anyway. We were the only two left from that photo, and now it's just me.' She gave a shaky sigh. 'She was such a firecracker, Morag. Always bursting with fun. Morag was the one I knew the best. She and I palled around together for a while.

'I knew about her mother and her family business and all

that. Everyone did in those days. But I sensed that she just wanted to be Morag when she was at the dancing, so I never let on. We had some good times together...' Rita got lost in her memories for a few moments.

'After they found Lizzie, it was—it was all just so sad. The ridiculous thing was they tried to stop us from going dancing while he was on the loose, and we all refused. But after Lizzie, we drifted away after all. It wasn't really a conscious decision. I didn't feel like going for a few weeks—all of a sudden months, then years slipped by. Music changed. Disco dancing came along—' Rita smiled, her eyes sad. 'All that pointing and shaking your hips nonsense wasn't for me. If you weren't going to be birled around the floor by a handsome gentleman, then what was the point?

'I took up Salsa—goodness me, it was quite a few years ago. I was in my fifties. I love it. Takes me back to those days when it was good. Sometimes, I picture Morag or Nan. I remember how we used to catch each other's eyes and give approving nods and winks when one of us was dancing with a particularly handsome specimen.

'But you wanted to know about the Shadow.' Rita shifted in her chair as though giving herself a mental shake. She took another biscuit but didn't bite into it.

'I've read quite a bit about the investigation,' Kirsty said. 'But it would be helpful to hear anything you remember from your point of view.'

'I saw him with Jetta. I had been chatting with her earlier that evening. Some young lad she had been quite hopeful about got engaged to someone else. She was raging at him for leading her up the garden path. A man interrupted us and asked me to dance. I didn't want to leave her, but she told me not to be so daft. He had on a good suit, and that meant he was working.

'A bit later that evening, I noticed that she was dancing with someone and was pleased she was getting back on the horse. I watched them for a bit, hoping to catch her eye. I remember that she looked happy. I've thought about that a lot over the years. Her eyes lit up, and she was laughing at something he was saying to her. Six hours later, she was lying on frosty cobblestones behind her tenements, strangled with her own stockings.'

Rita broke off a bit of biscuit, crumbled it between her fingers, and then gave Kirsty a tight smile. 'You'd think horror would fade with time,' she said quietly. 'But it doesn't really. How dare he? How fucking dare he?'

'Were you certain she left with the man you saw her with?'

Rita shook her head. 'Not at first. I was paying attention to Jetta, so I only got a brief impression of him. I wasn't there the night Nan died, but I saw Lizzie leaving with a man. I'd been stood up by my date so was blethering with Pat the Pot Man, deciding whether to go or stay on my own, when I spotted Lizzie. She was heading down the stairs, arm-in-arm with a young man.

'Again, I just caught a glimpse of him, but I recognised him. Some instinct propelled me to shout after her, but she didn't hear me. I ran down the stairs, but they were gone. The following morning, Lizzie was found. I know there's no use in *what ifs*, but I've often thought if I had just been a little faster—'

'He probably would have picked up a different woman,' Kirsty said.

'Perhaps.'

'You don't think so?'

'I don't know,' Rita said slowly. 'But I've always thought it curious that all three victims were in that photograph. You have to remember that it wasn't like today when there could be hundreds of pictures of any given night out and all manner of strangers in them. A photograph in those days was quite a precious thing. You might have a family portrait or a wedding picture—in fact, I remember feeling a little strange that there existed a photograph of me with relative strangers.

'And now four of them have been murdered.'

TWENTY-EIGHT

'I asked her why they didn't stop going dancing,' Kirsty said. 'Just for a while, just until they caught him.'

She paced the old, worn stones in the kitchen, rage coursing through her. Frej sat at the table, carving a small piece of wood with Kirsty's mum's potato peeler. There was no sign of Nathan.

'She said that if it was a choice between the risk of being murdered or being left on the shelf, there was no competition. They went dancing, knowing full well a killer was on the loose. They were playing Russian roulette every time they let a man walk them home. Jetta, Nan and Lizzie lost.

'Every few years, a murder case hits the news, and there's always an outcry because the victim was just going about her business. She did everything right. She wasn't drunk or on the pull. She was wearing sweats; she was just walking home. And I get it—it is fucking horrifying that there is nothing we can do to safeguard ourselves. But somewhere, buried deep in all that horror, there is a sliver of judgment. Because what about the women who are drunk? What about those of us who go out fully intending to bring someone lovely, or at least acceptable, home for the night? We don't deserve to get murdered, either.

'It is so devastatingly cruel that the very people we fancy and love and are supposed to fancy and love us are our biggest danger. Because Rita is right. At first, I was like, getting married isn't that important. Just skip dancing for a few months. And it's not—but we shouldn't have to choose between companionship and safety. It shouldn't be one or the other.'

Frej listened intently as he silently whittled. Kirsty felt her rage dissipate, then reform into something harder. Something determined.

When Kirsty was wee, she thought that the grand sandstone building of the Mitchell Library, with its fancy roof and brass dome, was a magical palace. A foundation stone was laid by Andrew Carnegie, and Kirsty couldn't help but hesitate as she passed the entrance, wondering if she could peer into 1907 and watch the ceremony. Nathan waited impatiently by the door.

'Can you even give me a hint as to what we're doing here?' Kirsty called, trying to keep up with Nathan's urgent pace as he pushed through the heavy doors.

'I may not understand how you get information from that doohickey you keep in your pocket, but I know my way around microfilm.' The lady at reception nodded to Nathan as they barrelled past. Somehow, he had become a regular.

'What's microfilm?'

'You were right that The Shadow case sure dominated the news for a long time. And it gets aired all over again on anniversaries and suchlike. Sometimes when another killer is caught, a bunch of articles suggest he might have also been The Shadow all along.'

'Yeah, there was a guy imprisoned when I was at school—
early nineties, maybe. Loads of people thought it was him. He
never confessed, though.'

'So when I was pulling out those details, I got talking to
somebody, and—just come. It's easier if she explains—'

'I'm coming, I'm coming.'

Nathan disappeared through a door in the wood
panelling. Kirsty was about to follow when she noticed a row
of framed pen and ink drawings displayed on the gleaming
walnut wall. A young woman with dark blond hair tied in a
sensible ponytail frowned over her glasses as she mounted the
final drawing, then stepped back to admire her work.

'These are straight, aren't they?' she asked Kirsty with a
distracted smile, her eyes never leaving her work.

'I think so.'

'Good. Last thing want is to be responsible for the first
work of Charles Rennie Mackintosh to be newly discovered in
decades, hanging squint.'

My pal, Charlie. Kirsty grinned as she recalled his startled
expression when she shouted at him outside the tea room. The
drawings were abstract, shapes and lines that somehow
conjured an image beyond their form. Kirsty stepped back to
take them all in, and her eyes widened as realisation prickled
over her. 'They were—just found, did you say?'

The woman nodded, her eyes shining with awe. 'In an
attic in a house in London where he and Margaret
MacDonald lived for a while. Chelsea, think. It was owned
by the same family for decades, and nobody had ever bothered to look in any dusty corners. The last member of the
family passed away a few months ago, and some distant relative arranged for it to be cleared out to sell it. We all nearly
died when we got the call. It's incredible to imagine what
else there might be hidden in cellars, wardrobes, and attics,
just waiting for somebody to stumble across it. I just *itch* at

the thought of what more there may be yet to learn about
him.'

'He was always late,' Kirsty blurted before she could stop
herself.

'I beg your pardon?

'*Kirsty*—' Nathan hissed.

Kirsty tore herself away with an apologetic smile.

'He was always late,' she repeated with a wink and scuttled
after Nathan. The woman stared after her as though she had
two heads.

A small door in the wood panelling led to a claustrophobi-
cally cramped spiral staircase winding down into the bowels of
the library. There was a cool heaviness in the air, and Kirsty
had to duck under several low beams. Finally, Nathan turned
into a small, cramped room stuffed with files and papers. A
neat wee woman with a dark grey bob, thick glasses and a
hand-knitted jumper looked up with a smile.

'You must be Nathan's cousin, Kirsty.' She held out a
hand. 'I'm Maureen. I've been looking forward to meeting
you.' Maureen's handshake was firm. She gestured for Kirsty
to take a seat at the oak table.

'Nathan tells me you are interested in the murders.'

Kirsty glanced at Nathan. 'The Shadow murders.'

Maureen gave a tight smile. 'Well, this is the thing,' she
said. She industriously laid out a series of photocopies and
newspaper articles and notices. Each proclaimed a slayer on the
loose, warned ladies to stay indoors or announced another
victim found. Ice settled over Kirsty as she took them in.

'These—these go back a lot earlier than the sixties.'

'The earliest mention I have found is from 1190.'

'1190?' Kirsty stared. '*Eleven ninety?*'

'And every few years since.'

'I'm sorry, I don't understand—how could these murders
possibly go back *eight hundred years?*'

Maureen smiled, but there was tension behind her eyes. 'Don't worry. I've had nearly twenty years to get used to the idea, and I'm not much calmer about it than you are. My best guess is that there has been some sort of society or family passing down this abhorrent *mission*, for want of a better word.'

'But since 1190?'

'Outwith royalty, very few of us can trace our lineage nearly back that far—but it's not beyond the realms of possibility. We all necessarily must have ancestors going back to the dawn of humanity. It's just rare that we can identify them.

'Why don't we start from the beginning? I'll give you an overview of what I know, and we'll take it from there?'

Kirsty nodded, her head spinning.

'Right.' Maureen put on a pair of small wire-rimmed glasses, signalling she meant business. 'There was a market held in July of 1190 in the grounds of the then-brand-new Glasgow cathedral. It's the origin of the Glasgow Fair holiday. People from all over the city and surrounding areas came to trade, feast, and celebrate summer. There are very few written sources from the time, of course, but the monks were fairly diligent record keepers. I found three sources that refer to two women murdered during the fair. They were each strangled with their own stockings.'

Maureen pushed two of the documents closer to Kirsty. Kirsty glanced politely, knowing she had no hope of reading either the archaic language or the ancient script.

'There seems to be no pattern to the dates. The next murders are fifty years later, then none for almost three hundred, followed by a gap of a hundred-and-twenty. Each time, the killer appears as if from nowhere. Many accounts specify he is known to no one. Bear in mind these were times when communities were tight-knit, and relatively few people travelled—strangers were uncommon. This stranger murders two, three, or four women, and then he disappears. He is never caught.'

'But—these couldn't be random murders with coincidental similarities?'

Maureen shrugged. 'I can't prove anything for certain—well, not yet, at least, I'm working on it.' Her eyes sparkled with determination. 'A few years ago, I went to a conference in Washington, DC. There, I met a forensic profiler who had created a database that helped catch the serial killer Ted Bundy and is still used today.

'Until the seventies, when Bundy was at large, a killer could murder somebody in Seattle, then commit their next crime in Montana or somewhere. Each murder would be investigated by separate police forces who had no idea the other existed. So they created a national database that could identify potential serial killers. Details of crimes committed all over the country are inputted to the system. It analyses them and alerts if two or more may have been committed by the same person. Am I making sense?'

Kirsty had watched a billion true crime documentaries. VICAP was not new information to her.

'Anyway, this man kindly allowed me to run the details of these crimes through a simulation of this database. It came up with an almost 100% match of being committed by the same killer.'

'But it can't have been.'

'No, not literally,' Maureen grinned. 'Again, I suspect a society or family which passes down the details of the victimology and methodology. They recreate the crimes throughout history so closely that it is as though it is the same perpetrator.'

'Often the victims know one another?' Nathan prompted.

Maureen nodded. 'They are generally single women. Unmarried women tend to form closer social bonds than—'

'Single women?' Kirsty repeated in surprise. 'In those days?'

'If you only read media from today, you would be forgiven for thinking that the rise of the single woman is a twenty-first-century invention. Throughout recorded history, up to a third of all adult women have been unmarried in this country.'

'But how did they—survive? Could they work?'

Maureen smiled. 'Once upon a time, *Spinster* was a title that commanded respect. It meant a woman who earned her own living. Initially, it referred to spinning threads and fabric, later becoming more generalised. These women,' Maureen gestured to the pile of notices and newspaper articles, 'were midwives, herbalists, healers, seamstresses, maids, writers, governesses, teachers. Several of the victims had been accused of witchcraft.'

'Witchcraft?'

'You must remember that for many centuries women could be accused of witchcraft for many reasons. You're probably aware of the hysteria that swept Scotland under James VI —who became James of England. He believed witches had conjured storms to the North Sea when his queen sailed from Denmark. Throughout his life, he remained paranoid that he would suffer a violent death at the hands of witches.'

'Yet, it was Guy Fawkes and his crew who actually tried to kill him.'

'To be fair, James did turn his attention to Catholic conspiracies once he moved to London,' Maureen says dryly. 'But the great witch-hunt was well underway in Scotland. Around three thousand people, over eighty-five percent women, were tortured or executed for witchcraft in Scotland over the next hundred years or so. Officially, the witch-hunting practice ended in the mid-1700s, but that doesn't mean it never happened again. We may no longer torture with thumb-screws, but slut shaming has the same *energy*, as my nieces say.

A common theme throughout the accusations was women who spoke out angrily or argued. It could indeed be argued that an allegation of witchcraft was an effective way to shut a woman up.

'Interestingly,' Maureen continued, 'although the population was much more evenly spread throughout Scotland in those days, the vast majority of witch trials took place in the Central Belt, particularly Glasgow.'

'The women of Glasgow aren't known for keeping their opinions to themselves,' Kirsty said.

Maureen smiled. 'I wouldn't doubt that is a factor, but my personal theory relates to the weather.'

'The weather?'

'A widespread accusation against witches was that they raised storms to kill crops or flatten buildings, or otherwise wreak revenge on their enemies—'

'And if every time there is a storm in Glasgow, a woman is accused of witchcraft—'

'That's a lot of women accused of witchcraft,' Maureen finished with a rueful smile. 'The point is, these women may or may not have been literally magic.'

'But you believe they could have been?'

'I don't put any limits on what I will or will not believe. My research has taught me to be open to almost any possibility. I haven't found any definite proof of the existence of magic. But the absence of evidence is not evidence of absence.'

Kirsty thought of the woman she saw burning on Duke Street all those years ago. The woman who was in so much pain. There was a storm then, she remembered suddenly. She could picture the woman's hair whipped up by the wind as she screamed her curses. *Good*, Kirsty thought. *I hope she flattened the lot of them.*

Something else flickered at the edge of Kirsty's consciousness. Something about that scene—something about the people watching? Kirsty frowned, but it was gone.

'Of course, for the most part, we are talking long before there was any organised police force or the sort of criminal investigations we would recognise today.' Maureen turned her attention back to the murders. She pushed her glasses up her nose as she rummaged for the next document. 'And for many of the years we are dealing with, if a woman's husband or father didn't report her missing, she simply disappeared. None of these women had living husbands, so only those with fathers or brothers were reported missing.

'What I am saying is I believe the killings we have found sources for may be the tip of the iceberg.'

Exactly what Kirsty had thought the other night in town. 'There is something so particularly horrible about the fact he uses their own tights,' she said with a shudder. She remembered Rita McLeod describing Jetta laughing at something the killer said. 'It's so intimate.'

Maureen took her glasses off and rubbed the bridge of her nose. 'I have a diary here—' She pushed more photocopies across the table. 'It belonged to Jeanette Murray, who was murdered in 1797. She was upper class and grew up in one of the mansions that lined the Saltmarket. She was highly educated for her time and a great fan of Mary Wollstonecraft, who wrote extensively on women's rights and how our Achilles heel will always be the love of men.

'Jeanette herself was a published novelist. Her tales of high society in Georgian Glasgow were quite popular. Unfortunately, her father ordered her books out of print upon her death, so she was forgotten. I believe she may have influenced Jane Austen, who was just starting to write in the 1790s.

'Regency England had a great deal of cultural fascination with Scotland. Many young people who fancied themselves fledgling literary minds were sent to live with Highland relatives for a year or two to experience the poetic wilds of the north. For example, Mary Shelley lived with family friends in Dundee, and Lord Byron grew up in Aberdeen.

'I believe the inspiration for the dashing hero of Jeanette's books was a man named Archibald Gillespie, the Earl of Kilsyth. He was a terribly handsome young man who grew up on the Saltmarket along with Jeanette. He abandoned their engagement to fight French revolutionaries. Jeanette was determined to find herself a replacement suitor before he returned to Scotland so that he wouldn't think she had been waiting for him. She writes in her diary that she would attend every ball, tea or luncheon until she was engaged.'

'And instead, she met her killer.'

'A tall, red-haired young man who spoke as though he were educated, according to her letters her sister wrote to the Lord Provost begging him for help.'

'You said she lived on the Saltmarket?'

Maureen nodded. 'Each victim from 1190 onwards appears to have met her killer within the oldest area of Glasgow, a village once known as Cathures.'

'That's where the cathedral and the Royal Infirmary are?'

'More or less—and down the High Street as far as Glasgow Green.'

'So the Barrowlands is smack dab in the middle of the hunting ground.'

'The sixties murders, the ones that the press called The Shadow murders, were the first to take place in the era of modern policing and media interest. Therefore, we know the most about those. I've approached the detectives who worked on it—only two are still alive, but they have steadfastly refused to speak to me for several years.

'One of the things that particularly frustrates me is the erratic nature of the dates of the murders,' Maureen continued. 'Try as I might, I just can't discern any pattern. Suppose it were every hundred years. I might be tempted to conclude that it relates to some kind of anniversary. I've searched for any conditions in common, heatwaves or particular constellations or planets in view. But if there is a reason why the murders happen when they do, I've not found it.'

TWENTY-NINE

It was one of those afternoons where the sun is scorching, but the air is Baltic when it goes behind a cloud. Kirsty found the Hokey Cokey of *taps aff* and taps on again exhausting. She sat in the garden, searching for anything she on the detectives who investigated the Shadow murders in the sixties.

Iain Kinnoch was a young uniformed officer when Jetta was murdered and was promoted to detective after the team expanded when Nan died. He now lived in a care home in a village just outside Glasgow. Kirsty crossed her fingers as she dialled.

'Hello?' It was a woman's voice, warm with a Caribbean accent.

'Hello there, I was hoping to speak with, or ideally visit, one of your residents, Iain Kinnoch. Is it possible to—'

'Who are you?'

The woman's voice was suddenly sharp. Taken aback, Kirsty's mind went blank. 'I just wanted to speak to—'

'He doesn't talk to strangers. Mind your business.'

'It's nothing personal,' Kirsty said. 'It's to do with a case he worked on as a young man. I'm just trying to—'

'I know what it is about,' the woman snapped. 'It's always the same with you people. Leave the poor man alone. He never asked for any of this.'

'I'm sorry, didn't mean—'

'Vultures, every one of you.'

The line went dead. Kristy shivered but didn't bother putting her cardigan on again. The Shadow murders happened over fifty years ago—were there so many "vultures" ringing anymore?

Kirsty opened the folder where she had saved all the Shadow information and skimmed through several news articles. Not a single detective associated with the case had given a direct quote to the media since late 1967. Had some decree from the police force forbidden them from speaking to the press to quell the attention?

Several columns and opinion pieces heavily criticised the police's failure to catch him. One article described a demonstration by female Glasgow University students outside the Southern Police Office in the Gorbals after Nan's death. It wouldn't surprise Kirsty if the force wanted it to disappear. But would any such decree still apply decades after retirement?

Kirsty sighed and toyed with her phone, waves of frustration rippling through her. She didn't know what she was doing. What were they playing at? It was one thing imagining they could bring down a killer—but a family or organisation of them who have been at it for centuries? It was absurd.

Her head spun with everything Maureen said, but she couldn't see how any of it helped them catch the guy out there now. They must have a whole infrastructure, she thought sourly. The boys' club to end all boys' clubs. Alibis and safe houses and witnesses who just so happen to go on holiday forever. Harry said the suspect had never been caught with any of the victims on CCTV. Although they found plenty of DNA on the victims' bodies, it was meaningless without a match. How very *convenient*.

The early evening sun lay low in the sky, and nerves darted through Kirsty. She thought about the hundreds, maybe even thousands of women, all over the city, getting all dolled up right at that moment, ready for a wee night out. Straightening hair and applying lashes, lining lips. Gritting teeth to shove feet into fabulous, excruciating shoes that were too good a bargain to worry about buying the correct size.

They might be hoping for a wee flirt with somebody nice-looking with great chat. Or somebody okay-looking with middling chat. Or, funny-looking with no chat, but it was the end of the night, and you'd had a few, and maybe he'd turn out to have hidden depths.

Or maybe he'll turn out to be a serial killer.

All the while, that lanky ginger prowled the shadows, circling his hunting ground. Waiting for the games to begin. What if Kirsty was the only one who could stop him, and she didn't know how?

Frej came to sit by her. He was still carving that wee bit of wood. There was something strangely hypnotic about his focus. Kirsty put her phone down, pulled her knees up to her chest, and rested her head as she watched him work. He was entirely, contentedly engrossed for minutes and minutes and minutes. She couldn't remember the last time her attention held that long without her brain zapping off into some random argument from years ago, what she would have for lunch or being suddenly compelled to check social media.

Finally, Frej looked up and smiled. He smoothed a tiny ragged bit of wood with his thumb and held out the carving he had made. It was a rose. Each petal was picked out in intricate, loving detail that was delicate and vibrant. It took Kirsty's

breath away. Her eyes widened, and she mouthed *wow*, hoping
the sentiment would translate because it was spectacular. Frej
shrugged with a bashful grin.

'*Fagr,*' he said softly. *Fah-r.*

He pointed to the carving.

'Far?' she asked. Her heart raced, and she wasn't sure why.

'*Fagr,*' he repeated, pointing to the flower and then to
Kirsty.

His eyes crinkled as he smiled. A shiver of joy ran through
Kirsty. Her heart danced, her breath caught, and she had a
horrible feeling she was blushing as she grinned at him like a
loon. Suddenly the only things in the universe she was aware
of were his lips.

Her phone buzzed, and they both jumped. It was a text
from Rita. *Got in touch with Pat the Potman from the Barrowlands. He's happy to talk to you, and he's working tonight.*

Kirsty hadn't been to the Barrowland Ballroom since she saw
Alice Cooper in 1998. She was underage, with a shocking fake
ID that claimed she was 42, but enough makeup and cheek
that the bouncer never even asked to see it. She and Harry got
wired into the Buckfast the minute they arrived. Kirsty passed
out and slept through the whole gig, so she'd still never seen
Alice Cooper. He had a brilliant support act, though, an all-
girl punk band from down south. They were worth the ticket
price alone, so it was all good.

She was pleased to see that nothing had changed about the
legendary venue. Other than the smell of smoke being replaced
by the smell of toilet. And the fact she wouldn't touch a drop
of Buckfast if you paid her. The tired grandeur was somehow
simultaneously faded and fired up into angry grunge.

The famous ceiling was chequered in some manner that
supposedly made the acoustics world-class. The disco ball was

still there, presumably a monument to dancing gone by. The ubiquitous gang of girls leapt around in front of the stage, their long hair ironed uniformly straight and cheekbones contoured to within an inch of their lives. A few older, hairy guys with bored expressions, grey stubble and well-worn leather jackets that screamed music journalist—watched disdainfully. A middle-aged couple bounced about with unselfconscious glee.

Some scruffy-haired indie boys were giving it laldy on the stage. There must be some kind of showcase affair, though Kirsty suspected this lot wouldn't be plucked into the dizzying heights of fame any time soon. They were gloriously terrible. All dull verses and screechy choruses about the kind of heart-break there was no way skinny wee arses like them could understand yet. Kirsty cringed as an amp emitted a piercing shriek that begged for mercy.

She, Nathan and Frej hung about the back, scanning the crowd for an elderly man who met the description Rita gave of Pat the Pot Man. She said he dyed his hair jet black and was known to wear silk smoking jackets like Hugh Hefner. Kirsty suspected he'd stand out in a crowd, but there was no sign of him.

'I'm gonna go talk to some people,' Nathan announced and disappeared.

Frej seemed fascinated by the throng, the screechy guitars, and the bass thudding from nearby speakers. He moved with the beat, his face lighting up with a grin as his hips—Kirsty would hesitate to use the word *gyrate*. But let's just say it would be much more sensible if she looked the other way.

The Rolling Stones played the Barrowlands in the early sixties. Kirsty remembered reading about it on some anniversary or other. She wondered if she could figure out how to peer into then and watch their set instead of the monstrosity currently murdering their guitars onstage. Sadly the Shadows stubbornly refused to appear on command.

'Scuse me?'

The young guy collecting empty glasses looked around with the practised patience painfully recognisable to anyone who'd worked with the public.

'Sorry to bother you, but you don't happen to know if Pat is due in tonight?'

'Who?'

'Old guy, been working here since the year dot. Apparently, he's got jet-black hair?'

'Oh aye, we just call him Old Yin.'

'Bet he loves that.'

The kid shrugged and grabbed another couple of pint glasses to add to the precarious pile wobbling up the entire length of his arm. 'Says he doesnae care as long as we don't call him late for dinner. Whatever that means.'

'Is he in tonight?'

'Fuck knows. Comes and goes as it pleases him.'

'See if you see him—'

'Aye, aye—' The kid dismissed Kirsty with a wave and disappeared into the crowd.

The torturous set ended, and the indie boys bowed as though they'd just played Wembley. They bounced around the stage and spread their arms to accept the non-existent adulation. Kirsty couldn't help but wonder if a bit *too* much self-esteem had been instilled in the youth of today.

When they finally vacated the stage, a guy wandered on alone. Kirsty figured he was crew—or indeed just lost. He was barefoot, wearing battered jeans and a moth-eaten T-shirt, and generally appeared to have just rolled out of bed and onto the stage. A few whoops and hollers broke the silence. Even Frej seemed to have picked up on the new energy that zinged in the air.

The kid hadn't played a note, yet there was something about how he ambled around the stage. He dragged a stool to the mic and casually adjusted the height as though he had all the time in the world. He belonged up there. He owned it.

He perched on the stool, and after a moment's contemplation, he began to play a hypnotic rhythm. Slow at first, then building, almost excruciatingly slowly. Kirsty felt it thrum through her bones, harmonising with her heartbeat. Then he began to sing.

She had expected some kind of reggae or hip-hop, but this was blues. Real blues. *Old blues.* Blues that do deals with the devil on dusty Alabama crossroads. His voice was deep, throaty, and soulful—and had no business coming out the mouth of a skinny toerag from Glasgow. It filled the space with a heartrending story of loss and loneliness. It held the ironed hair gang, the cynical journos, the bouncy middle-aged couple in its thrall.

It was nothing short of phenomenal, and Kirsty felt honoured to experience it. Frej was mesmerised. A Viking with a mancrush was a sight to see.

The kid's set might have been six minutes or six hours. When the last note finally died in the air, it was as though the audience woke up from the kind of collective trance that princesses are prone to in fairytales. There was a heavy silence as they processed the loss of that final note, and then they erupted in a feral roar of screams and cheers, applause and stamping.

The skinny toerag nodded awkwardly and scuttled off the stage. Kirsty turned to grin at Frej. Her mouth went dry as she spotted him coming up the stairs.

Him.

The lanky ginger. The Shadow.

She blinked, unable to accept it for a second, but there was no mistaking him. Lanky. Ginger. Tick.

He placed a cigarette back in a silver holder, his neat grey suit tailored impeccably. He met Kirsty's gaze for an instant, and the coldness in his eyes sent ice seeping through her veins.

They were empty. Bleak. Blank voids where warmth, compassion, and love should be.

Kirsty squeezed Frej's hand and nodded. He casually moved towards our guy. She scanned urgently for Nathan to alert him, but the crowd was packed. There was no sign of him. *Shit.*

She was scared to lose The Shadow, so she joined Frej, and they fell into step on either side of their prey. He faltered, glanced from Kirsty to Frej—then he swerved backwards, swung around, slid down the metal bannister and clattered out the door.

Fuck.

They chased, but neither of them quite managed his slick bannister move, so he got a head start. He had just disappeared onto the Gallowgate when they reached the doors. They belted after him down the road, across the High Street in a hail of angry honks and slammed brakes, dodging crowds along the Trongate, then they swerved left down King Street.

The streets weren't too busy on a weeknight, but they scattered a crowd of skinny-jeaned guys, and Frej nearly got battered by the walking stick of an old lady he startled. The Shadow sprinted over the bus station, past the Clutha pub and onto the bridge, Frej and Kirsty in hot pursuit. *You'll regret straying onto my territory*, she thought in satisfaction as they hit the South side of the river.

Sure enough, a few more zigzags around quiet streets, and Kirsty spotted two of Agnes's old associates hanging about outside the Laurieston pub. Old Mick and Wee Mick, the discrepancy of which bothered Kirsty more than it should for many years.

'Can you not be Big Mick,' she would ask Old Mick with an earnest smile.

They'd be standing sentry outside the flat as those in debt to Agnes queued up to pay their weekly fealty. Kirsty always sat outside with the Micks. She hated being in the flat, hearing grown adults sob and beg.

'Ah'm no' big, but—,' Old Mick would wheeze. He'd had chronic emphysema since his twenties, but it never seemed to hold him back. 'He's just awfa' wee.'

'Then you be young Mick.'

Wee Mick had a snuffly laugh on account of him having no teeth. Agnes paid for him to get falsies because she said he was showing her up gurning about the place like a plague victim. He said they hurt, so he never wore them.

'Long time since I've been young, darlin',' he'd wheeze.

'Mick!' Kirsty bellowed now from across the street. 'Him—'

That was all she needed to say.

Old Mick smashed his nearly full pint glass against the side of the pub and bottled The Shadow in the face. The Shadow screamed, shrill with rage and pain. He clutched his face, trying to hold it together.

Frej grabbed him, flung him over his shoulder and looked expectantly at Kirsty for instructions. The Shadow wailed, blood splattering the pavement. A police car screeched by, siren wailing, but the occupants either didn't notice or didn't have time to care. A young guy in a tracksuit leaned against the pub door, smoking, entirely unconcerned.

A bit stunned, Kirsty hesitated, trying to catch both her breath and her thoughts. Or at least one or the other.

'He should lean his head back,' the smoking guy observed mildly as The Shadow yowled.

'That's a nosebleed, ya tube,' laughed Wee Mick. 'No' a fuckin' Glesga smile.'

Blood poured through The Shadow's fingers. He needed a hospital. Kirsty thought about wee Morag, lying in that gloomy lane all on her own on a frosty night, her tights knotted around her neck. If this evil bugger wanted stitches, he could whistle for them.

'You owe me a pint, doll,' said Old Mick.

THIRTY

'I looked for you for ages—' Nathan strode furiously up the garden path. 'I found Pat, and you were gone—'

'We've got him,' Kirsty blurted

'What?'

'Him.' She nodded towards the garden shed where Frej dumped The Shadow. Bangs and thuds sounded from inside. 'We've got him.'

'You're saying the killer is in there?'

'I'm sorry we didn't find you. We would have lost him.'

Nathan's eyes narrowed. He stared at the shed containing his daughter's murderer. 'What are we going to do with him?'

'I tried phoning Harry, but he's not answering.'

'You want to turn him over to the police?'

'I don't know. I suppose that's the right thing, but.... '

'But?'

'But he doesn't exist now. Maybe they can still arrest him without ID, I've no idea, but at best, they could only charge him with three crimes, and that's if they get the evidence we know they don't have. We know he is responsible for at least six.'

'At *least*.'

'He could press charges against us.'

Kirsty gestured to the shed, and the blood splattered on the garden path from his shredded face. The impact of what she was saying settled heavily in her, curdled in her guts. 'There won't be justice that way.'

'So what do we do with him?' There was a hardness in Nathan's voice.

'The white light,' she said. She started to shudder, but she gritted her teeth. She had no time to be a fanny now. She could break down later when she had cleared some space in her diary. 'I've thought about it, and it's the only solution.'

Kirsty had rehearsed this wee speech a hundred times in her head as they waited for Nathan, but even so, saying it out loud gnaws at her. 'I'll turn him to dust.'

'You can live with that?'

Frej reached over and covered her hand with his. She was fairly sure he'd gathered the gist.

'I don't know.' Her voice caught in her throat, and she forced herself to breathe slowly. 'But I'm going to do it anyway.'

The garden was still and silent, as though nature held its breath. An almost full moon cast a silvery glow over them. The sky was alive with stars.

'No one will ever know,' Nathan said. 'He'll disappear, just like he did in the sixties.'

'No more women will die. At least, not from him.' Kirsty forced a wobbly smile. 'The moon is our only witness.'

Nathan looked up. The velvety black sky was alive with stars, the full moon glowing a dazzling silver. 'She'll keep our secrets,' he said.

Frej nodded at the moon and whispered something in his language.

'Do you know how to do it?' Nathan asked.

'Not really. It's only ever happened in the heat of the moment. But if we open the door, he'll go for me and I think it will come.'

'And if it doesn't?'

'Then feel free to step in before he kills me.'

'Okay.' Nathan nodded. 'Let's do this.'

He went to the shed door. Kirsty and Frej got to their feet. Frej backed off a few steps, confirming he had an idea of what was happening. He stared at her intently. He muttered something under his breath that might be some kind of prayer. Kirsty forced a wobbly smile, and he gave a *thumbs up.*

Nathan took hold of the rusty old bolt on the shed door and hesitated. For a horrible moment, Kirsty worried he'd make some big heartfelt speech about the scales of justice and how The Shadow needed to answer to a higher power for what he's done. They had about three seconds left before Kirsty lost her nerve.

A determined look flashed across Nathan's face. He kicked the lock off the door, and the serial killer burst out, fuelled by adrenaline and hatred.

Kirsty didn't get the chance to draw breath before he lunged at her, fury raging in his eyes like fire on ice. Terror shot through her like lightening—*it's not going to work, I don't know what to do, there's no time—*

Then she raised her hands. The white light shot from her fingers with a sharp crack. The Shadow howled with twisted pain, drew back—

But he was still there.

He was still fucking there.

How wasn't he dust?

He came at Kirsty again. Frej swooped in from behind, grabbed him by the scruff of his neck and held him about half a foot off the ground by his own tie. There was no way Frej knew, but there was delicious poetry in watching that scourge of humanity gurgle and choke, just like his victims. He kicked his legs, pathetically flailing.

'No fun being strangled, is it?' Kirsty sneered.

The Shadow glared, his gasps hoarse and tortured as Frej twisted his fist slowly to tighten the noose.

'I think this is what they call the shoe being on the other foot. How do you like it?'

Kirsty nodded at Frej to loosen his grip fractionally.

'I say, I've had quite enough of this,' The Shadow spluttered, and Kirsty laughed. His accent was indeed refined. Not quite English, but it was a voice of family ski trips and board games, roaring fires and riding horses. 'I don't know what you mean by all this chasing me and locking me up, but I won't have it. If you don't let me go at once, I shall telephone the police.'

'Will ye fuck?' Kirsty snapped.

Only a posh white guy would have the cheek to think he was in a position to issue orders. He had half a face left and was dangling a foot off the ground by his tie. Frej looked at Kirsty, asking permission to break his neck.

She hesitated.

It was stupid. She had been willing to turn him to dust, but somehow, that was—*magic.* It wasn't quite real. Breaking an actual human body was—

She needed to work herself up to that one.

'Just—give me a sec,' she muttered, revulsion dripping over her.

''He killed Morag,' Nathan said.

That was one vote in favour, then.

Kirsty turned to The Shadow. 'What's your name?'

He was staring at Nathan. A slow grin spread over his face. 'Oh, you're friends of Morag's?' he sneered. 'Feisty filly, that one. She put up quite the fight both times. I do like her.'

'I asked you a question.'

'I've given her much thought over the years.' His grin turned lascivious, and he sniggered. 'A great deal of *personal* thought. She is quite the woman.'

Pure, acidic rage rose in Kirsty like bile. Was this fucker telling her he *wanked* over her gran's murder? She could barely breathe for loathing. Frej waited for the signal.

'Your name,' Kirsty spat through gritted teeth. 'You're so bloody proud of yourself. Tell us who you are.'

The Shadow grinned and cocked his head to one side, his eyes glittering like black diamonds. 'They called me Owen once,' he whispered.

Kirsty nodded to Frej. 'Kill him.'

Frej snapped Owen's neck with his bare hands. The sickening crack echoed through the still night. Kirsty's breath caught, and her stomach twisted as Frej dropped him. He crumpled to the ground like a used tissue. Kirsty clamped her hand over her mouth to stop herself from screaming when—

'Cooee!'

A woman's head appeared above the high red brick wall and Kirsty nearly puked with horror. She was probably fifty or so. Her steel grey hair was pulled into an elegant chignon that made her look like she should be sipping a cappuccino in Paris.

Instead, she perched on a ladder—it must have been a ladder, the wall was a good seven, eight feet high—bearing witness to Kirsty and her pals bumping off a murderer in the middle of the night.

'You must think we're so rude!' the woman trilled as Frej swiftly rolled the broken body into an unruly rose bush.

'We've been meaning to have you in for a wee glass of wine for I don't know how long, but with the children's exams, then my husband was in New York—he's in banking, you see.' She rolled her eyes as though indulging her husband's daft wee hobby. 'So he's forever nipping back and forth, you know what it's like. I really think the jet lag can't be good for him, but you can't tell them, can you? Is this your husband?'

She blinked expectantly at Nathan.

'He's my cousin,' Kirsty said quickly. 'From the States. Near Chicago.'

'Oh, we've been to Chicago,' she gasped. 'We loved all the, you know, the cow statues in the streets. Neil, that's my husband, well he just thought they were marvellous. I mostly shopped till I dropped. It's not New York, but you make do, don't you? Listen, I don't mean to bother you this late. You'll be wanting your beds. It's just I was out watering the peonies. You have to wait until the sun has gone or else they'll just scorch, poor darlings.'

'No, we can't have that.' Kirsty's voice sounded shrill in her ears, but the woman didn't seem to notice.

'I heard you out here and thought to myself, I just couldn't let one more moment go by without saying hello.'

'We were rehearsing a play,' Kirsty blurted. 'Well, a skit, really. It's for a family reunion. That's why Nathan's come over.'

'How smashing!' The woman clapped her hands together in glee. 'I do a bit of am-dram myself now and then. I'm your gal if you ever want to chat treading the boards.'

'Yes, we'll come for gin and tonics,' Kirsty shouted like a demented robot. 'But we have to get to bed now. Nathan is very tired because of the jet lag.'

She rolled her eyes merrily. 'My Neil is a martyr to jet lag, so I know what it's like. I'll leave you to it. Night, night.'

'Sweet dreams,' Kirsty half screeched.

The woman finally disappeared down the ladder. Kirsty didn't know if she wanted to cry, laugh, or puke.

Frej ushered them towards the house, evidently intending to take care of the body himself. Kirsty shook her head because they were in this together. She didn't get very far articulating her argument when she heard a noise from the rose bush that chilled her to the core.

Another crack.

They turned to find Owen on his knees by the rose bush, snapping his head back into place as though fixing a dislocated shoulder. He grimaced and groaned, then looked up with a manic grin. The congealing blood across his face glistened in the moonlight.

'Will people STOP doing that,' he screeched.

In one fell swoop, he vaulted over the garden wall and was gone.

THIRTY-ONE

'No.' Frej reached for Kirsty, but she backed away. 'No. I just need to—no.'

She wasn't going to chase Owen. She would have no hope of catching him even if she wanted to. But she couldn't breathe. She needed to get away. She needed to be alone.

Frej took a step as though to follow her. She shook her head, and he stopped, concern swimming in his eyes.

'Kirsty—' Nathan began. 'Let us at least—'

'I'll be back,' Kirsty stammered. 'Promise. I just need—just need a wee minute.'

She ran. Around the side of the house and onto the road. Her trainers slapped against the pavement as she sprinted through the silent night, passing sleeping houses, bars, and shops shrouded in darkness.

She ran faster and faster, desperately trying to find that rhythm that cleared her mind. Her lungs burned, and her legs trembled, but she pounded on and on. She swerved left, then right, vaulting over the railing around Queens Park as though it were nothing, then raced up the path to the flagpole. A swan hissed at her and a dog's bark echoed in the moonlight. She leapt onto the platform around the flagpole from the path below, clearing at least three metres straight up.

Kirsty drank in the view as she caught her breath. Her brain whirred like a possessed waltzer. Half-thoughts, snatches of feeling, fragments of horror zipped and sizzled and seared across her mind. The white light and the crack of Owen's spine snapping back into place rattled around and around until Kirsty was dizzy.

What was he?

What was she?

The city spread out before her, lights twinkling in the blackness. The Campsies barely an outline against deep purple clouds. Her city. A city that had ricocheted from poverty to riches and back again; that was famous for being one of the friendliest and most dangerous places in the world. A cultural capital of Europe that had an outbreak of bubonic plague in the twentieth century. A city riddled with vibratey time holes and lepers who play *Simon Says* with wee girls and maniac serial killers who can't be killed.

A strange, icy sense of calm enveloped Kirsty. She looked up, and the stars were dazzling, celestial fireworks twinkling a hundred colours, filling her with awe and strength. The night was still, but a gust of wind swirled around her, whipping up her hair, whispering something she couldn't catch.

A glittering sound crackled, like a fire that had almost burnt itself out, leaving only red-hot coals to shimmer and snap. The air itself was alive, fizzing with magic.

Kirsty thought of Mrs McCafferty's words. *Just focus on the next step.* Could she do that? A fox screeched in the dark.

The Shadow had gone to the Barrowlands that evening to find another victim. *Owen.* Kirsty pictured him coming up the stairs, all smooth and suave in his tailored suit and his silver cigarette case.

He might have been running his victim's tights through his fingers right now, slowly approaching as she cowered in terror. He might have been displaying her body, ready for some poor bugger to stumble across in the morning. Instead, he was hiding somewhere in the dark, trying to put his face back together. *That was something.*

They hadn't won the war. Kirsty wasn't even sure what the war *was* yet. But they won a wee battle.

The gates at Victoria Road were locked, but she vaulted them without missing a beat and wound her way through Govanhill towards home. She passed the bus stop where she once winched a boy called Scott, who insisted on sticking his tongue in her ear, and it had sounded like a washing machine. She passed the wall where she knocked Harry's front teeth out, playing with a great big pole the night before he was supposed to play Joseph in the school nativity play.

She passed a row of small brick sheds behind Agnes's tenement. They were once outside toilets, then middens, and now bike shelters. Once upon a time, Kirsty would climb onto their jaggy tiled roofs and sit curled in a wee ball, counting to a hundred over and over.

Mrs McCafferty's flat was shrouded in darkness. Kirsty was more confident than she wanted to be that Mrs McCafferty wasn't tucked up in bed with her curlers in. She leapt lightly onto the stone windowsill under Mrs McCafferty's front window.

Mrs McCafferty was—something. She was connected to all of this, somehow. The way she ran when she saw Kirsty coming. The portrait of her from the 1800s. The way Owen leapt over a seven-foot wall without missing a beat. They were —whatever they were, they were the same thing.

And Mrs McCafferty was the last person to see Morag alive.

Except for Owen.

Kirsty crouched on the cool stone. She placed her hands on the glass and pressed firmly upwards. There was nothing to get a handhold on outside the window, but—

Kirsty felt the pressure of the lock above, then she felt it give way. The sash window flew open with a clatter and Kirsty cringed. She would make a rubbish cat burglar.

She heard a faint noise in the close. Someone was approaching the front door. Without thinking, Kirsty reached the top of the sash window. She pulled herself up and stepped onto the stone ledge above the door. It was barely centimetres wide, but it was just enough for a toehold. She clung to the rough, red sandstone, bracing one foot against the bay window behind.

She would think about the fact she was basically clinging to the side of the building like an insect some other time.

Mrs McCafferty stepped into the night. She wore a black polo neck and slim black trousers. Her white hair tucked under a black beret reminded Kirsty of Audrey Hepburn in a movie Morag used to love. She walked nimbly up the road in the direction of town.

Too nimbly. It was after 4 a.m. Mrs McCafferty was hardly away to meet her pals at Bingo. Kirsty held onto the narrow ledge to drop lightly onto the front step. Then she started to follow.

They cut up Crown Place and onto the Old Rutherglen Road before joining Crown Street. They crossed the inky black river shimmering in the moonlight and reached the edge of Glasgow Green. Mrs McCafferty headed north. *Towards the Barrowlands.*

The venue would be long closed by now. Was there a late-night meeting of the bionic freak murdery club? Kirsty wasn't sure if she could handle any more Owen in one night.

But she kept following Mrs McCaftery.

Just to see where she's going. She would watch, what she could, from a distance. Then she would come back with Frej and Nathan tomorrow.

There had been an event on at the Green. The grass was ankle-deep in rubbish. As they wandered up the road, a small hoard of happy, drunk youths yowled a tuneless rendition of something or other.

Mrs McCafferty was moving at a brisk walk, quickly enough to cover ground but not so fast as to attract attention. Mrs McCafferty seemed focussed, even tense. She wove her way through the inebriated young people and occasional sober pedestrian, intent on getting where she was going.

As they approached the Trongate, a cloak of inky blackness draped over the city. Prickles of fear crept down Kirsty's spine. She looked around, every sense on high alert. The air grew icy. Candles flickered in lanterns lighting the way up to Glasgow Cross.

The lift-stopping-too-fast feeling washed over Kirsty. She shivered, fear scuttling over her, but she didn't turn back. She reached for a bus stop to steady herself and smothered a scream when it evaporated under her fingers.

A horse snorted, its breath misty in the night air. The clip-clop of its hooves echoed on the cobblestones as it pulled a small hooded buggy up the hill. Kirsty felt her way slowly forward, her heart thudding in her ears.

The soft lanterns barely pierced the shadows, but Kirsty sensed people around her. She heard coughs and farts and smelled the odd whiff of stale sweat or tobacco breath. Horror curdled in her guts.

A horrific thwack resounded through the still night. It was followed by a painful grunt and crack, then a low rumble of jeers. Kirsty's blood ran cold. The man was hanging from wooden gallows, just in front of where the Tollbooth pub was a moment ago or several hundred years from now.

The night was freezing and clear. The man was silhouetted by moonlight as his body jerked agonisingly under a rough hemp hood. A line of soldiers stood beneath him. Redcoats and black tricorn hats were only just discernible in the dark. Their bayonets were drawn.

The hanging man writhed and twisted, his choking gurgles ringing through the air. The hangman's rope was designed to break the neck and cause instantaneous death. But if it went wrong, the prisoner was condemned to minutes and minutes of excruciating strangulation.

Instinctively, Kirsty moved forward. The lift-stopping-too-fast feeling got stronger. The air itself seemed to close in on Kirstyand she had to fight for breath. The soldiers' laughter echoed around her.

She couldn't see them clearly. They were Shadows, drifting in and out of the ether, their laughter distorted, bayonets taking form and fading. It was real but not real. It was now but also then. She was inside a Shadow.

She could feel and smell and hear the horses, the soldiers and the hanging man, but when she looked down, her trainers were on modern pavement. She blinked, and she could see the red paint of the Tollbooth pub glowing through a red coat. Black plastic rubbish bags glistened under orange streetlights beneath the gallows.

A crack split the sky. White light flashed through the air, and the hanging man crumbled to dust. The soldiers' shocked, terrified calls filled the air as their formation scattered. Kirsty stumbled backwards—

And crashed into the bus stop.

She clutched at the plastic pole as the pressure eased in her chest. Big, gulping breaths of manky city air with a strong note of old rubbish and a touch of urine were a sweet relief. She staggered onto the wee bench and sat a moment, leaning over her knees, catching her breath.

A bus pulled up, the door opening with a clang and a hiss. The driver sighed, tutted grumpily when he saw she wasn't boarding and pulled out again. An ambulance roared by, with no siren but blue light flashing urgently. A drunk guy sang a heartfelt howl of a cartoon theme tune from somewhere just out of sight.

The white light. That was the white light. The same one Kirsty had. The same one that didn't bloody work on Owen a few hours ago. It worked on the hanging man. He crumbled to dust, just like the boar and the Viking.

Was it Mrs McCafferty?

Kirsty put her face in her hands and rubbed her weary eyes. She didn't know anything. She started out this evening knowing nothing, then hunners of mad shit happened, and somehow she now knew even less. She was trembling, half from fear and overwhelm and half from exhaustion and hunger. It had been a long bloody night.

It was dawn. The light was grey and pale, and a rubbish truck mades its noisy way up the back lanes. A couple of young lassies in nurses' uniforms came out of the 24-hour Tescos, munching filled croissants. Kirsty's stomach grumbled. She would get a breakfast roll before she did anything else.

'Gonnae gies a pound for a wee drink?'

The guy staggered back and forth as though on an invisible boat, filthy tracksuit and sores on his neck suggesting he didn't take as good care of himself as he should. 'Jist a pound, tha's aw need. Jist a wee drink,' he wheedled.

'I've not got my wallet on me, pal,' Kirsty said sympathetically. He looked as though he could do with a wee drink.

'Aye, no bother,' he replied agreeably enough. He stopped suddenly and jerked as though he'd heard something. Kirsty froze, waiting for Mrs McCafferty to come flying round the corner on a giant glowing bat and zap them both to kingdom come. The guy pointed two fingers at her.

'You have a good time, pal,' he commanded and wandered off into the night.

THIRTY-TWO

The breakfast roll revived Kirsty, so she started walking. Dr Solveig Ljotrsdóttir never replied to her email, but Kirsty needed somebody, somehow, to explain something. If that something was the Icelandic language, then so be it.

Office workers streamed out of Central Station, yawning over takeaway coffees. Night shift workers dozed on the bus home. Kirsty marched up Buchanan Street to Bath Street, over the motorway. Past the library where Maureen was probably hard at work and into the leafy West End.

Even at this early hour, it promised to be a scorcher. There was a party atmosphere in the artisan café in Finneston, where she grabbed a fancy coffee. She passed Kelvin Hall and headed along the grand, tree-lined boulevard that divided the university and Kelvingrove park, then up the hill into the university grounds.

Grey, modern extensions built from concrete were spread all over the hill. Giant yellow diggers and orange barriers stretched all the way to Byres Road, suggested more to come. But the heart of the university was the imposing, gothic stone

square that dated, at a conservative estimate, from hunners of
years ago.

'Hello? knocked, but there was no answer.' Kirsty opened the
door gingerly and peeked in. 'Sorry to disturb you, but I'm—'

The cramped office was gloomy. It was lit only by a tiny,
frosted window and a small lamp with a dark green shade.
Kirsty blinked as her eyes adjusted. She took in the floor-to-
ceiling bookcases, every square millimetre of space crammed
with books, papers, and files. A bronze, jewelled dagger sat
casually on a shelf atop some dusty, leather-bound books next
to what looked horribly like a human skull.

'I did not say enter.'

'I beg your pardon?'

'You knocked but did not wait for me to invite you to
enter.'

The woman sat in an old-fashioned wooden desk chair.
On the large mahogany desk in front of her was spread what
Kirsty could only describe as parchment, yellowing and
tattered. Kirsty spied a few symbols that reminded her of Frej's
tattoos, and her heart leapt.

Dr Solveig Ljotrsdóttir was tall, her strawberry blonde
hair pulled back in a messy bun. She wore a chunky, dark blue
jumper, frayed and moth-eaten, over a long tweed skirt and
lace-up ankle boots. She looked like an extra in some Victorian poverty-porn film and must be boiling in this weather.
Yet somehow, the woman's unnerving gaze made Kirsty feel
like she was the oddly dressed one in her jeans and leather
jacket.

'Oh—wasn't sure if—just thought that—'

Solveig gestured to the parchment. 'You have disturbed
me.'

'Wow—what is that?'

The faintest outline of some kind of map was drawn in a fine, shaky hand, surrounded by symbols.

'My work.'

Dismissing Kirsty, Solveig turned back to the desk. She picked up a magnifying glass.

'What are those symbols?'

Solveig ignored her.

'It's just that my friend has similar tattoos. I was wondering—'

'I don't think so. Close the door on your way out.'

'Look, get that you've got your work to do. I'll wait until you're finished, but I'm not going anywhere.'

'My work will never be finished.'

'You'll need the toilet at some point.'

Solveig stared impassively.

'I really need your help.'

'Why should I care? I do not need yours.'

'It's a bit difficult to explain. People are in danger.'

'People are always in danger. It is the nature of life.'

'I need to learn some Icelandic. Urgently. Aren't you an Icelandic teacher?'

'Amongst many things.' The tiniest flicker of interest sprang to life in Solveig's deep blue eyes. 'I have never heard of an urgent need to learn Icelandic.'

'I need to be able to understand somebody. He can't speak English.'

'A man.' With a smirk, Solveig turned away again.

'Yes, but not like that.'

Well, not entirely like that. Kirsty's face grew hot, and she was glad of the shadowy office.

An email pinged on Solveig's laptop. The laptop looked incongruous amongst the parchment and the skull and whatnot. Kirsty was about to say so when she noticed that Solveig had paled.

Kirsty leaned over to look at the laptop screen. Solveig was watching a video of the Viking brawl from the other night. *Jeezo, folk were getting their arms broken, and some teapot was filming it for YouTube?*

'You must leave,' Solveig snapped.

'No, wait—that's why I need your help. Because of what's happening in that video.'

'I beg your pardon?' Her voice was like ice.

'I was there—let me show you—' Kirsty gestured to the laptop. 'May I?'

Solveig's eyes were cold, but after a moment, she nodded. Kirsty scrubbed through the video until she found a frame of herself. Axey Man was coming at her, and Frej stepped into his path, protecting her. Her stomach gave a flip. She hadn't noticed that happening at the time.

'That's me,' she said. 'These men—I need to know who they are and what they want with—'

There was a clatter as Solveig leapt to her feet so violently her chair nearly tipped over. She was as white as a sheet. She backed against the bookcases, her eyes never leaving the screen.

'How did—it's not possible. How is he—?'

With horror, Kirsty realised that Solveig's eyes had filled with tears. She clamped her hand over her mouth and shook her head. She was muttering to herself under her breath.

In the same language Frej spoke.

'Who are you?' Kirsty asked.

'My name is Solveig, daughter of King Ljotr of Børgin,' Solveig said finally. 'Wife to Halfdan the Fearless, shield-maiden and queen. Frej—Frej is my twin brother.'

THIRTY-THREE

'There was a thunderstorm as we sailed into the Clyde,' Solveig began that evening. She turned to Frej and asked in their language if he remembered. He nodded.

It was only a few days ago for him.

A chill was in the air, but Kirsty was toasty around the fire. They were into hamburgers Nathan barbecued. He might be determined to call them sandwiches, but the boy made a good burger. Kirsty had slept away most of the day but roused herself as evening fell to contribute corn-on-the-cob, marinaded with lime juice and chilli flakes the way she'd learned in Mexico once.

'A ferocious thunderstorm, which many of our people believed was the gods warning us away from the Celtic lands. But we were not coming to invade. We wanted to create a treaty between our lands in Dumbarton and the trading centres of Govan and Partick. Forces from Northumberland had been sighted deep in what is now the Borders. We felt that the northern peoples should band together for cooperation and protection.

'Today, people imagine those days were filled with mind-less violence and endless war, but we often negotiated first.' She smiled. 'Humans do best when they look out for each other. That is something I have learned.

'I saw a woman standing alone on the banks of the Kelvin River, just where it flows into the Clyde. I gave the command for the fleet to stop.'

'You mean where the Riverside Museum is now?'

'On the other side of the Kelvin. The near bank if you are coming from the sea.'

That was another decrepit lot. There were flats to the west, but the strip of land directly on the riverbank had been empty as far back as Kirsty could remember. *There was a reason they didn't build on the holes of Glasgow.*

Kirsty and Nathan stayed out of the twins' way earlier as they sat at the kitchen table, clutching one other's hands and catching up in their language. Kirsty didn't have siblings, but she knew what it was to lose family. She didn't mind admitting she'd become a bit misty-eyed when he bellowed with joy and grabbed Solveig in a bear hug that nearly knocked her off her feet. Now they were together, Kirsty could see the family resemblance in their long straight noses, reddish-blond hair and deep blue eyes.

'Ulf is an impetuous, hot-headed man. Our father was taken to Valhalla during the siege of Dumbarton. He left explicit instructions that Frej and I should jointly step into his place as leaders and that Ulf should remain war chief. Ulf was furious. He believed that he should have inherited the crown, and he took every opportunity to undermine Frej and me.'

'Crown?' Nathan repeated. 'You guys are royalty? Should we bow?'

Solveig smiled. 'Crown is somewhat metaphorical. Our father was called king, but we were such a small—tribe, suppose is the word, that his role was more like a mayor.' She grinned cynically. 'Or CEO, perhaps.'

'Wasn't it unusual for any crown to be passed to a daughter?' Kirsty asked. 'Wouldn't he have been expected to nominate only Frej as his successor?'

'My father understood that Frej and I have abilities that complement one another. Left alone, I am like Ulf, but Frej and I together are decisive and compassionate.

'Men and women in our culture took on roles according to individual ability. Of course, women were limited by pregnancy and breastfeeding, but gender was not the defining quality that determined one's purpose in life. If a woman had abilities that suited her for politics or battle rather than childbearing, that is what she did. That is what I did.'

She gave a dry smile. 'We had not invented the patriarchy yet.'

'So you are a queen?' Nathan pressed. He looked overwhelmed. He was of a generation that took forelock tugging to monarchy for granted.

'So to speak,' Solveig said. 'But every day was a struggle to maintain order when Ulf was determined to challenge us at every turn.'

'What does Ulf look like?' Kirsty asked.

'He is about the same height as Frej, with dark hair, and he wears a burgundy cloak.'

Axey Man.

'He was trying to kill Frej.'

Solveig nodded. Frej reached for a corn-on-the-cob and frowned at it, bemused. 'Frej told me. Frej had little chance of holding on to power against Ulf without me. He is too kind.'

'So he wasn't a human sacrifice? The fire, I mean.'

Solveig smiled. 'Frej believes Ulf may have persuaded the others that a sacrifice was necessary for their triumph in

Govan, so they were not tempted to object. His true intention, however, was to rid himself of Ljotr's son and heir.'

'You were already, uhh, gone by then?'

Solveig nodded. 'When I saw the woman alone by the banks of the Kelvin, I issued the order that we would camp there for the night. I wished to help her, but I also hoped the delay would allow me to persuade Ulf to proceed more cautiously. The King of Strathclyde was mighty at that time. Frej and I felt that a better outcome could be achieved by creating a treaty for trade and cooperation rather than attempting to invade.

'As we pulled our ships high on the shore, the woman approached me and begged for my help. She seemed desperate and terrified. Of course, I offered her protection, but she said she needed me to come with her. I agreed I would come once the ships were secure and camp was built.

'She took me by the hand and pulled me into the forest. I don't remember her hand leaving mine. I only know that a strange, vibrating sensation came over me—'

'Like a lift stopping too fast?'

'I did not have that frame of reference at the time, but yes. And then it was not raining any more. I tried to turn back to camp, but— it was gone. Everything I had ever known was gone.'

'You must have been terrified,' Kirsty said. The fire crackled and glowed, reflecting in Solveig's eyes. It almost seemed as though her hair was alight, and despite her thread-bare jumper and skirt, Kirsty could see the Viking warrior queen she was.

'I would not have survived without Lailoken. He lived in the forest, a wild man even in those days. I had made a fire, found berries and a rabbit for food, but the people would have killed me if I had ventured into the town dressed as was. He—' she smiled. 'He was like my tour guide. I owe him very much.'

Kirsty glanced at Frej, guilt trickling through her. He was a king, and now he was sitting in her garden munching charred corn on the cob with a confused frown. She didn't know if he understood that it was her fault. She didn't know if he would hate her when he found out.

'Lailoken was extremely powerful,' Solveig was saying. 'He could control wind, water, and fire like nobody else had ever seen. He was the real man that inspired the character Merlin from the King Arthur stories. He lived in the forests of Partick for many centuries.'

'Hold on a minute, what?' Kirsty asked. A giggle bubbled up in her. 'Merlin? Merlin the Magician? The old guy with the long beard and the poky hat?'

'That is the cartoon version of him, yes.'

Pure hysteria took over, and Kirsty was in stitches. The venerable sage who advised King Arthur and his Knights of the Round Table was some mad wee guy fae Partick. Her tummy ached, and she couldn't breathe. She curled over on the grass, howling. *Here, pal, you'll pure be king wan day, nae bother. Ah had a mad wee dream about it. Gies a tenner?*

The others had no idea what was so funny, but Kirsty's laughter was infectious. Soon they were all greetin', wiping tears from their eyes, clutching their sides.

Nathan was doubled over. Solveig held her tummy. Frej's deep chortle rumbled through the air as tears streamed down his cheeks.

'So, Lailoken helped me for many years,' Solveig continued before dissolving into another fit of giggles that set them all off again.

The sun lay low in the sky, bathing them in an orange glow. The fire gave off a cosy heat that drew them in close. *These people would notice if I disappeared for a year and three months.*

'You must remember that there were very few mirrors in

those days.' Solveig finally managed to pick up her story. 'And no clocks or calendars. It took me many years to realise that I had stopped ageing.'

'Wait—you didn't time travel?' asked Nathan. 'You have been alive this whole time?'

'You must be knackered.'

'We sailed into the Clyde two summers after our siege of Dumbarton, which has since been dated to approximately 870. During the harvest after Lailoken found me, he and I travelled to Cathures. They were building what would become Glasgow Cathedral. That was a little before 1200.'

'So you travelled four hundred years?'

Solveig nodded.

'And you have been alive ever since?'

'Yes. And yes, sometimes I am knackered.'

'What have you been doing for nearly a thousand years?'

'Many things,' Solveig said dryly. 'I have travelled. I have studied. I have survived. I have tried to learn what this is, what I am. What we are.'

A chill ran through Kirsty as she took in the implications. *We.* What they were.

'So is that what happens?' she asked slowly. 'You travel through, and then you stop ageing? Forever?'

Would Kirsty sit here in a thousand years, telling her story to some other wee idiot who had stumbled across all of this? Would she be alive in *a thousand years*? She could just imagine Morag telling one of her pals, *oh, that's Kirsty, taken that immortality. She's a pure martyr to it.*

'And we can't be killed?' she asked.

'We stop ageing, but some of us can be killed. Only in a particular way.'

'The white light?'

Solveig nodded. She rolled her eyes at her brother's attempts to eat the cob itself and gestured to him to put it down. Frej still looked hungry, so Kirsty handed him a packet of crisps.

'Exactly. I believe the white light undoes the spell that keeps us immortal. It transforms the person into their 'correct' age, so to speak.'

'So if they were born hundreds or thousands of years ago, they would be turned to dust,' Nathan said. 'I think that pig in the park was a boar. I looked it up. They've been extinct in Scotland since the thirteenth century, but they were likely to have been found in the grounds that became Queens Park.'

'I did it to one of the Vikings from the other night,' Kirsty said. 'I didn't mean to, but you must have known him. I'm so sorry—'

Something flashed in Solveig's deep blue eye. She looked warily at Kirsty. 'You have it?'

'Do—we don't all have it? It's not part of the—this whole thing?'

'No,' Solveig said shortly. She asked Frej something in their language, and he replied. Solveig nodded. 'Birger was an idiot,' she said. 'Don't worry about it.'

Oh well, as long as the guy Kirsty murdered was an idiot.

'I have seen others turn into skeletons or simply age for a few decades.'

'And then they just carry on their life as an older person?'

Solveig shrugged. 'The sudden ageing is traumatic to the body. Not everyone survives it.'

A cold, heavy feeling settled over Kirsty. She heard the reverberating crack as Owen snapped his neck back into place. 'But it doesn't work on everybody,' she said.

Solveig frowned and started to shake her head, but Nathan interrupted.

'Have you figured out what this is? The actual travelling part.'

He was still hoping to can get home and watch Morag grow

up. Kirsty's heart contracted with sadness. Her gut told her he was going to be disappointed.

Solveig was silent for a few moments, considering. 'The first reference to what may be a time hole comes from St Mungo.'

'My pal went to his school,' Kirsty interjected.

'Kentigern, or Mungo as he became known, lived to a very old age, especially for his time. At least his eighties or nineties. He witnessed a great deal of interesting history during his life. In his later years, somebody, we assume a priest or a monk in his order, wrote down his memories. I suppose we might call it a memoir today. It is called the Book of Kentigern.'

'I've never heard of it.'

'Hardly anybody has. Nobody is certain that it exists anymore if even it ever did. I suspect that the church hid it because it contained references to magic. Many of us believe that Mungo's grandmother was a witch.'

Long shadows danced on Solveig's face; for an instant, she looked as ancient as she was. Kirsty shivered. Frej moved closer, and Kirsty was grateful for his warmth.

'Over the centuries, I have met people who claim to have seen parts of the book or met others who did. I believe it was kept in a crypt on Iona for a time. But I have searched every inch of the island many times over for several centuries, to no avail.'

'Didn't your lot plunder Iona?'

'We did not usually steal books,' Solveig smiled dryly. 'One of the stories told by those who claim to have read the Book of Kentigern is a tale from when he was a small child. He describes how he witnessed a man disappear into thin air. He tried to go after him and felt a strong vibration as though he were standing inside a large bell. I believe that is what he meant when he spoke of a bell that never rang. He felt drawn forward into the vibration, but his mother pulled him back to safety just as a terrible storm blew up.'

'Wasn't his mother St Enoch?'

'She was called Teneu during her life.'

'I like her shopping centre. And you think *her* mother was —a witch?'

'It is a theory. But Teneu was known to survive two attempts to execute her while pregnant with Kentigern. At least two of the miracles attributed to him, creating fire with only words and bringing a bird back to life—these are things I have known witches to do. I understand Kentigern believed his grandmother created the vibration he felt, but I can't know more unless I find the book.'

Frej spoke up then, asking something in their language.

Solveig replied with a sad smile. 'He asked about my husband. Halfdan disappeared at the same time as me. He tried to follow the woman and me, calling after us, but when the rain stopped, he was also gone. I do not know what become of him.'

THIRTY-FOUR

olveig left shortly afterwards, and Nathan turned in. Kirsty suspected he was coming to the same conclusion about the irreversible nature of their travel and needed to be alone to take it in. Kirsty wasn't ready to sleep. A hundred million thoughts and questions careened around her brain.

Immortal. She couldn't wrap her head around the enormity of it. It wasn't exactly her style. She had always been more of a *live fast, die young* kind of gal. She'd never been one for eating her veg then tucking herself up with a good book at a reasonable hour.

She'd felt guilty for years, and it turned out it would have been a waste of time. Kirsty had spent a good thirty-odd years staying out all night, existing for weeks on toast and takeaways, dabbling in her fair share of pharmaceuticals. And now she was going to live forever.

Take that, vegan yoga nutters.

She hugged her knees close to her chest and buried her face in them. She had a horrible feeling that her vast array of cynical quips wouldn't get her through this one.

What would they *do* with all that time? What about climate change? Would the Earth explode in a fiery mass, killing off humanity, her, Frej, Nathan and Solveig cutting about a scorched planet ruled by cockroaches?

And Mrs Bloody McCafferty correcting their grammar.

Her chest felt tight. She was about to dive headfirst into a full-on panic attack when Frej tossed another log on the fire and sat next to her. They weren't quite touching, but Kirsty felt the presence of his solid warmth. She could breathe again.

She couldn't process what they might be doing in five hundred years, but she knew what they needed to do now. They needed to stop Owen. They needed to track down Ulf and the Vikings. Kirsty would *not* spend eternity waiting for Frej's psycho uncle to pop up with his axe every two seconds.

Warm shivers shot through her. Frej's hand lay right next to hers in the grass. Only their knuckles grazed, but it was as though a billion tiny fireworks lit her every nerve.

Maybe there was something else to do first.

The fire crackled and spat. Kirsty was afraid to look at him. What if it was an accident? What if he was just sitting so close to keep her warm?

She finally forced her gaze to meet his, and the liquid desire in his eyes made her breath catch. He trailed his fingers maddeningly lightly across hers. Over the back of her hand and up her forearm, drawing circles and swirls as though tracing invisible tattoos. His eyes never left hers, and she felt mesmerised, her every sense on high alert.

Gently, he pushed her back against the soft grass. The night air filled with the scent of wildflowers and smoke and Frej. Kirsty reached for him, but he grinned, softly placed her arms by her sides and whispered something she guessed meant *be patient.* He lay on his side, propping himself up on one powerful elbow and drank the sight of her in, his gaze tingling with curiosity and anticipation.

The burning log toppled over with a crash. They jumped and chuckled together. His laughter vibrated through his thin T-shirt, sending ripples cascading through her as he dipped his head to kiss her quickly. It was so fast it was almost as though she imagined it, except for the echo tingling on her lips. He ran his fingers lightly down her neck, over her shoulders and collarbone.

He paused at the collar of her sundress, then dipped painfully slowly beneath the thin fabric. She moaned and arched her back to press herself into his touch. He stroked her hair with his other hand, kissed his way gently along her brow, over her temple, ear, and jawline. Kirsty squirmed as the hot tip of his tongue found her neck and gasped as his fingers finally worked their way under her bra.

She grabbed his face and pulled it to hers. Their lips and tongues met and twisted together, clumsy with need as his thumb teased her nipple. She hooked her leg over his waist, shoved his joggers down, desperate to feel him closer. She yanked his T-shirt over his head and half sat up to kiss her way over his pecs, salty with sweat, covered in a fine smattering of red-gold hair.

Frej pushed her back against the grass. He slid the straps of her sundress and bra over her shoulders and yanked them low. Rough now, impatient and ravenous, he hungrily kissed his way over her chest, burying his face between her boobs. He squeezed and stroked, licked and kissed his way over first one and then the other, his tongue like tiny flames. A fine, icy mist of rain broke over them, making Kirsty's skin simultaneously hot and cold, every nerve standing to attention yet melting into him all at once.

His hands moved over her waist, dragging her dress, too damn slowly, over her hips. His lips followed, licking and nipping their way along an invisible winding path ever lower.

Kirsty buried her hands in his thick hair, gasping and moaning and giggling as he teased and tickled and maddened.

Then her dress was off, and he knelt between her knees like a hungry lion.

He lifted her ankles to rest on his shoulders, holding them firmly against his hot skin. He turned to lick a tiny soft patch of skin just behind her ankle bone. It sent shockwaves through her so strong that she jerked, and he grinned.

He kissed the other ankle and then made his way up her legs, alternating kissing one then the other. He followed his lips with his fingers until he held her hips firmly as he nibbled his way along her thighs. She bucked and writhed, needing him more, needing him closer, needing him *there*—

Frej paused, centimetres away, then popped up to kiss her tummy. Kirsty growled with frustration and felt his chuckle vibrate on her skin. He was crouching, her thighs around his neck as he very gently opened her with his fingers, and time seemed to stand still.

The first lick nearly sent her over the edge, but Frej wasn't nearly finished. He buried his face in her, eagerly devouring as hot waves crashed again and again. She had no idea if she was screaming or gasping or howling like a wolf as every fibre of her melted like lava.

Kirsty was still shuddering as he flopped on the grass next to her. He gave her a soft peck on the lips and rolled on his back, appearing entirely satisfied with life. Kirsty needed to take care of him, but she didn't think she could physically move. She'd do it in a wee minute.

'I'll do you in a wee minute,' she promised through a deep yawn, giving his willy a wee pat to show good faith.

THIRTY-FIVE

The next thing Kirsty knew, it was morning. She was cradled in Frej's arms, and her great-grandfather stood over them, shaking his head with horror.

'You knocked Agnes up in a lane behind George Square, so I'll have none of that judgmental pish from you,' Kirsty said sternly.

'I'm going to make pancakes,' he sniffed, as though he'd never dream of judging. 'I need to go get buttermilk.'

The corner shop was just a few minutes away, so it was a race against time to wake Frej with her tongue and straddle him for a rough, frantic quickie in the grass. And then another in the cold, cobweb-ridden shower that rattled Kirsty's bones and left her a trembling mess. All she'd say is that if this was what rowing across the North Sea did for a boy's stamina, she was all for it.

They stood in the shower for a while afterwards. Icy needles of water soothed their fiery bodies. Kirsty leaned against Frej and felt every delicious sensation.

This was usually her cue to exit stage left. *Well, nice to have met you*. She'd give a comically awkward grin, trying to pull off the impossible balance between chilled yet not cold.

About half of them instantly went distant and weird lest she got ideas about being their girlfriend. The other half got smushy and weird, so they could pretend they had a girlfriend for a couple of hours before deciding they'd had enough and telling her to go. Kirsty did her level best to skedaddle long before finding out which was which.

The usual script wasn't exactly possible now. Strangely though, there didn't seem to be any awkwardness. Frej was as steady and warm as he always was, strolling out into the sunshine in the frankly spectacular altogether, to gather up their clothes.

A niggling force of habit ordered Kirsty to grab her pants and wish him a nice life, but before she could get the words out, he gave her a *thumbs up*. It made her giggle, and the next thing she knew, Nathan was making a show of banging loudly when he returned with the milk.

'Solveig said she could help organise papers and whatnot for Frej and me,' Nathan announced. Kirsty and Frej tucked into fluffy pancakes drenched in maple syrup. 'We are to go to her office today.'

Under the table, Frej lightly traced around Kirsty's kneecap with his finger, and a shiver ran through her. She could think of about twenty things she'd rather Frej do today that didn't involve getting a passport. However, if the boys were here for the duration, they needed to officially exist.

Kirsty couldn't help thinking there was a lot Solveig hadn't told them last night. Solveig had been around for eight hundred years, so it wasn't unreasonable it would take a fair few chats to get fully up to speed. Even so, Kirsty sensed she'd held back a few pertinent points. *Like who sent her that video of the Viking fight on Buchanan Street.*

Kirsty had taken a look through the news online, and the rammy was being reported as standard Saturday night shenanigans. A handful of witnesses mentioned that a few participants appeared to be in fancy dress. Nobody commented on the white light thing. Presumably, because nobody who saw it could believe their eyes.

But somebody thought that Solveig needed to see the video.

Kirsty hailed a cab, and they dropped Frej off at the university to spend the day with Solveig. She handed the driver a couple of ten-pound notes as she and Nathan clambered out on Duke Street. Nathan couldn't wipe the grin off his face as the taxi pulled silently away.

'A taxi cab powered by electricity,' he muttered in wonder. 'That's swell.'

The afternoon was gloomy with the promise of rain. Traffic inched past towards the Tennants Brewery and the city centre. A couple of boys were doing bike tricks on the pavement, much to the chagrin of several pedestrians. A man in a dark blue thaub sweeping the front step of his corner shop shouted at the boys to be careful, and they informed him at great volume that he was a bandit. He chuckled and went back inside his shop.

Kirsty tried to orientate herself. They needed to cross the road and head maybe one more block east. Nathan obediently followed her as she concentrated, trying to conjure up a long-ago October afternoon.

There it was. The café where Morag brought Kirsty for ice cream that day was now a dry cleaner, but the large window was much the same. She and Nathan stood in front of it, and

Kirsty stared intently at the road, but all she could see was modern traffic. She sighed, impatience and frustration needling at her.

Relax, don't pay attention, let them come.

'I think Morag knew something more about all of this than she ever told me,' she murmured. The traffic started to shimmer and fade. 'She was the last person to have seen Owen in 1968 and possibly the first now. She and Mrs McCafferty were never pals, but she went with her that night. I thought she just wanted any company, but now I'm starting to think—'

Kirsty grabbed Nathan's arm as she spotted a man on an enormous white horse.

He nodded. 'Yeah, I see him.' A young guy ambling past in gym gear looked up in surprise. 'Not you, buddy,' Nathan said. 'Keep walking.'

At first, it seemed odd they couldn't hear the horse's heavy clip-clops against the tarmac until Kirsty remembered there was no tarmac beneath its hooves. The rider wore a long, thick velvet robe of deep sky blue with a fur collar and gold brocade trim. His hat, a kind of puffed cap, was a darker blue. Light brown hair fell in waves to his shoulders, and his beard was trimmed neatly into a point, almost as though he had a very long chin.

'He looks like the Sheriff of Nottingham,' Nathan said.

'Whoever he is, he looks pleased with himself.'

The streets were lined with people in rags. They watched silently as the fancy man rode by on his big horse.

'I think he's the duke,' Kirsty murmured. 'The original one the street was named after.'

'The Duke of Duke Street?'

'The Duke of Duke Street.'

A double-decker bus honked.

The scene shimmered and faded, replaced by a solemn line of prisoners in black, each man's wrist tied to the waist of the man in front. Heavy rain lashed them as they made their miserable way towards the gallows. A tram clanked its bell, a horse whinnied in fear as a cannon went off in the distance, and a nun in a huge, heavy-looking wimple collected herbs in a large woven basket. Kirsty sighed in frustration.

'Tell me what we are looking for.'

'We're looking for a witch. Morag showed me a Shadow one afternoon when I was a child. A witch was burned at the stake. Morag took me out of school and brought me all the way to Duke Street when there were plenty of cafés round our bit. I think there was a reason she wanted me to see her.'

Nathan considered. 'You think Morag ever kept a diary or wrote letters to a friend? Maybe she wrote something down about what she knew that we could find?'

Kirsty made a face. 'She wasn't one for diaries, and all her friends were local.'

'Some weather this!' A lady in a beige anorak, furiously shoving a canvas shopping bag on wheels along the pavement, stopped with a pained expression. Kirsty hadn't noticed the drizzle, but the woman was right. 'Fine bloody July!'

'Can I help you with your cart, ma'am?' Nathan asked.

'I can manage!' the woman informed him indignantly, but Kirsty was longer listening because she could see the fire.

A green hatchback with a broken wing mirror honked its horn as flames flickered to life around it. The red-faced driver gave a white van man the finger, but Kirsty let her gaze drift into the fire. The hatchback faded, and the flames leapt higher.

Prickles of fear rushed over Kirsty, and she had to stop herself from reaching for Nathan's hand. The fire grew bigger and hotter, the heat blasting at Kirsty through the centuries. But it wasn't just fire. The air itself seemed to sizzle, to tingle with something Kirsty didn't understand, but every instinct warned her to fear. Her heart thudded painfully as she caught sight of—

Her. The witch. The woman they accused of witchcraft.

An executioner, cowardly beneath his heavy black hood, stood sentry at the fire's edge. A group crowded around, ignoring the wild wind and the dark, threatening sky rumbling overhead. The women wore long dresses and tunics in dark earth tones. They had starched white collars and caps, while the men's hats were large and black with buckles that put Kirsty in mind of Guy Fawkes. *The 1500s.* The height of the hysteria whipped up by James VI's paranoia.

The old woman tied to the stake was fully conscious, feeling every crackling, white-hot flame. Kirsty thought of every time she'd burned herself on cooker rings and baking pans and once falling drunkenly face first into a lit birthday cake. She could barely conceive of the excruciation and terror unfolding before her eyes, yet ice-cold terror nipped at her like a million tiny daggers.

Stunned fear was etched on the crowd as they watched in hushed, fearful silence. *If this was the height of the witch hunts in Scotland, why did they look so horrified?* Wasn't this cruelty commonplace? *Something wasn't right.* Something was different about this burning.

The woman's rags were filthy, and her long white hair was matted, whipped up by the furious wind. As the bottom of her skirts caught alight, she thrashed back and forth, screeching curses and revenge in a deep, rasping voice. She howled, and the timber stake creaked. Lightening cracked the black sky, the crowd screamed and—

And Kirsty knew that voice.

Her blood turned icy and pounded in her ears. As the flames licked her blistered, bleeding legs, the old lady's screeches got louder, sharp with agony. Kirsty shrank back, desperate to look away and pretend it wasn't real, and the scene started to fade.

But she couldn't let go. Not yet. Not until she knew for sure.

The woman turned to face Kirsty and laughed maniacally. Her eyes gleamed and glittered black. Kirsty stared, horror clawing at her throat until she could barely breathe, unable to tear her eyes away until—

Finally, mercifully, Mrs McCafferty's screams dulled to tormented gurgles, and she was engulfed in flames.

THIRTY-SIX

A sharp bang behind Kirsty made her jump a mile, her nerves jangling on edge. The dry cleaner, red-faced and indignant, thumped again on the glass window.

'Hoi yous! Away fae there or you'll come an' wash ma windae—'

Kirsty raised a shaking hand to wave in apology, and he thudded again for good measure. 'Fuckin' reprobates!'

'Did you see her?' Kirsty and Nathan started walking up towards High Street. Kirsty was trembling, her knees wobbly, and she was grateful when Nathan slipped his arm through hers. 'The woman in the fire.'

Mrs McCafferty.

Mrs McCafferty.

Mrs McCafferty used to shout at Kirsty and Harry for making noise in the street under her window. She was burned to death in the 1500s. She told Agnes off for using Glaswegian slang. There was a portrait of her from the 1800s. She led Kirsty into an execution at Glasgow Cross in the 1700s.

She was the last person to see Morag alive.

Nathan nodded. 'I can't see very clearly. It's like—don't know if you ever removed a photograph from the dark room before it finished developing?'

Morag once had a Polaroid camera. Kirsty loved watching photos develop from hazy outlines to a squint corner of good-ness-knows-what. She was forever getting in trouble for wasting expensive film.

'I know what you mean.'

'The little I could see looked pretty horrible.'

'It was Mrs McCafferty.'

Nathan stared.

'In the fire. Burning to death.'

'Morag's friend?'

'The woman Morag was with the night she died.'

Nathan was silent a moment. 'The one who had the photograph of Morag and her friends in her apartment?'

'Yeah.' Dismay curdled through Kirsty. *Why did she have that photograph?* Was it some kind of *trophy*?

'So she's—like Solveig?' Nathan said. 'And us?'

'And Owen.'

'The folks standing around the fire looked like Thanks-giving pilgrims,' he said with a frown. 'That was 1621. I know that from second grade.'

'I think it was part of the witch-hunts that Maureen talked about. After James VI thought witches tried to kill him and his wife with storms on the North Sea. So any time from the early 1500s, for around a hundred and fifty years.'

'So this lady has been alive since then.'

'At least. We know that killing us doesn't work. She could have been burned at the stake dozens of times.'

Kirsty took a deep breath as the horror shrouded over her. *Mrs McCafferty could have been burned at the stake dozens of times.* No wonder she was so crabbit.

'Well, we need to go talk to her right away. We need answers from her.'

Kirsty shook her head. 'She's been keeping her secrets for longer than your country has existed. We can't just pop around for tea and start interrogating her. If she gets any inkling that we know anything—' Kirsty sighed. 'It's not going to go well for us. We need to be more careful.'

'So what do we do?'

They turned onto High Street, and chills darted at Kirsty as she realised they were in Owen's hunting grounds. *Was he out there?* Was he hanging about some manky pub or swanky wine bar just out of sight? Sidling up to an unsuspecting lassie, whispering seductive patter honed by fucking centuries to lure her to her death?

Was Mrs McCafferty helping him? Was she the Myra to his Ian, the Rose to his Fred? And how, in the fresh, buggering hell, would they take on the pair of them if she was?

'I need to ask Morag.'

'I beg your pardon?'

'Morag.' Kirsty nodded. Then again, more firmly. 'Hear me out. A few days ago, I saw a couple of Shadows. I was excited because I recognised them. It was this amazing entrepreneur and one of Glasgow's most famous artists. I yelled something to them, and they heard me.'

'They didn't just look up at a noise in their time?'

Despite everything, Kirsty couldn't help but grin as she shook her head. 'No, they heard. He drew me. '

The sketches on the wall at the library. The newly discovered series. They were impressions of a woman with Mackintosh's rose design on her bum. 'I shouted about the tattoo on my bum, and he drew it. He must have heard me. I don't think many women were getting bum tattoos in his time.'

'You shouted to a strange man about your behind?'

'I don't feel like that's the headline here, Nathan.'

'Okay, but even if he heard you, you don't know if he could have talked back. You really think you can have a whole conversation with Morag in another time?'

'I don't know. But there's only one way to find out. And it's Morag. She'll tell me anything she can if she can. It's worth a try.'

For days, Kirsty camped out in the waste ground by the Ghostie Soldier's Grate, with the ghostie soldier keeping her company.

After a few false starts, Kirsty got the hang of relaxing her eyes to peer into time. She and Nathan shared sandwiches in companionable silence, watching waves of migrants, Highlanders, Irishmen, and Jews beg, scuffle, and survive. Gangs gathered on corners, and starving children swarmed gleaming carriages pulled by liveried horses. Mammies tossed bread and jam out windows to waiting children. A grand lady in a pale pink dress with a long train and veil gave imperious orders. Workers, in hand-dyed tunics, canvas dungarees and mustard bell bottoms, marched across the bridge into town for their day's toil.

But no Morag.

If there was any rhyme or reason as to what they could see when, Kirsty couldn't figure it out. As hours turned into days, centuries drifted to and fro. Carriages faded into carts, then surged into hand-cranked cars with leather hoods. Sometimes, Kirsty could only make out indistinct forms, and at other times she could discern brass buttons, spots and worry lines. Occasionally there was nothing to see, but they could hear coins jangling in pockets and squeaky pram wheels or smell horses and soot and babies who needed a change.

'People are just the same, aren't they?' Kirsty muttered on the third day as they watched a couple of peasants in tunics shyly work their way up to a winch. 'I mean, they're dressed differently, and the kind of work they do all day long is different. But no matter the century, they're all just cutting about. Looking after kids, falling out with pals, fancying folk, having a laugh.'

'Yeah, when you get used to the cars and outfits and whatnot, folks around now are the same as when I grew up. People like to imagine that we were all noble and dignified then, but we got scared and stupid and selfish too.'

Nathan carefully folded the greaseproof paper he had wrapped their sandwiches in. 'I remember walking across George Square one time when the air raid siren started up. It was after the Blitz, but we got occasional warnings until the war ended. Everybody started running for the shelter, but this lady grabbed my lapel. She launched into a story about how her daughter just wanted to go dancing and to the pictures instead of helping out at home, and she couldn't decide how best to punish her.

'I kept trying to steer her towards the shelter, but she wasn't interested. When I broke in to tell her I was going underground, even if she wasn't, she shouted that she was sick and tired of the war and wouldn't put up with it for a single second more. Then she turned to march away indignantly and crashed into a lamppost.'

'Do you reckon there were people who refused to quarantine or wear masks during the Plague or Cholera outbreaks?' Kirsty mused. 'Just wandered the streets warbling about they didn't believe in it, and it wasn't going to get them anyway?'

'I'd bet my bottom dollar.'

'I can't decide if I'm relieved or depressed.'

Kirsty had tried calling out to see if she could get anyone to look around. She started with children, figuring they were most likely to accept her as a ghost or an imaginary friend and not be frightened. She was almost sure she caught the attention of one or two, but it was hard to be sure. Even the leper man had kept his distance, ringing his mournful bell without looking in her direction.

After a few days, they got the hang of focusing their aware-ness on summoning Morag's lifetime. It became clear that they couldn't see their own lifetimes. Kirsty could see everything until the eighties when she was born, while Nathan couldn't see anything between the twenties and 1946 when he disappeared.

They watched silently as the horrific urban deprivation of the fifties and sixties unfolded, then as slums were cleared to leave gaping holes where lives were once lived. Girls in fifties school uniforms, then beehives and Mary Quant skirts, skipped past on their way to the dancing. None was Morag.

'We know she was there,' Kirsty said in frustration after the fourth day. Her head was pounding from peering into the ether. She blinked and yawned. One of her eyes twitched, and her vision wavered from the strain. She tried to imagine explaining to an optician why she suddenly needed glasses.

It couldn't be that they couldn't see anyone they knew. Kirsty glimpsed a little girl in ringlets and a smock dress chal-lenging some boys to a fight in the late twenties who was defi-nitely Agnes. Nathan went quiet when he spotted her being driven away from a gang execution in the sixties.

Kirsty had seen other faces she recognised. Harry's parents as newlyweds—Harry was the *image* of his dad as a young man. Wee Mick and Old Mick as young Teddy Boys—horrify-ingly, Old Mick was quite hot in a James Dean kind of way. At one point, she thought she'd mistaken the rule about not being able to see yourself when she spotted a wee girl in plaits skipping rope. It was like looking into a mirror, but a lump formed in her throat as she realised it was her mum.

But no Morag.

'If she's hiding from us, I'll wring her—' Kirsty cut herself off as she couldn't decide whether to laugh or cry. Owen already wrung Morag's neck.

'You should go home,' Nathan said with a yawn. 'Frej will be back from Solveig's. You should relax and spend an evening with him.'

'So should you,' Kirsty said, squeezing his arm. 'You look exhausted.'

'I'm a hundred goddamned years old,' he grinned, though his shoulders sagged. 'And think Frej would prefer an evening with you.'

Kirsty shrugged. A tiny sliver of hurt she'd ignored for days flickered to life. She hadn't really seen Frej since—

Since.

Which was fine. She hardly expected him to follow her around, holding her hand forever more or anything. She just—

This is why you take your pants and wish them a nice life, she reminded herself sternly.

Her world may be spinning off its axis with time travel, white light, and ancient serial killers, but some things never change.

'That fellow is smitten,' Nathan proclaimed with a grin. 'I've known that since the first day you brought him home.'

'I'm not sure a Viking is capable of being smitten,' Kirsty muttered. She pulled her knees to her chest and frowned at the stupid vibratey time hole. A man in a burnt orange tunic, with animal furs wrapped around his calves like leg warmers, squinted worriedly at the sky as though judging the likelihood of rain.

'Just assume it's gonnae pish it down, pal,' she yelled. He looked up in fright and backed away in a hurry.

'You okay, kiddo?'

'Frej and I have never even had a conversation.'

Nathan shrugged. 'Words don't matter. I couldn't understand Agnes's accent for months after we met. But when that special thing is there between two people—' He grinned, lost in a reverie Kirsty did not want to think about.

'Do you think it's odd Solveig hasn't really spoken to us again?' *Time for a change of subject.* 'I know she helped you two out with passports and stuff, but she's been researching all this for centuries. She must know so much more than she's told us.'

'She wasn't in Glasgow in the sixties,' Nathan said. 'I asked her, and she spent a few decades in California after the war, so she doesn't know anything about The Shadow.'

'Funny that she's always ended up back here. I mean, eight hundred years—you'd think she'd have had enough of the weather.'

'She said she wanted to stay close because of her research. If she's trying to figure out something that happened in Glasgow, then it makes sense she needs to be in Glasgow.' He grinned. 'But I think she's lying. I think she sticks around in case her husband shows up someday.'

'Her Viking husband? You honestly think Solveig still fancies him after eight hundred years? I can barely remember who I was pumping eight hundred hours ago.'

'True love lasts forever.' Nathan's smile didn't quite reach his eyes. 'Whatever an old cynic like you thinks.' He frowned into the distance, his shoulders drooped as though suddenly too heavy for him.

'Do you want to see Agnes? I warn you, she's changed a good bit since the last time you saw her.'

He smiled, that faraway look still in his eyes. 'You know that photograph of Gloria from the newspaper in that radio doohickey you carry around?'

'My phone?'

'The picture from her hundredth birthday. Well, she hasn't changed at all. Not really. She's got that white hair and a wizened little face, but she's still the same girl who used to ride my handlebars home from school. The track up to her house was full of craters and mud, so all her hairpins would fall out, and her Mom would be spitting mad. That girl is still right there in her eyes.'

'Agnes is just round the corner,' Kirsty said. 'If you want to visit her, I think you should. You don't have to tell her everything. You could pretend to be one of your nephews or something. I can wait here.' She grinned. 'Though I'd like to see her face when she lays eyes on you.'

Nathan didn't answer.

'So you don't think Solveig is avoiding us?'

'I think that time passes differently for her than for us,' Nathan said. 'I think if you've been alive for eight hundred years, then keeping us waiting a few days doesn't mean a lot. She's been alone all this time, and her brother just appeared. I understand that her priority is to spend time shooting the breeze with him before she starts filling us in on the ways of the universe.'

Kirsty nodded. Her great-granda was awfully wise for twenty-something.

'There she is!'

Nathan clutched her arm as they stared.

Morag wore a wraparound dress in a bright paisley pattern with a large collar and floaty sleeves. Her sandals were a sort of espadrille weave, and her eyeliner was bold and winged. *The seventies*. Kirsty's mum must have been six or seven, but Morag was alone. She was in a hurry, glancing at her slim gold watch as she looked both ways to cross the road opposite the waste ground.

'Morag!' Kirsty yelled. 'Gran—over here!'

Morag rummaged in a large leather handbag as she strode past them.

'Morag,' Nathan hollered, his voice hoarse with emotion. He staggered back a bit, clearly overcome at laying eyes on his daughter. 'She looks like my mother,' he breathed in wonder. 'She looks exactly like my mother.'

'MORAG—' Kirsty tried again, but Morag disappeared around the corner. 'She didn't hear us.' Tears of frustration threatened as disappointment crashed over her. *After all that, she just kept walking.* 'How could she not hear us?'

'None of them has heard us,' Nathan said with a dejected sigh. 'I'm sorry, but they haven't. I can only just see them most of the time. I don't think we can communicate with them.'

'But Charles Rennie Mackintosh drew my bum. How could he know my bum existed?'

'I saw those drawings you're talking about, Kirsty. They're abstract. There's no way you could be sure what he meant to depict.'

There was a painful lump building in Kirsty's throat. There was no time for dramatics. She tried to swallow it down, but a strangled sob burst out. 'I wanted to talk to her.'

'I know, kiddo.' Nathan put his arm around her and ruffled her hair. 'So did I.'

'I don't know what to do if I can't ask Morag,' Kirsty mumbled, her voice wobbling. 'I don't know—don't have another plan.'

A pressure built in her, pressing down on her chest so hard she could hardly breathe. She pictured all the young women in Glasgow, heading out to nightshifts, laughing with their pals, and doing YouTube tutorials to learn the perfect winged eyeliner. And Owen, lurking in every shadow. Invincible. Fucking immortal.

'He's going to just keep going. He's been killing for over a thousand years and has not had enough. I need to stop him and don't know how.'

THIRTY-SEVEN

Back at the house, there was no sign of Frej and the flicker of hurt burst into a flame. He was avoiding Kirsty. There were no two ways about it.

Which was fine. Message received. Nae bother.

She and Nathan picked up some mince on the way home because there was nothing like mince and tatties when you're feeling hopeless.

I could just not do all this, Kirsty thought as she peeled potatoes. Meat and onions sizzled in a pan. The sky was grey, but candles flickered and the kitchen was cosy.

They set out to solve Morag's murder in case it turned out to be the magic mission that would send them back to our own times. That was always a fairy tale. Morag would still be dead whatever they did. Catching killers wasn't their job, and catching ones that couldn't be killed was definitely a hiding to nothing.

They hadn't even heard from Harry in goodness how long. Kirsty put the potatoes on to boil for mash. *So much for sharing information.* Not much of what they had found out would be of any use to him. Kirsty tried to picture earnestly explaining to the police how witches can bring forth storms, and the killer they are after has been at it for a millennium.

'One of the victims might have inspired Jane Austen,' she'd tell them. 'Ooh, any chance of collecting forensic evidence from the original Glasgow Fair? Yes, in 1190. William I was on the throne, if that helps at all. Not the Conquerer, our William I.'

She could forget about all this, walk out the door and get on the next plane. She could catch up with pals in Vietnam or go skiing in New Zealand. None of this had anything to do with her. If Morag wanted Kirsty to know what she was mixed up in, she would have told her.

If you been around over the past ten years, she would have, that shitey wee voice whispered. Kirsty focused on chopping carrots. She'd had it up to here with the shitey wee voice.

'Can I use your phone to call Solveig and tell Frej dinner is ready?'

Nathan's excitement over using an iPhone broke through Kirsty's misery guts. She talked him through putting in the passcode and pulling up Solveig's number. He shook his head in awe as it rang.

'Hey, if this screen can feel what number I'm pressing, you think that if touched a movie screen, Rita Hayworth could feel it?'

'No, I do not, you mucky wee perv.' Kirsty was grinning despite herself as he wiggled his eyebrows in a manner she had a horrible feeling was supposed to be salacious.

'Good afternoon, this is Nathan Williams speaking. May have the pleasure of speaking to Solveig Ljotrsdóttir?'

Kirsty had explained approximately a hundred times that nobody but Solveig would ever answer her mobile.

'Oh, she's not?'

Kirsty looked up in surprise. Who answered Solveig's mobile?

'I'm trying to locate her brother—perhaps you have met him, he—oh, I see.'

Nathan frowned. A sliver of worry unfurled in Kirsty's stomach. Followed by a pathetic hurt. If Frej wasn't with Solveig, where was he?

'Well, thank you kindly for your time, ma'am—'

'Wrap it up, Nathan,' Kirsty muttered. 'Where is he?'

'Solveig has been out of town the past four days,' Nathan reported. 'She left her telephone with her colleague to field any work calls.'

Kirsty frowned. That didn't make sense. Solveig could forward work-related calls if necessary, but who went away for four days without their mobile?

'Her colleague said she was called away on urgent family business.'

'Something to do with Frej?'

Nathan shook his head. 'Frej has definitely been here in the past few days. He's been coming and going but I made him oatmeal yesterday morning when you were still asleep.'

And he left before Kirsty woke up.

'Well, who else could Solveig be related to that has urgent business now?' she asked, hoping her pathetic desperation wasn't showing on her face. 'Did she lie to her colleague, maybe? Make up an excuse?'

'Their uncle?' Nathan suggested.

'Maybe. But that doesn't explain where Frej is if she's been gone for four days.'

Hurt flipped into worry, and pins and needles prickled through Kirsty. Frej could take care of himself even if he weren't immortal, but her unease lingered. He could hold his own in any fight, but nobody ever taught him the green cross code. Just because a double-decker bus might not kill him, it would still sting. He didn't speak English, was baffled by the concept of private property—and if anyone got the slightest idea of what he was—

Kirsty took a shaky breath, visions of that bit in *ET* where scientists nearly killed him with their fascination dancing through her mind. *What would the government do if they knew that immortal Vikings were on the loose in Glasgow?* Frej could be tied up in some historian's basement somewhere, being forced to explain whether or not he'd ever sailed up the Mississippi River.

'Hey, look—'

Solveig had created a rune-to-English dictionary for Frej to start learning English, and it was lying on the kitchen table. Nathan picked it up, frowned at the upturned page, and handed it to Kirsty.

There was a sketch, in wobbly biro, as though drawn by someone not used to holding a pen. Kirsty frowned, trying to figure out what looked familiar about it—

'Is that—the Barrowlands?'

Nathan nodded. 'Looks like it to me.'

It was a rough sketch of the sunburst-shaped sign. Underneath, in careful, unsure letters, was the word *ME.* And an arrow.

THIRTY-EIGHT

The streets were lively as Kirsty and Nathan made their way up the Gallowgate. Office workers heading home, tourists clutching souvenirs from the People's Palace, gatherings of early evening drinkers. A gaggle of football fans sang their way up the Gallowgate.

Frej was a head and shoulders taller than just about everyone in Glasgow, but there was no sign of him. They scouted the road around the front of the Barrowlands and tested all the front doors, but each one was chained shut. Ignoring the shouts of market traders that they were closing for the day, Kirsty beckoned for Nathan to follow her into the back of the venue.

The stage door was open, emitting bursts of music that suggested a sound check.

'Should I keep a lookout?' Nathan asked as Kirsty stepped into the shadowy corridor leading backstage.

'No, stay with me.' Kirsty had seen enough horror films to know that nothing good came of amateur detectives splitting up.

She had been backstage at the Barrowlands once before.

Years ago, she and a pal flirted with the crew of some indie band who were hot for five minutes and managed to blag themselves an invitation to the aftershow drinks. They stood awkwardly at the edge of the sweaty crowd in the cramped green room for about half an hour. They sipped warm bottles of lager and batted away roadies intent on mauling them to the best of their drunken ability. They tried desperately to make eye contact with the lead singer in hopes of mauling him to the best of their drunken ability. A security dude informed them they were making the lead singer nervous, staring him out like that, so they needed to go. He confiscated their warm lager before escorting them to the door, and that was the end of their careers as rock groupies.

None of that helped a great deal now as Kirsty led Nathan through narrow, dingy corridors, vaguely hoping one of them would lead—somewhere. The walls were covered with peeling gig posters, a handful of framed photos of famous bands who'd played the venue, and equipment in metallic boxes was piled up here and there. The corridor led up some stairs, down some more, and around a few sharp corners. Kirsty was beginning to wonder if they had stumbled into one of those funfair ghost houses, and any minute now, a clown would leap out and eat their heads. Finally, they turned one more corner and found themselves at the side of the stage.

The stage lights were blinding, even from where they were tucked in the wings. Various powerful lights switched on and off, presumably tested by some unseen lighting designer. The band onstage looked vaguely familiar. Artfully terrible haircuts, head-to-toe in black, slouched over their mics and instruments; they could have been literally any moody indie band of the past twenty years. They played a blast of music, and Nathan jumped a mile.

Shielding her eyes from the light, Kirsty could just about discern a handful of figures standing around, your standard band staff and hangers-on in uniform black. Her heart leapt as a huge shadow moved, but then the laminate of the huge shadow's Access All Areas pass caught the light. It was a burly crew guy balancing a bit of a drum set on his shoulder. There was no sign of Frej.

Kirsty sighed and shook her head. As the lead guitarist played a piercing scale, Nathan stared like a deer in headlights. After a second's delayed reaction, he nodded. Kirsty motioned that they should go, and they headed dejectedly back through the endless corridors.

'What did he mean he's here? He wrote *me* and pointed here, but he's not here. Where is he?'

'Maybe we missed him?' Nathan said. 'He could be back at the house wondering where we are?'

Kirsty stopped dead as she spotted a young man walking towards them, carrying a couple of wooden shakers. He was barely taller than Kirsty, lithe, skin-and-bones, in a tight black suit with a slim tie. His shaggy brown hair reached his collar, and lips that—

No way.

Kirsty stood aside to let the whole band pass. She stared at the shower of self-conscious, skinny wee boys in their neatly pressed suits. Each fringe was less flattering than the last.

'They don't got barbers where they come from?' grumbled Nathan, as the ginger one gave him a wink. *The ginger one.* He died young, didn't he?

'Alright, darlin'?' drawled the one with the darkest hair in a London accent as he passed them. He was all in white but for a black cord waistcoat buttoned tight, and he carried a gleaming black guitar.

'Keith!' Kirsty blurted.

The young man looked around in surprise. 'How d'you know my name? Have we met?'

'See if you ever find yourself up a palm tree in Fiji? Gonnae be careful?'

'Yeah, alright, will do.' He gave her a little salute and disappeared around the corner after the others.

'They're a band,' she explained to Nathan as they made their way back through the empty market to the main road. 'They are extremely famous, even now, and they played here in 1964. They definitely heard me.' Kirsty shook her head in wonder.

'I don't think too much of their style.'

'Bet you anything your sister is a fan,' she grinned. 'But listen—the magic, or whatever it is, it's stronger here. It's as though the veil is thinner.' She thought about what Kenny said about Sauchiehall Street being a sacred area. Maybe Cathures was too. Maybe that was why Owen hunted here.

'Could be why Frej came here,' Nathan said. He stopped short. 'Hold up, I know why Frej came here.'

'What?'

Nathan was grinning in the direction of The Drum pub across the road. It took Kirsty a minute to see what he was looking at.

When she did, her first reaction was to burst out laughing. Partly from relief because there was Frej, entirely safe, bold as brass and large as life. And also because the sight was so gloriously absurd that Kirsty was speechless.

There was a group of women crowded around the pavement outside the pub. Shimmery dresses and glittery bronzer, they were cackling with laughter, downing pints and generally looking as though they'd stepped out of fairyland to cut a bitch. One even wore silver wings as she chugged what looked worryingly like a pint of white wine. Kirsty had no idea whether it was the fancy dress or fabulous style, but she thought she had found her queen.

And there was Owen.

Trying desperately to get at them, calling out wild declarations of love like some woeful, wimpy Shakespearean hero. Except he couldn't because Frej was cheerfully getting in his way. The most literal cock block of all time.

It was like at playtime in primary school, when you finally got hold of the ball, and a bigger kid would get up in your face, waving wildly over your head. Except, in this case, you were an ancient, immortal serial killer, and a Viking was shimmying in your face to stop you from getting anywhere near a potential victim.

Owen ducked and dove and finally smashed into Frej as though playing the squashed tomato game, but he all but bounced off Frej's solid abs. And Frej? Frej was loving life. He was grinning from ear to ear, thoroughly enjoying the game. He laughed his big booming laugh and waved to Kirsty, pleased as punch, as Owen yowled with frustration.

The women had no idea what was going on but were highly entertained regardless, alternately jeering and encouraging Owen's frantic attempts to chat them up.

'Mon, pal, I believe in you!' one of them whooped. 'You can't want your hole that badly if you give up that easily! Tell me again how beautiful my eyes are.'

They dissolved into giggles as Owen rammed into Frej again and howled.

He was protecting women. That was why there had been no other murders. For days and days while Nathan and Kirsty were trying to make contact with Morag, Frej had taken it upon himself to frustrate a centuries-old serial killer. Kirsty was confident most men would condemn Owen in the strongest, most earnest terms if asked, but only Frej would bop him on the nose as he lunged for the woman with the fairy wings.

Kirsty's heart contracted with an unfamiliar feeling.

And then she saw Morag.

THIRTY-NINE

It was cold when Morag was. Frost twinkled on the pavement, and she wore a toasty coat trimmed with fur that made her look like an old movie star. The man accompanying her touched her elbow to steer her past the pub towards the High Street. She wore strappy dancing shoes. Her feet must have been freezing.

The man half-turned as they crossed the High Street, and Kirsty's blood ran cold.

It was Owen.

A crowd of glamorous dancers in bright dresses and sharp suits queued outside the ballroom. Large, wide cars rumbled down the road, their rounded curves well-polished. A tram clanged its bell as it pulled to a stop. A wee boy in short trousers and a flat cap scampered to the back of the tram to hop on without paying, his knees scuffed and blue with cold.

Frej's laugh and Owen's screeches faded and distorted in Kirsty's ears. The lift-stopping-too-fast feeling washed over her so strong her knees nearly gave way. She could hear Nathan shouting, but Morag and Owen were disappearing down the Trongate. Kirsty couldn't lose them. Her heart pounded, and revulsion flooded her as she spotted him leaning down to say something to Morag.

She ran to catch up with them, and icy air filled her lungs. Goosebumps prickled over her bare arms. It was the dead of winter.

Hand-lettered shop signs swung in the breeze. Buildings, stained with soot, wavered and twisted before her eyes, and the uneven stone bricks of the pavement danced beneath her feet. *She wasn't supposed to be here.* The air itself was thick and undulating as though it were raging water.

Kirsty glanced behind and glimpsed a modern grey and purple bus pulling away from the Sydney Street stop. The sparkly women dashed across the road in front of it, one of them laughing at something or other. Nathan yelled *Kirsty,* and it was echoey and distant.

Every nerve jangled, every cell screamed at her to go back where she belonged, but she couldn't lose Morag. The air got thicker, heavier, pressing on her windpipe and chest. She swallowed a scream through gritted teeth. Every breath was a battle as Kirsty fought through a world that shimmered and swayed.

But she couldn't lose Morag.

He didn't get her tonight, Kirsty reminded herself. She knew Morag would survive because she would meet her in about thirty years.

Even so, her heart pounded with terror as she clawed her way after them. It was like being caught in a strong current. The air shoved and rollicked and undulated around her. Buildings oscillated, and faces of passersby twisted and swayed as though in funfair mirrors.

'Five pence for all the news!'

A boy manning a newspaper stand waved his papers at folk passing by. He couldn't be more than fifteen, but he wore a thick overcoat, neatly knotted tie and trilby hat. He looked like a wee man as he accepted coins from an old guy in a pin-striped suit and bowler hat.

'CH-53 helicopter found—no survivors. Jinky says we should have won!'

'I know what's going to happen in The Prisoner.'

At the tram stop, a young man on a bike called to a group of laughing women in thick winter coats. Trams were queued down the Trongate, green and mustard yellow and cream.

'Gies a cuddle, and I'll tell you.'

'Oh, away, you're havering.' A woman in a navy coat and pillbox hat shook her head and laughed.

'It's that cold. I'll take a cuddle anyway,' another woman yelled, and the man nearly fell off his bike.

Morag and Owen turned down King Street and stopped a little way from a bus that sat idling on the stand. The pressure pressed on Kirsty's bones as she half-ducked behind a large black car to watch.

Owen loomed over Morag. She looked so wee as she said something and gave him a cheeky grin. The bus driver flicked contentedly through a large newspaper. Kirsty willed him to look up, to shout, to help her.

Morag's expression changed and Kirsty's heart twisted. Fear flickered across Morag's eyes, and she took a step backwards. Owen moved forward.

'My Da'll be raging if I'm late.'

Morag's voice drifted across the road. Her *Da*? Was she talking about Nathan?

Kirsty couldn't hear Owen's reply. He leaned close and ran his finger down the side of her face and across her throat. Kirsty screamed.

The scream, a ragged howl of fury and terror, tore from her throat and seemed to warp in the air.

They can't hear—

A second or two later, it reached them. Owen looked

around in surprise and irritation. Morag kicked him in the shins and ran.

Yasss, she's away! Because of Kirsty's scream. Her scream distracted him and saved Morag. Relief coursed through Kirsty, but not for long as Owen gave chase.

His legs were longer, but Morag was smarter. She zigzagged over the frosty pavement, nimble in her dancing shoes, leaving him to slither and skid with angry shouts. Morag glanced behind her with a smug grin as she led Owen into a back lane off the Briggait.

The lane where she would be found dead half a century later.

No! Kirsty's voice caught in her throat. *Not there—*

The pressure clawed at her, pressed on her windpipe, her every nerve strained and screaming. She gritted her teeth, howled and staggered with a strangled groan. Reaching for the filthy, soot-blackened corner of the building, she yanked herself closer. The pressure drove her back, tried to ram her away, but she fought against it.

She needed to see what happened.

A terrifying blackness erupted. Owen's laughter twisted through the air, and the universe shuddered. The force hit Kirsty with an agony that ripped at her bones.

Morag! The blackness swirled, pounding a powerful pulse that rattled existence. Kirsty couldn't see her.

'Morag!'

The blackness faded, and someone emerged—but it wasn't Morag. It was a woman about Kirsty's age. She had flaming red ringlets piled on her head. She wore a lilac, empire-waisted dress under a midnight blue velvet cape, and she held a dainty cream shoe in her hand as a weapon. She staggered back against the wall, dishevelled and sweating. A shaky smile of relief broke through, and she gave a strangled sob.

'Compliments of Jeanette!' she roared at the blackness. Her voice trembled with fury and grief and satisfaction.

Jeanette? Jeanette Murray. The novelist. Her friend, or sister, tracked down the well-spoken young man who swept her off her feet when her sweetheart went to war and—

A shrill, desperate scream pierced and Jeanette's friend shimmered and faded. A woman with dark, waist-length hair. She wore a baggy, floor-length dress belted with a rope from which hung a large, wooden crucifix and clutched her face. Blood poured from a fresh wound.

Chills dashed over Kirsty as she spotted Owen in a navy blue tunic and hose, laughing maniacally as he advanced. He was holding what must be the woman's woollen stockings. She gritted her teeth and flew at him, shoving with all her might until, with an irritated screech, he disappeared into the blackness.

Kirsty backed away against the filthy wall, horror clawing at her as she realised what she was seeing. *The gaps.* The tens and hundreds of years when Owen was missing from time. Women who had figured out he couldn't be stopped, couldn't be killed. Who understood just enough about the vibratey time hole to know that at least her friends would be safe, shoving him desperately into forever. None of them with any way of knowing that she was heaving him into the path of her future sisters.

Sure enough, there he fucking was.

In Jacobite-era Highland regalia, Owen swung around the corner, chuckling with childish glee. He was pursued by a black woman in a heavy brown dress with a laced corset, a white cap only just clinging onto her hair. She yanked his kilt up and booted him in the balls. He yowled, doubled over with agony. Immortal or not, that didn't sound fun. The woman took the opportunity to bundle him into the blackness with a triumphant grin.

She stepped back, breathless with frightened triumph as, in another time, the blackness swirled again. Owen doffed his feather cap, swirled his kilt and took off into whatever time he was in now. Kirsty screamed. The white light flew from her fingers with a resounding crack, but he was gone.

The screaming hopelessness of it all descended over Kirsty, and white-hot fury churned in her guts. *All those women.* Centuries and centuries of his victims, of those who thought they were stopping him. All for nothing. Time and time again, he had been shoved into the mists of time. Time and time again, he popped right back out, like a fucking Jack in the Box.

He wasn't even *fussed.* He chuckled as he came out and cracked on without missing a beat. *It cost him nothing.*

The air pressure was excruciating. Kirsty staggered back out of the alley without knowing where or when she was. Morag's bus rumbled to life and pulled away from the stand. Crackly music emanated from a nearby window. *Hello, Goodbye.*

She was still in 1968, but there was no sign of Morag. Kirsty needed to get back to The Drum. She needed to get home.

Her rage was palpable. It coursed through her veins, throbbing and corroding.

This ended with her.

Kirsty didn't know how, but Owen's days of terror were numbered. They could tear him limb from limb. Frej would be well up for that. Let Owen try to put himself back together when they had thrown one leg into the North Sea and the other off the bloody Eiffel Tower.

A ferocious wind whipped Kirsty's hair, and fat, icy raindrops pattered mercilessly. Great gusts battered through the square, scattering debris, shop signs and someone's hat. Tiles flew from rooftops like hailstones. There was a horrifying crash as a tram toppled over into the side of a building. An ominous rumble reverberated as the first building succumbed to the storm. Wind whistled and howled and shrieked, great powerful furies almost as raging as Kirsty felt.

It was her.

Her rage, frustration, and helplessness took form in black clouds and wrathful wind. The storm was in her and of her. It ravaged from her very core, emanating onto the world where it shrieked and howled like a living, apoplectic creature.

The Great Storm of 1968.

'Stop it!' she screamed, but the wind whipped her words away. It was dangerous. *She* was dangerous.

People were going to be hurt. People were going to *die* tonight because Kirsty had lost her temper. She waved her arms wildly. White light was instantly swallowed by the darkness. In the distance, a tenement crumbled to the ground. Desperate screams and yells of warning filled the air, and a baby cried.

She couldn't stop it. It was beyond her. It was destructive and lethal, a force that started within her but was more powerful than her.

'I'm sorry.' Horror and regret burned through her like acid. 'I'm so sorry. I can't control it.'

The wind wailed, and icy rain poured. A great gust nearly lifted Kirsty off her feet. The pressure pounded so intensely that she felt her skull could crack under its power. She fought and screamed, clawed and yanked. The universe screeched at the seams, agony ripping her every cell.

At the Trongate, the wind shoved Kirsty into a wall, wrenching her shoulder painfully. She shouted in pain, held her arm against her side and lurched onwards. A fire had broken out on the High Street, and a fire engine's bell pealed weakly through the racket of the storm. Folk sheltered in doorways. A three-wheeled truck overturned in front of the Tollbooth Steeple, apples and oranges rollicking wildly across the cobblestones.

Kirsty spied a flash of purple and the relief was so sweet she wanted to cry. Gale force winds battered her in 1968, but incandescent at the edge of her vision was Billy Connolly as Bonnie Prince Charlie. The mural commemorating his 75th birthday, well into the twenty-first century, was splashed across the side of a building. Camp and fabulous, the costume was resplendent with bikes in bums on his shoulders and bananas poking from his tea-cosy helmet like horns.

Kirsty gritted her teeth and flung her through the lift-stopping-too-fast feeling. The very fabric of her felt ripped to shreds from the inside, and she screamed with agony. She was thrown violently onto the pavement with such force that she whacked her head on the tarmac. Everything went black.

FORTY

Kirsty woke to the sound of a Christmas carol warbled in harmony with an ambulance siren. Her body throbbed from head to toe, and her shoulder shrieked with pain. She moved her fingers and touched cool metal.

Machines beeped, babies cried, and an imperious voice shouted about the appalling wait. The ambulance siren drew near and stopped. Heavy doors heaved open, and an efficient rabble of orders was called as thuds and clangs filled the air. Kirsty had been here before. One of the gorilla guys tried to pre-game a gym night out with rubbing alcohol once upon a time. Kirsty and Kenny had sat here on hard plastic chairs all night, keeping him company as he regretted everything. Kirsty was in Glasgow's Royal Infirmary in the twenty-first century.

She forced her eyes properly open, cringing at the bright fluorescent lights. She smelled antiseptic and floor bleach and a faint scent of puke. She was on a stretcher, the curtain of her cubicle open. A drip was attached to her arm, but she appeared otherwise intact.

Kirsty tentatively scanned her body. *Nothing missing.* She

wiggled her fingers, toes, and nose and stretched her head from side to side. Her head pounded, and she ached as though she'd gone a few rounds with Kenny, but all in all, not bad. She'd had worse hangovers.

The caroler appeared to be in the cubicle next door, a loud male voice slurring *Jingle Bells* at the top of his voice. A doctor with a blonde ponytail paused as she passed, rubbed her temples, and snapped to attention as another ambulance siren approached. A young woman paced up and down the corridor, trying to soothe a screaming baby. She wore a red ski jacket over her pyjamas, and as she turned to start another lap, Kirsty glimpsed her red-rimmed eyes.

'Hello there.'

A nurse appeared. He had a neatly clipped beard and rimless glasses he kept pushing back up his nose. He grabbed the chart from the bottom of Kirsty's stretcher and skimmed it quickly with a resounding yawn. 'Sorry,' he grinned.

'I'm actually fine. I could just get out your hair, to be honest—' Kirsty struggled to a sitting position.

The nurse darted forward and gently pushed her back against the pillow. 'Just you take it easy. The doctor will be along to take a look at you in a wee minute.'

Kirsty gave her firmest smile. 'I shouldn't waste your time. You'll be needing the bed for sick people.'

'You were found unconscious on the street on a freezing morning,' Beardy Nurse said. His voice was gentle, yet Kirsty couldn't help but notice she was lying down again. 'Do you remember what happened?'

She remembered. A wave of hot guilt flashed at her as she remembered the storm. Her storm.

'I just tripped over and went flying on the pavement.' Kirsty gave a weak attempt at a laugh. 'Wee nap sorted me right out. Thank you for your—uhh, service.'

'My what?'

'Do we not clap you anymore?'

'Don't let me stop you,' Beardy Nurse said with an easy grin. 'I could go a wee round of applause now and then. Doctor will be along in a minute.'

'There's no need.'

'Aye, there is.' His smile didn't falter, but a steely edge to his voice told her he wouldn't be taking no for an answer. 'Couple of your tests showed up a wee bit unusual.'

Kirsty bet they did.

'Probably nothing to worry about, but better safe than sorry, eh? Seeing as you're here anyway.'

Could she be diagnosed with *just nipped to 1968 to witness several women try to murder an immortal serial killer*? Were there pills for having started the most destructive storm in living memory? If there was a cure for immortality with white light that shoots out your fingers, Kirsty bet it wasn't on the NHS.

There was no reason to give some hard-working doctor the shock of their life. She was confident they had plenty of stabbings and car crashes to be getting on with. But there was no arguing with Beardy Nurse, so Kirsty smiled sweetly.

The moment he was out of sight, she gritted her teeth and forced herself to sit. A wave of dizziness hit, but it passed quickly enough. Okay. *I can do this.* Shoes. Where were her shoes? Her trainers were lined up neatly beneath the stretcher and—

The drip. Apparently, Kirsty could handle turning folk to dust and giving the order for someone's neck to be broken, but removing a wee needle from her arm was too much. She had to do it, and she had to do it without fainting. She had no idea how immortality and time travel might show up on whatever tests they'd done, but she had a funny feeling she didn't want to hang around to find out.

Closing her eyes, Kirsty turned away and picked at the

plaster holding the needle to her arm. If she could just get the plaster off, the needle would be nae bother. *Right?*

'You trying to do me out a job?' Beardy Nurse was cheerfully unperturbed by busting her mid-escape as he firmly guided Kirsty to lie back down. 'You don't appear to be dehydrated, so I can take this out if you want, but if I catch you trying to skedaddle again, I'll handcuff you to the stretcher, okay?'

'You can't hold me here against my will. I'm a functional adult and am refusing treat—'

'Car crash just came in, so doctor will be another wee minute,' Beardy Nurse continued breezily as though Kirsty hadn't spoken. 'I'll get you a cup of tea if you promise to behave.'

'I don't want a cup of tea.'

Actually, she could murder a cup of tea, but it wasn't worth risking an ET situation if immortality showed up in tests.

'Will I send your pal in?'

'What pal?'

He shrugged. *Nathan?* Kirsty wondered. *Frej?*

'She's in here,' Beardy Nurse said. 'She's being troublesome, but I've told her the doctor won't be long. Maybe you can persuade her to behave.'

Beardy Nurse stepped aside. Kirsty supposed she was lucky she was in the right place because her heart stopped dead. It was good that she wasn't attached to one of those beepy machines, as she would have probably fused the whole hospital.

Smiling shyly from the bottom of the stretcher was Morag.

FORTY-ONE

'I shouldn't have followed you,' Morag said quickly.

Kirsty blinked. Morag. Twenty-something Morag was here in the twenty-first century.

'I didn't mean to,' she continued. 'You seemed lost and I was worried. I wanted to thank you for distracting him, then I saw you collapse and—have you got a concussion?'

'I hope so,' Kirsty said.

The guy in the next cubicle reached a crescendo with *Jingle Bells* and fell mercifully silent. *This—wasn't possible.* Solveig explained there was no nipping back and forth in time; you came through, skipping over months or decades or centuries, and that was it. Yet Kirsty would meet Morag in the eighties. She had a whole childhood and adolescence still to come with her.

Or did she?

Kirsty held her hands in front of her eyes. She stared intently at one, then the other. They didn't appear to be fading from existence. She tentatively poked herself. Nothing but the same aches and pains she felt a minute ago. She wasn't sure what fading from existence would feel like. Pins and needles, maybe? A bit of a queasy tummy?

'So this is the future. I feel as though I've walked into the Tardis,' Morag said. She looked around, eyes snapping with curiosity. 'Why are they wearing pyjamas?'

'I think they're called scrubs. I don't really know why they wear them. Presumably, they're comfortable for long shifts.'

'Yes, but pyjamas. People can see them.'

'I suppose if you're lying here with your leg falling off, you're not really paying attention to the fashion sense of the folk sewing you back together.'

Morag sniffed dubiously, looking so much like Nathan for an instant that it took Kirsty's breath away.

The caroler started up again, this time a bastardisation of *Merry Christmas Everybody*. Somebody a few cubicles along yelled at him to *gies all peace*. He roared about the birth of Christ and peace on earth, which was significantly worse than his Slade impression.

'Do you never think of a wee dod of lipstick?' Morag stared critically at Kirsty's face. The look was so familiar that a lump formed in Kirsty's throat. 'I order one from a magazine in America,' continued Morag. 'It's the very same brand Grace Kelly wears. Tommy says it brings out my eyes.'

Trust Morag. Only she could be in an Emergency Department fifty years in the future and worry about whether or not Kirsty had done her face.

'We need to get out of here,' Kirsty said. 'Can you get this needle out of my arm?'

Morag screwed up her nose, and Kirsty remembered she was as squeamish as Kirsty. They once spent a whole morning on the kitchen floor, taking turns screaming and dry-boaking as they tried and failed to extract a tiny splinter from Kirsty's big toe. Finally, Agnes came home and yanked it out without even using tweezers. 'It's really important a doctor doesn't see me.'

'Why not?'

Kirsty thought about the plastic corridors, the hazmat suits, and ET almost being killed with curiosity. One day, Morag would love ET so much that she'd buy Kirsty a giant blow-up one for my Christmas. They would sit him at the dinner table and apologise profusely when Agnes refused to serve him a mince pie. But not quite yet. 'Imagine if a normal doctor examined Doctor Who.'

Morag's eyes widened, and she nodded. Kirsty picked the plaster off, closed her eyes and turned away. Morag squealed with disgust, and Kirsty felt a sharp pain as Morag yanked the needle clumsily. Blood spurted from the wee dot on Kirsty's skin. They flapped in horror, Morag boaked, and Kirsty stifled a scream as she covered the gaping wound with the plaster.

Kirsty hopped off the bed, slipped her feet into her trainers and beckoned for Morag to follow. Beardy Nurse appeared, followed by the harassed-looking doctor frowning at a printout.

'And she's conscious?'

Beardy Nurse nodded.

'Oriented?'

'Seems to be.'

Kirsty tried the door to her right, but it was locked.

Harassed Doctor shook her head. 'There must be some mistake.'

There were no other doors. *Shit*.

Morag slipped into an empty cubicle. Kirsty followed and pulled the curtain over. They stood in silence, barely daring to breathe. After a few moments, Kirsty peeked out the gap in the curtain. The coast was clear.

'This way—'

To Kirsty's surprise, Morag slipped out and beckoned her

to follow. They walked briskly up the corridor and approached some double doors. Kirsty was sure they would be trapped, but Morag fell into step behind a doctor and caught up as he flicked his ID at the lock.

'Lovely evening, isn't it?' She smiled at him. Kirsty had no idea fluttering eyelashes were an actual thing, but Morag did it, and the doctor looked dazzled. 'I do like your pyjamas.'

They were in. They scuttled down another corridor, round a corner, past a waiting room and a nurses' station. Kirsty's headache was gone. All the pain was gone, and she felt fine.

'Hurry,' Morag hissed.

She disappeared down some wide stairs, and Kirsty had to run to catch up with her. There was a blast of icy air, as though they'd walked into a fridge. Kirsty's stomach heaved as she realised—

'Have you brought me into the morgue?'

'Shh—'

They flattened against a doorway. A couple of porters passed the far end of the corridor, pushing a mercifully empty stretcher.

'Where are we going?'

'I said *shh.*'

Morag listened keenly for a moment—then beckoned, and she was off again. The corridor was dimly lit, and a heavy silence hung in the air. One more corner, and they faced a thick set of metal doors. Footsteps approached and Kirsty's heart fell. She mentally gave herself over to the wrath of the Beardy Nurse, but Morag's face lit up.

'Thought yous were feart,' she shouted. 'Who's ready to face the Grey Lady?'

'Get lost. There's no such thing.' The tall guy in a Sikh turban laughed.

A middle-aged Caribbean lady rolled her eyes. 'I've got a

lot better things to do than silly initiations,' she said. 'Can we get on with this nonsense so I can get back and do my job?'

'I'm on my way to a party, as you can see,' Morag continued brightly. 'I'll get slagged rotten if I haven't done it before my next shift, so let's get on with it, shall we?

'This is my auntie,' she added, gesturing at Kirsty. Kirsty was about to object, then remembered she was indeed over a decade older than Morag. 'She didn't believe me when I told her that all new staff at the Royal have to venture into the tunnel to meet the Grey Lady, so I dragged her along.'

'Well, let's get moving,' the Caribbean lady said.

'My auntie will come in with me, so we don't take up any extra time.'

'That's cheating!'

'We'll go first if that's alright,' Morag continued blithely so I can get going to my party. Who's got the key?'

The Sikh guy fished in his uniform pocket and unlocked the metal door. It opened with an ominous creak, revealing sheer darkness. A drip echoed from somewhere deep in the shadows.

'I'll tell the Grey Lady you're all looking forward to meeting her,' Morag grinned. She blew a kiss as the door clanged shut.

Inside, it was even colder, the stone walls hard and damp. Even once Kirsty's eyes adjusted, she could barely make anything out. They appeared to be in some sort of tunnel. Morag reached for my hand and marched confidently ahead.

'How do you know about this? Did you know those people?'

Morag laughed, her voice echoing around the gloom. 'That was a lucky break. I knew about the initiation. My pal Jetta was a nurse here, and she told me all about it. She snuck me in once and lent me her spare uniform so I could do the initiation.

'I wanted to see if the Grey Lady is a Shadow, but never saw her. I suspect she's just a daft story medical students scare one another with. That's how I knew my way, and I took a chance there must be a few new recruits most evenings.'

'What would you have done if they hadn't shown up?'

'No idea.'

They fell silent for a few moments, concentrating on picking their way through the darkness. Kirsty had read about the tunnels that ran beneath Glasgow. Some were built to protect phone lines during the war, but many were much older.

'Jetta was murdered.' Morag's voice echoed in the darkness. 'Last year.'

'I know.'

'By the man you saw me with this evening. They call him The Shadow.'

'His name is Owen.'

'Are you trying to catch him? Are you a detective? Is that why you followed us?'

'Something like that.'

'The police tried to shoot him.'

Kirsty tried to figure out what they might be walking under. They'd changed directions at least three times. If Kirsty wasn't mistaken, they were heading towards George Square.

'The police tried to shoot Owen? They knew who he was? But the case is unsolved.'

Kirsty thought of the elderly detectives who ignored her messages and refused to speak to Maureen all these years. The angry woman who refused to let Kirsty visit the detective, Iain Kinnoch, in his care home. Did Iain Kinnoch know who Owen is?

'Officially.' Morag's voice dripped with scorn. A terrific rumbling sounded overhead. Kirsty jumped a mile, but Morag laughed.

'Queen Street,' she said.

'Of course.'

'Who are we to each other?' Morag asked. 'You look exactly like my mother.'

'I do not,' Kirsty snapped, appalled.

'You've met her, then.'

'Yes.'

'You can't be a niece or cousin. We don't have any other relations.'

'I'm your granddaughter.'

Morag blinked. 'No, that can't be. Be careful,' she added as she climbed a rickety staircase. 'These bricks are crumbling.'

'Well, I am,' Kirsty shouted.

They reached a heavy metal door. Morag yanked an ancient bolt that gave way with a bone-tingling screech.

'Did I get old?' she asked. She opened the door, and they were hit by a blast of freezing air.

'No,' Kirsty said. 'You're a lot of things, but you're never old.'

They emerged onto George Square. Twinkly lights blasted through the darkness, and screams and yells filled the air as an enormous, brightly lit Ferris wheel slowly turned. A drunk Santa tried to climb a lamppost while a couple of polis shouted at him to get down. Well, that explained the caroller in A&E.

It appeared that it was Christmas.

FORTY-TWO

'Kirsty!'

Joy exploded across Frej's face. He bounded down the path and enveloped Kirsty in a bone-crushing bear hug she never wanted to be released from. He swooped her off her feet. She wrapped her arms around his neck, burying her face in his shoulder, feeling his heart beat against her. He still smelled like herbs and an Islay malt.

Finally, he loosened his grip just enough to let her lean her forehead against his. Their noses smooshed against each other as Kirsty breathed him in. Her daft hurt at not seeing him for a few days after their mini shagging marathon melted away. Kirsty ran her hand down the side of his face, along his jawline and the stubble that was just long enough to be soft. Then it was all getting a bit soppy, so she tweaked his earlobe and he laughed.

'I missed you,' he said softly.

'I missed you too,' she whispered—

Hold on, what the what?

'You speak English?'

Frej chuckled and put her down. He kissed the top of her head and breathed in her hair. 'We have much to catch up on.'

'I am Frej,' he added in a lilting Scandinavian accent, turning Morag.

'Morag McIvar,' she said with her patented cheeky grin. 'Pleasure.'

Frej blinked and glanced at Kirsty. 'Morag?'

'Like you said, a lot to catch up on.'

Frej took Kirsty's hand and led them to the front door. The porch was clear. The aggressive rhododendron had been tamed into submission and the path cleared, swept and washed. The rotting wood of the doorframe had been replaced, sanded and painted.

Inside, the grand hallway had been restored to its former glory. The wide staircase was repaired and polished, the stained glass window overlooking the landing sparkling with morning sunlight. A warmth and energy danced in the air as though the house had come back to life.

A large fire roared in the fireplace in the good room—the room where Kirsty slept wrapped in Harry's jumper that first night. A man—judging by his height and blondness, he'd have something to do with Frej—snoozed in the big armchair next to the bookcase.

'Nathan is in the kitchen,' Frej said

They followed Frej down the hallway that led to the big kitchen at the back of the house. The smell of lentil soup and baking bread hit Kirsty and her stomach just about turned inside out with hunger. Nathan stood by the cooker, stirring several gigantic copper pots.

Morag hung back as Kirsty and Frej stopped in the door-way. Kirsty had filled her in on Nathan's story in the taxi. She hadn't said much.

'Nathan,' Frej said.

'Just a wee minute,' Nathan murmured, and Kirsty grinned. *Frej learned English, and Nathan learned Scottish.*

'Gotcha—' He triumphantly extracted a bay leaf from the soup with a pair of tongs, turned around with a smile—

Which froze on his face as he caught sight of Kirsty.

'Kirsty?' His eyes glistened with tears. He broke into a gigantic grin.

'I'm home,' she laughed.

'Kirsty! I'd almost given up hope—'

Kirsty got her second ferocious hug.

'Ahh, kiddo,' he said finally, wiping his eyes with the back of his hand. He squeezed her shoulder. 'We missed ya.'

'I was only gone a night,' she said wryly.

'Solveig believes that time in the vibratey holes does not exist,' Frej said.

He rubbed Kirsty's back as Nathan hugged her again. The kitchen was brightly lit and toasty warm. Kirsty couldn't help but remember the last time she returned to this kitchen after a spot of time travel. She'd been faced with a mutant mint plant and hunners of shagging mice.

'So the world outside marches on while we are in there,' Frej continued. 'That is how one year passed when you came through to rescue me—'

'And two and a half years passed when you were in 1968,' Nathan added.

'Two and a half years!' Kirsty yelped. She looked from one to the other in shock. 'I've been gone for two and a half years? No wonder you missed me.'

Frej slung his arm around Kirsty's shoulder and pulled her close. 'We did.'

'What happened?' Nathan asked anxiously. 'Did you find her? Did you talk to her?'

'Well, that's the thing.' Kirsty stepped aside with a grin.

She was still freaked out by all the potential consequences of Morag being there, but she couldn't help but be thrilled Nathan was going to get to meet his wee girl after all.

Confusion and shock, and finally, joy spread across Nathan's face. Morag smiled awkwardly as her father grinned at her like a loon. She stepped forward and held out a hand.

'I take it you're the married GI bastard who abandoned my pregnant mother?'

'Yeah, that's me.'

'Well, I'm your long-lost daughter.'

'Morag,' he breathed, staring at her in awe. 'Glad to meet you.'

They shook hands firmly.

'We managed just fine without you,' Morag blurted.

'I know you did. You look like my mother,' Nathan shook his head in wonder. 'That's Millicent Williams right there in your eyes. She was a swell lady. Made the best apple pies you ever did taste.'

'Your lentil soup is burning.'

With a panicked look, Nathan dashed to the cooker and removed the pot from the heat.

'I don't look like any of the McIvars,' Morag says as Nathan added cold water to the pot and stirred. Kirsty could see emotions having a high old time across his face. He'd be a terrible poker player, that boy. 'Agnes always said she didn't know where I came from.'

'She did know where you came from,' Nathan said, shoving a wooden spoon in the sink with a clatter. 'You came from me. She shoulda told you that.'

'My mother's a nightmare,' Morag said. 'If you never figured that out, you're dafter than you look.'

Nathan chuckled despite himself. 'Yeah, I figured that out.'

Frej slipped his warm hand into Kirsty's and squeezed.

Nathan doled the soup into bowls, the smell making Kirsty's knees go weak. Morag seemed a bit perturbed at first, but after a moment, she tucked in too.

The back door opened. Two guys came in, one with poker-straight, white-blond hair down to his bum and the other with a dark blond Mohawk. The white-blond one said something to Frej in Norse, and Frej nodded. The guys head into the hallway.

'What did he say?' Kirsty asked.

Frej and Nathan exchanged a look. 'We should have asked your permission—' Frej began. 'This is your house.'

'Asked my permission for what?'

'We offered them room and board in exchange for helping to babysit Owen,' Nathan explained.

'You've been following Owen all this time?'

'Frej and I kept it up between us for months, but it's a lot easier with a rota, and—' Nathan hesitated and glanced at Frej. 'And they needed help surviving the twenty-first century.'

'Owen?' Morag demanded. 'The Shadow, you mean? But the black mist— thought that would—I didn't think he would be a problem anymore. That was the whole point.'

'He gets out.' Kirsty explained what she saw in the lane. 'He was shoved in, five, six times, at least.' She nodded to Nathan. 'The gaps Maureen talked about. He wasn't killing then because he was trapped in the time hole.'

'I thought—' Morag slammed her spoon down. 'I thought I'd got rid of him forever.'

'Your plan saved women in your time.'

'But not the women of now?'

Kirsty flinched. Nathan turned away quickly. *Morag was one of the women of now.*

'Well, that won't do,' she said firmly. 'There simply must be something permanent that can be done about him.'

Kirsty nodded. 'I agree.'

She looked at Frej and Nathan and Morag. She could see her reflection in the kitchen window. They all wore identical determined expressions.

'Somehow or other, this ends with us.'

Stuffed with soup, bread, and red wine, Kirsty yawned and found herself slumped against Frej's shoulder. Morag was excitedly telling an enthralled Nathan all about the time she won her school spelling bee with the word *malfeasance*. Frej beckoned Kirsty to follow him upstairs. He led her to her favourite room in the house.

The room was at the front of the house and was the perfect balance between spacious and cosy. Pleasingly square, there were flowers carved into the cornices and the wallpaper was dusky pink with a rose motif. It was a guest room when Kirsty was a child, but she used to sneak in every chance she got to play, colour, or read on the little window seat over-looking the road.

'I hope it is okay I chose this room,' Frej said quietly. Light snow fell outside, and a small fire crackled in the grate. 'I don't know—it felt like you. Of course, we can change if—'

'It's perfect.'

The fire was the only light in the room. It silhouetted Frej's powerful form as he stood respectfully back, letting Kirsty wander around the room, taking it all in. The flames cast dancing shadows, and Frej's hair glowed golden as he watched her silently. Her every cell sparkled to life as she took in his expression, the desire and longing swimming in his deep blue eyes.

Kirsty felt shy, suddenly. It had been two and a half years. She couldn't expect him to—he's hardly going to have—surely he would have had loads—

Then suddenly she didn't care anymore. He was here, and

he was hers now, and that was all that mattered. Her stomach churned with nerves and lust as she drank him in, savouring the exquisite anticipation for just one more moment—

'Come here,' she whispered.

He approached agonisingly slowly, sending flames flickering deep in Kirsty's core. The fire snapped and spat. Frej stopped close enough. Kirsty could feel his warmth, hear his ragged breath as he stared at her intently, ravenously. He leaned forward and softly nuzzled her neck just below her ear. He followed it with a kiss and a lick. Kirsty gasped and reached for him.

She brought his face to her and kissed him, gently at first, then deeper and deeper as they melted into one another. He lifted her, and she wrapped her legs around his waist, her hands twisted in his thick hair. One arm wrapped around Kirsty's waist, holding her tightly to him, and the other stroked her bum through her jeans.

Kirsty squirmed as he teased her. His breath was hot on her neck as he pressed a finger between her legs. She gave a choked scream and flung herself backwards onto the bed, bringing him tumbling on top of her.

They laughed as the old bed gave an ominous creak. Frej lifted his jumper over his head. Kirsty straddled him to run her hand down his chest, then slowly unbuttoned his jeans, rewarded with a deep moan. She teased him, stroking firmly through his jeans, feeling him harden as he groaned and shifted his hips to beg for more.

Kirsty reached into his jeans to wrap her fingers around him. She held her hand still a moment, enjoying the thick, solid feel of him. He ran a warm hand over the small of her back, traced her waist and slipped his fingers into the front of her jeans. Kirsty swallowed a scream as he pushed the flimsy fabric of her pants aside and gently stroked in tiny, maddening circles.

She leaned over him, nibbled his shoulder and firmly ran her hand up and down his length. The catch of his breath when she cupped his balls made her smile, and she tugged and stroked as she found her rhythm. He gasped and muttered in his language.

Kirsty pushed him farther back against the bed and yanked his jeans down, dipping her head to kiss the tip as he gave a strangled cry. He gathered her hair into a ponytail, tugging gently. Her tongue swirled around the head and down and up the length, following with her hands to squeeze and suck and lick until he was tight and growling and hopefully seeing stars.

She struggled out her jeans and underwear, clumsy with need, and straddled him. He took hold of her hips and ran his strong, warm hands up over her boobs and across her stomach. Kirsty slid herself back and forth along the outside of his length, teasing herself against his hardness as hot flames sprang to life inside her. Finally, she raised her hips to slowly take him in, enjoying his muttered, incoherent pleas as they started to move together.

Frej had such a lovely willy, Kirsty thought afterwards. It was decidedly proportional to the rest of him but not absurdly huge. It was a bouncy, friendly one with a smattering of freckles and a slight bend that gave it character.

She rested her cheek on his tummy, which was cool with sweat, contentedly watching it settle back down. Boys were always so keen to show off their big daft erections. But there was something so intimate, so soft and vulnerable about it afterwards. Kirsty trailed her nails over his hip bone and watched it give a sleepy twitch. She kissed her way back up his chest and nestled in the crook of his arm.

'This is normally my cue to leave,' she whispered, trailing her fingers over the ruddy gold hair on his chest. The fire was glowing embers, and Kirsty was warm next to her human heater. He reminded her of those adverts for hot porridge where the kid shone orange all the way to school.

He played with her hair, twisting tendrils around his fingers and then letting them fall back across her shoulders.

'What? Where do you want to go?'

Kirsty chuckled. She recalled from her summer in Stockholm that Scandinavians tended towards the literal. 'No. Normally, I mean. This bit—the lying together afterwards all glowy and melted. It makes me uncomfortable. Usually, about now, I'm fumbling around in the dark trying to find my knickers and my other shoe without waking the dude.'

Frej shifted and propped himself on his elbow. 'Why?'

Kirsty shrugged. 'I don't know.' *She did know.* 'I suppose I always figure boys are distracted by the prospect of boobs, then, you know, by the sight and feel of boobs—'

'Yours are very distracting,' he murmured, leaning down to plant a kiss on each nipple.

'So it's about now that they'll start to notice I'm—'

He frowned. 'You are what?'

'I don't know. That I'm just me.'

'You are just you. And I am just me. Who else would we be?'

His puzzled frown gave her the giggles. All those times over the years she had stubbed a toe trying to escape some strange bedroom suddenly seemed utterly absurd. Kirsty was just her. Who else would she be?

'I started a storm,' she blurted. 'A terrible storm. One of the worst in history.'

He nodded. 'You are very powerful.'

'People were killed. Half the city flattened. Hundreds of people were made homeless, injured. Because of me.'

Frej trailed a finger gently down the side of Kirsty's face. 'Did you intend to cause harm?'

'Of course not. I didn't—know I could do it. I was just so furious and heartsick, watching all those women think they had triumphed over Owen. The way he was so completely unscathed, so unstoppable—the anger became the storm.'

'Then you must learn to control your power.'

'But the suffering caused—it's awful, it's—'

'The past is not bad or good,' He kissed her hair. 'It only is. We must not sorrow at what we cannot change.'

'Alright, Yoda.'

'What?'

Kirsty chuckled sleepily.

'Learn what you must learn and move into the future,' Frej added. He yawned, curling himself around her like a giant Viking question mark. 'The past is set in stone. Only the future is to write.'

Frej's breathing became deep and even as he fell into a deep sleep. Kirsty stared at shadows dancing on the ceiling as her mind slowly unwound. *Morag doesn't stay here.* She must have gone back in time to marry Tommy, have Kirsty's mum, and live to raise Kirsty. Whatever was to come was already in the past for the Morag Kirsty had known.

Promise me you'll never help them, pet.

Was this why Morag told her that?

Could've been a bit mair fuckin' clear if so, Granny. Kirsty chuckled into the darkness. Frej stirred, muttered in his sleep.

Shoving Owen into time didn't work; that much was clear. Kirsty needed to figure out a permanent prison. A jail that she controlled.

As she drifted into sleep, the beginnings of a plan formed in her mind.

FORTY-THREE

'I want to go with you,' Frej said.

'You can't. I've told you why.'

They crowded around in the driveway of Kirsty's house. The snow had been falling heavily all day, softly blanketing the world in white. Now, the sky was clear overhead, stars dazzling through the blackness.

A taxi pulled up, and Harry's eldest sister Rachel popped out. She was done up to the nines, her blonde curls piled on her head, multicoloured feather earrings brushing her shoulders.

'You look fab, Rach.' Kirsty hugged her and waved to Jacqueline, Caroline and Siobhan, who crowded in the cab. 'Thanks for this, guys. You're sure you're okay with—'

Caroline waved her electric blue fur stole. 'Away, hen. If there's one thing we can do, it's put the lassie-mafia to work.'

'I've not had a proper night out in ages,' Rachel grinned.

'You were out last week!'

'That's ages!'

'This is my cousin, Morag.'

Morag washed and pressed her green dress this afternoon,

and then Kirsty summoned the power of YouTube tutorials to help her with *modern makeup*. Rachel gave Morag a hug, and the others peered curiously at her. *The Finnegan girls had known Morag all their lives—would they recognise her?*

'Will I do?' Morag asked anxiously.

'You look smashing.'

'Remember, if you see him—' Kirsty cautioned

'We get Morag out of there, and we call you.'

'Are you sure you don't want one of us to stay with you?' Jaqueline said, her eyes filled with concern. 'I've got a decent right hook from all my CrossFit.'

'I'm sure, but thanks.'

Morag gave Kirsty a quick, tight hug. She squished into the backseat next to Siobhan, who squeezed her hand. The taxi crunched slowly over the icy road and disappeared around the corner.

'He's been bundled out of enough pubs by you lot that word will have spread anyway,' Kirsty muttered, more to reassure herself than anyone else. 'He'll think of another way to get women alone sooner or later, but this should buy me enough time.'

Another cab pulled up, and Nathan hopped out, brandishing a large printout. Kirsty waved to Maureen. The librarian waited in the backseat, her eyes snapping with excitement. 'We've got it,' Nathan said. 'We checked it already, and the coast is clear. The van can follow us.'

'The Micks will be here any second.'

It turned out that the Micks moonlighted in their retirement as removal men. When Kirsty explained she needed their help, they had been more than happy to *forget* to return the lorry to the depot after their shift today. 'Anything for you, darlin', Old Mick shrugged, holding a hand up as Kirsty started to say more. 'You need us. That's all we need to know.'

'The owner definitely won't report it missing tonight? We

don't have time for the pair of you to be hauled off to jail tonight.'

'Aye, aye nae bother,' Wee Mick had promised. 'He pays peanuts and asks no questions. We'll have it back in plenty of time to move a nice family to Bearsden in the morning.'

'I don't like leaving you, kiddo,' Nathan said. The Micks' lorry rumbled to a stop behind the taxi. *NO JOB TOO SMALL* was emblazoned on the side in jaunty green paint. 'Owen doesn't even—'

'I need you to organise these guys,' Kirsty said. She couldn't meet his eye in case her resolve wavered. 'Nobody knows the old bomb shelters like you do.'

'Well, just make sure you—'

'I will.'

Old Mick hopped out. He opened the back doors of the filthy lorry, and the Vikings clambered in.

'You look mair like Agnes every day, pal,' he observed. Kirsty made a face. She didn't want to think about how alike she and Agnes were.

The detective Kirsty reported Agnes to had said something similar. The whole station had been buzzing with the news that Agnes McIvar was on the chopping block, but he seemed to understand what Kirsty had done. He reached across the interview table and awkwardly patted her hand.

'I bet she's known she's met her match in you a long time,' he said.

'I just want justice for the Finnegans,' Kirsty had muttered. 'I don't care about anything else.'

The back of the lorry was piled high with iron rods. Kirsty was reasonably confident that some building site or factory would be looking for them in the morning. It would be too late by then, so she hoped they had good insurance.

There was also an array of tools, a couple of welders' torches and several sacks of rice and dried beans. White-Blond

Viking eyed a torch with interest, and Solveig snapped at him in Norse. He meekly sat.

Frej hesitated by the doors.

'Kirsty,' he began.

'I'm not going to explain this to you again.' Kirsty's nerves made her snappier than she intended.

'But if I just—'

'Frej, she said no,' Solveig shouted. Kirsty flashed her a grateful smile.

'I'll see you afterwards,' she promised. 'Midnight, remember?' she shouted to Solveig. 'You must be gone by then.'

'It won't take us so long,' she said, eyeing the pile of supplies critically. 'We will be back here in two hours.'

'Good. Good luck.'

Kirsty gave Frej a quick hug. The lorry doors slammed shut behind him, and Kirsty gave them a whack for good measure. Wee Mick started the engine, and the lorry slithered a couple of times on the ice.

And then Kirsty was alone.

Forty-Four

Fresh snow muffled her footsteps as she walked lightly along the pavement. Owen was a few metres ahead of her. He wore a green and gold scarf tucked snugly into the collar of a long, dark overcoat. *He looked dashing*. Kirsty's stomach turned as he strode confidently across the road without a care.

He wasn't handsome. His face was middling at best. But his style, the way he carried himself. The confidence borne of centuries of getting his way was chillingly charismatic.

A woman waited at a bus stop. She wore a fuchsia bobble hat and a silver fake fur coat. She glanced up and gave Owen an approving once-over as he passed. Darts of horror scuttled down Kirsty's spine, but the woman looked back at her phone and continued scrolling. Owen walked on.

Kirsty had found him just where the Vikings said he'd be. They had been following him for two and a half years. They knew his routine. Horror curdled in her as she watched Owen emerge at 10 p.m. on the dot, just like they said.

They reached Argyle Street. Owen turned left, heading east. They passed a drunk serenading a busker, a handful of

late-night shoppers grabbing last-minute gifts, and a rowdy
work's Christmas night out.

'None of yous have even seen my willy!' a young guy with
a fiery red beard yelled indignantly. He turned to storm off and
skidded on some ice. With the infinite grace of the very pissed,
he glided into the side of WH Smith in an inadvertent
arabesque position. His colleagues dutifully applauded.

Owen slipped into a pub.

Showtime.

Inside, the pub was rammed with festive revellers. The
music was loud, and the chat was louder. The bar area heaved
with glittery bodies, red-faced, cheerfully slurring, cackling
with laughter. A woman wearing sequinned reindeer antlers
over her blue hair danced around her handbag, happily lost in
her own wee world. A big red-faced guy cut about, optimistically waving mistletoe in every punter's face, chortling when
they told him to get lost.

Owen approached a group of women in the corner. Kirsty
watched as one of them smiled at his charming opening line.
Her friend nudged her and pointed to something on her
phone.

Owen's photo. The woman's smile faded, and she coldly
turned away from him. Morag and the Finnegan sisters had
been doing their job. *Good start.* Now it was time for Kirsty to
do her job.

She approached a random group near the bar. A wee guy
with dark hair gelled into spikes told a heartfelt story to a
couple of women. One seemed interested, giving him wide-
eyed nods as he gesticulated. The other gave him the odd
encouraging nod but mostly looked over his shoulder for
someone more interesting. Her glasses were steamed up, and
she looked like she was

dreaming of toast and jammies. Kirsty gave her a hopeful
smile.

'Sorry to be a pain, but some roaster is making a pest of himself—mind if I stand here a minute?'

'Not at all. Which one is he?'

'I don't want to turn around. Tallish, brown hair,' Kirsty improvised wildly. 'He's wearing—a shirt.'

'I see him.' Her lip curled in disgust. 'Looks like a roaster indeed.'

'Oh god, my ex is here as well,' Kirsty gasped. 'It's not my night!'

Owen slithered through the crowd. Everywhere he looked, he got another cold shoulder. Irritation flashed in his eyes.

'Our first date, I got so drunk I tried to climb up stairs that weren't there,' Kirsty said.

Glasses Woman burst out laughing. Owen glanced over. *Bingo.*

'Then, on our second date, I accidentally hit on the barman,' Kirsty continued. 'Pure didn't mean to, just couldn't stop talking when he was taking our orders, and he was all like, *you seem nice, but are you not on a date with this guy?* I went *oh, I'm not a one-man woman*, which isn't even true but it sounded funny in my head. They both just stared at me. Then I ate all his chips. I really judge him, to be honest.'

Glasses giggled. 'What for?'

'There was a third date.'

A hand rested lightly on Kirsty's arm, and it took everything in her not to flinch. 'I'm terribly sorry to interrupt—'

Owen stared at Kirsty as though she were the only person in the bar. He glanced at the floor and then at her again as though her eyes were magnetic. Icy tentacles of fear slithered around Kirsty, but she kept her gaze steady.

'I know it's not the done thing to approach a woman anymore, and of course, I'll leave you alone if you prefer. It's just I would never forgive myself if I didn't at least try to speak to the most beautiful woman I've ever seen.'

Urgh. It was a bit much, even if Kirsty didn't know he was an ancient monster. Glasses subtly made a boaking face over his shoulder.

'I'm making an idiot of myself.' Owen grinned bashfully, a hint of a blush as he stepped respectfully back. His eyes never left Kirsty's. 'I'm so sorry. I'll leave you to your evening.'

'It's okay,' Kirsty said at the last second. 'We were just chatting.'

Glasses rolled her eyes indulgently. 'You're trouble,' she mouthed at Kirsty. Kirsty gave a *mea culpa* grin. Owen stepped infinitesimally closer, and revulsion crawled over her.

He didn't recognise her. She hadn't thought he would, but her heart hammered all the same. Thank heavens for misogynists who don't pay attention to women's faces. Owen turned to Glasses and held out his hand. 'What can get you both to drink?'

'Ooh, a bottle of champagne,' Kirsty said quickly.

'Any particular kind?'

'The most expensive.'

He raised an eyebrow, then nodded and disappeared into the crowd.

'He's no' really buying us a bottle of champagne.' Glasses made a face.

Kirsty shrugged. 'Suppose we're about to find out.'

'I don't like champagne.'

'Neither do I.'

A few minutes later, Owen popped the cork and poured it with a flourish.

'Are we celebrating?' he asked. He raised his glass in a silent toast.

'That remains to be seen,' Kirsty smiled. 'But so far, so good.'

Owen sipped his champagne. A frown flickered across his

face for the briefest fraction of a second as he stared intently at Kirsty. Nerves leapt into her throat.

'What?'

He leaned forward slowly, staring into her eyes as though peering into her soul. Her heart fluttered like a panicked bird trying to escape. Owen reached out and touched Kirsty's cheek.

'Eyelash,' he whispered. 'You should make a wish.'

Kirsty leaned forward to blow gently on his finger. *Boak.*

'Each of them carries both male and female sex organs,' announced the spiky-haired guy chatting up Glasses' pal. 'Even the Australian ones that are as big as snakes. They can actually mate with themselves. Which would make life easier, eh? Haha.'

He actually said *haha.*

'And how do they ruin forests again?' asked Glasses, evidently deciding that earthworm chat was a better bet than Owen's patter.

'Perhaps we could go for a walk?' Owen asked softly. Kirsty could barely hear him over the rabble. 'It's so noisy here, and the moon is beautiful tonight.'

The other woman's eyes widened in recognition as she looked at Owen. *Shit.*

'Hold on a minute, yous should stay here,' she shouted over the crowd. 'We don't have to talk about earthworms.'

'It's okay,' Kirsty muttered.

Morag and the Finnegan sisters had certainly been productive. Kirsty tried desperately to send silent vibes that she was the one exception to the *Keep Women Away from the Lanky Ginger* rule of the night. 'Owen here is an old friend. We haven't seen each other since, uhh, Rachel and Gus's wedding, have we?' Steeling herself against revulsion, she slipped her arm through Owen's. 'We're going to meet some uni friends at another pub across the road.'

The woman hesitated, unsure but clearly uncomfortable. 'Why don't we all go?' she said.

Spiky Hair looked at her as though she was mad, but Glasses was catching on. She knew Owen and Kirsty weren't old uni friends. 'Yeah,' she said quickly. 'Any old friends of yours are friends of ours. We'll come.'

'Could you just give us two secs?' Kirsty smiled winningly at Owen. He headed for the door, and Kirsty leaned closer to the women. 'I know who he is,' she hissed quickly. 'I'm undercover. There's backup waiting for me outside.'

The women nodded with relief, but Spiky Hair frowned. 'What are you talking about? I'm Specialist Crimes Division. What's your officer number?'

'I'm on—Fraser's team,' Kirsty snapped as authoritatively as she could muster. 'Stuart Fraser.' Hopefully, Spiky Hair was too wee to be a Taggart fan.

'Who?'

'Stuart,' she added. She'd once winched a police officer called Stuart at The Garage. 'Over and out.'

She retreated quickly and joined Owen at the door. 'Sorry about that.' She shook her head with a rueful shrug. 'My friends can be a bit—'

'That's quite alright. I understand how it is.'

Kirsty reached for the door, but Owen stepped in her way. Nerves twisted with disgust as he leaned so close she felt his breath warm on her ear.

'I know your friends very well,' he whispered. 'In fact, I've got your Viking.'

FORTY-FIVE

White light flashed from Kirsty's fingers. A guy yelped as the table he was standing at smouldered. Owen screeched, holding out a faintly blistered hand.

' I TOLD you to stop that,' he whined. 'It HURTS.'

'It's *supposed to,*' Kirsty yelled, blasting him again and kicking him in the shin for good measure. An umbrella drying by the door burst into flame, and people screamed. 'Where is Frej? What have you done with him?'

'Oh, enough of this,' Owen snarled.

White light flashed from *his* fingers. An almighty gut punch took Kirsty's breath away before Owen blasted her again.

'Yous two, OOT,' roared a gigantic barman with a bushy black beard like a pirate's. 'There'll be nae fuckin' fireworks in my pub.'

He opened the door and booted Owen out into the snow. Kirsty was about to sweetly thank him when he yanked her by the collar and flung her out too. She supposed that was fair enough.

She staggered on the freezing pavement, still a bit winded and wobbly. Owen leapt high into the air and kicked her in the face. Her head snapped back and her nose exploded with blood.

'You ARSEHOLE,' she howled. He flashed her with white light again. It may not pulverise her, but it stung like a bugger.

She flew at him, a feral rugby tackle. She nutted him in the nuts and he shrieked. He yanked her hair, and she bit his hand and rammed his hip with her shoulder, sending him sprawling over a pile of bin bags.

Kirsty ran, slithering and sliding on the glazed pavement. Owen scrabbled free from the rubbish. A few crisp packets and a bit of lettuce clung to his overcoat as he yanked her arm half out of the socket and spun her like a helicopter blade. He let go, and Kirsty slammed into a jewellery shop window at the bottom of Buchanan Street, setting off a screeching alarm.

'That's a lassie, man,' a muscly young guy wearing a Santa hat objected. 'You cannae fight a—'

Kirsty took another flying leap and thumped Owen's head with both fists in mid-air, sending him teetering to the ground.

'Oh right, forget that, she's fine,' Santa Hat muttered quickly.

By the time they reached the top of Buchanan Street, they had attracted a crowd. A couple of polis had their battering sticks out ready. *Maybe Kirsty was McIvar after all.* She jumped onto Owen's shoulders and battered him about the ears. He bit her calf and flung himself backwards like a toddler having a tantrum, smashing Kirsty head-first on the pavement. Her skull clanged, and she saw stars.

'Some'dy phone her an ambulance!'

'He's bleeding more,' someone else observed. 'She got half his ear off a minute ago.'

'Are they doing a play?'

'Right, that's quite enough,' one of the polis guys piped up. 'Time we all calmed down, eh?'

Kirsty was on top of the subway station in a single bound, only half aware of the awed gasp that garnered her. She slipped and was struggling to get a foothold on the frosty glass when Owen slammed into her from behind. He hauled her over his shoulder, lifted her above his head and—

Kirsty twisted, yanking his hair to loosen his grip. She flung herself wildly, flying through the air in a deranged doggy paddle. She collided with cold stone and clung, taking a second to catch her breath and—

She was on the Buchanan Centre.

On the side of it.

Clinging to the glass above the doors like a spider.

Jesus Joney.

She didn't have time to ponder that any further. Owen was right behind her. He lunged for her, those ferocious black-diamond eyes glittering. Kirsty steeled herself against the serious boak at her arachnoid qualities and scuttled upwards.

Owen's ragged breath was just behind as Kirsty sprung over the side of the roof, a bizarre euphoria pumping through her veins. Reaching the edge, she jumped into oblivion and landed on a greenish roof of an older building. This one was slanted, but it barely slowed her down. She skipped and galloped and *frolicked,* swinging round chimneys, hopping fire ladders and whizzing over glass domes.

The city was spread below her, twinkling, nestled in glistening snow. Kirsty belted over gleaming glass buildings, crumbling brick buildings, and majestic sandstone buildings. The city snoozed far below her. *Her city.*

Poverty and riches and warmth and danger. Cultural capital, bubonic plague. Vibratey time holes, lepers who play *Simon Says* with wee girls. And maniac serial killers who can't be killed.

She'd see about that last bit.

Stars dazzled, wind swirled, and the air glittered and crackled.

Spotting the river glistening in the moonlight up ahead, Kirsty paused for an instant. She slipped behind a chimney stack to take a second to orientate herself. They were going in the wrong direction. They'd come too far south.

'You look just like her,' Owen crooned. Kirsty couldn't see him, but he was nearby. *She could have impaled him on the spiky bit on top of the Princes Centre*, she thought with dismay. *Too late now.* 'It's almost like fighting with her again.' He gave a salacious chuckle and Kirsty shuddered with revulsion. 'Do you understand yet? Have you figured it out? I could help you. I would do that for her.'

Kirsty hesitated, temptation slithering through her.

'Will ye fuck?' she yelled and took off again.

Owen scuttled after her. She spotted the roof of St Enoch's shopping centre, grabbed onto a fire escape and vaulted herself over.

The road was too wide.

Shit—

Kirsty flailed desperately in mid-air, visions of going splat on Jamaica Street dancing through her head. At the last second, her fingertips grasped the roof. She gripped desperately, legs swinging wildly.

One finger slipped, and she swallowed a scream. She gritted her teeth and hauled herself back onto the roof, where she turned and—

Watched as Owen went splat on Jamaica Street.

FORTY-SIX

'Oh, mammy!' howled a man on the street. 'He needs a doacter! Is there no' a doacter anywhere?'

Owen lay deathly still, his broken body sticking in horrifically unnatural directions.

That won't keep him down for long. Kirsty hopped over the side and did her spider routine down to the pavement. One day, she might manage it without getting the heebie-jeebies. She ran to Owen and the hysterical passerby.

'I'm a doctor,' she announced.

The elderly man, with thick white hair and large red nose, looked her up and down doubtfully. 'Are you sure?'

'Quite sure,' Kirsty snapped, affronted that he dared question her non-existent medical qualifications. 'Step back, please. I'll take care of him from here.'

'You shouldnae move him, think his neck's mebbe broken,' the man shouted in alarm.

Given that Owen's spine was currently zigzagged over the kerb, Kirsty didn't need non-existent medical qualifications to know there was no *maybe* about it.

'*You* shouldn't move him,' she corrected imperiously. 'I'm qualified. Now stand back.'

The man shuffled back with clear misgivings. Kirsty reached down and unceremoniously hoisted Owen over my shoulder like a sack of coal.

' I—don't think you should do that,' he whispered faintly. 'Do you mind?'

Kirsty gestured haughtily for the man to get out of her way and marched into the night with an ancient serial killer draped over her shoulders.

She stuck to the back streets because—well, for obvious reasons. Shadowy side streets behind the shopping centre, across the car park, past the alleyway where Morag was found and where Kirsty watched multiple women boot Owen into oblivion. He was starting to stir by the time they got close. Kirsty briefly crossed her fingers and hoped that Nathan's directions were accurate.

Just beyond the Barrowlands, she spotted the manhole cover. It had been cleared of snow. On it, a rune Solveig had explained meant *here* was painted in glossy hot pink. Kirsty tossed Owen on the pavement. He wriggled a bit, emanating bone-tingling cracks and pops as his spine started to snap back into place. She managed to stuff him into the hole before he was properly conscious.

She didn't hear him land at the bottom, which was a good sign. Nathan did exactly as she asked. The stench of rancid water washed over her, and her stomach turned. She climbed down the rusty, rickety ladder.

The ladder went down seemingly forever. Kirsty's arms and legs weakened as the adrenaline drained in the cool darkness. The world above receded as she climbed ever downwards. Silence pounded in her ears.

Not long now. Just keep it together a bit longer.
Then you can fall apart.

By the time she spotted Owen, he was crawling away. Kirsty strolled after him. Her cuts and bruises from the fight were healing with tingling itches but she was pleased to note that Owen was clearly still in pain. She wondered if it was to do with age, or just that a five-storey drop to go splat on Jamaica Street will take it out of anyone.

Kirsty resolved to avoid finding out any time soon.

The tunnel walls were stone, a jagged, uneven shape, contrasting the flawless custom-built cylinders above. These were the deepest, oldest tunnels. Heaviness hung in the air, the weight of the city carrying on its business far above. The darkness was so thick it was almost like a tangible thing, swirling around them, whispering treacherous promises that it would keep their secrets.

Kirsty could only just discern Owen in the glow of the luminous line painted roughly along the wall. Owen started to crawl faster, gaining energy, springing back to life before her eyes.

At a fork in the tunnel, Owen clambered to his feet. He swayed a touch as he rolled his neck, working out the final kink. The luminous rune reading *this way* shimmered above his head. Kirsty poked him sharply in the back.

'Keep going,' she ordered like a sergeant major.

Owen whirled around and belted Kirsty so hard she flew against the stone wall. Pain exploded in her skull like fireworks. She slithered to the ground. Before she could move, Owen yanked her hair and whirled her against the other wall. Sickening cracks echoed around the stone walls.

Owen threw back his head and laughed. The sharp, maniacal sound bounced round and round. 'You little *bitch*,' he cackled. 'I'm going to enjoy this.'

Agony shrieked through Kirsty like lightning as she wriggled from his grasp and ran. Owen's white light blasted her over and over, sharp electric shocks that rained down on her like acid. Her shattered legs gave way. Kirsty dragged herself with her arms, then scrambled back to her feet when she could. It was excruciating. She screamed with abandon, hearing her pain ricocheting over and over. She forced herself ever forwards, as fast as she could—

There it was!

Kirsty screeched with relief and bounded the final few steps. Owen grabbed for her with a growl of loathing—Kirsty swerved violently. He lurched past, and Kirsty slammed the prison door behind him.

'Actually, *I'm* going to enjoy this,' she corrected.

The bolt was heavy. Kirsty could barely grasp the gigantic chain, but Owen was blinded by rage. He flung himself wildly against the solid iron, which gave Kirsty precious seconds to wind and clip and bolt the lock the way Solveig showed her.

She collapsed on the filthy, damp ground, a safe distance from the prison, and let herself tremble violently for a few seconds. Owen barked and bawled, violently worrying at every inch of the prison. It seemed, however, that Viking construction was high quality and the bars didn't even wobble.

Kirsty's heart was still racing. She was drenched in sweat and congealing blood, and she had a couple of bones yet to heal, but Owen was locked away. Banged up. In the nick.

Kirsty staggered back a couple of steps, laughing with hysterical relief.

'Welcome to purgatory, Owen.'

He screeched, an incoherent howl of choler and loathing.

'Seems to me that a wee bit of time alone with your thoughts is just what you need.'

Owen scampered back and forth, searching in vain for weaknesses in the cage. The tunnel was a dead end. The Vikings had reinforced the walls and ceilings with bars so there would be no burrowing his way out. The lock was complex and medieval. Solveig designed it. Kirsty didn't ask how many people she'd had cause to imprison in her time. Only Solveig and Kirsty could ever open it.

A small stream trickled along a sunken gutter at one side of the cage. It was a leak from the nearby Molendinar Burn, which ran above ground in this area when Mungo established his cathedral. The rice and beans would keep Owen going for a while. Solveig explained that they continued to eat and sleep mostly out of habit. While food provided energy, they could go for days or weeks without it if necessary.

'Maybe a few centuries of reflection will help you to see the error of your ways,' Kirsty smirked.

Owen froze, and Kirsty instinctively shrank back. He was listening, his eyes alert, darting to and fro like a trapped animal. Which he was.

A slow smile spread across his face.

'You weren't supposed to do this,' he sing-songed. 'You're going to get in *trou-ble*.'

'I don't recall asking anyone's permission.'

Owen threw back his head and laughed. His deranged shrieks reverberated around the tunnel and through Kirsty's bones. She started to walk away.

'Ooh, he's angry,' Owen guffawed. 'You're not going to like it.'

FORTY-SEVEN

Tiredness landed differently when you were immortal. Kirsty didn't have gritty eyes; she hadn't needed to yawn. She felt more spacey than sleepy.

Her body fizzed as it healed and restored itself. It was itchy as hell. Solveig had warned about the itchiness. Her best guess was that was something to do with the turbo-charged healing process. It was a pain in the arse but better than the alternative, Kirsty supposed.

But Owen was trapped. It was a permanent prison that Kirsty controlled. He wouldn't escape until Kirsty figured out how to kill him. Sometimes, the simplest solutions were the best.

After what felt like an age hiking back through endless tunnels, Kirsty heaved the manhole cover to one side and emerged into a bright, frosty morning. The air was sharp and invigorating. Pristine snow twinkled in the sun.

Frej sat on the pavement.

'Breakfast rolls?' he asked, holding a hand to Kirsty.

'He said he got you,' Kirsty whooped, running for him. 'Owen said he had my Viking.'

'Oh, he's got Snorri tied up.'

'Who?'

'With the long, pale hair.'

'He's not my Viking.'

'How would Owen know that? Snorri will escape when he wakes up. Owen is not very good at tying knots.'

'So—so then—' Kirsty couldn't quite believe it. 'Everything is okay? Owen is banged up, and everyone is safe.'

'I think so.' Frej smiled and leaned in to kiss her.

'In a minute,' she grinned, gathering a handful of snow into a ball. It hit him square between the shoulders. He whirled around with a whoop as Kirsty pelted him with a second snowball.

His return fire nearly knocked her off her feet. She grabbed an armful, leapt high and dumped it on his head. He laughed, threw himself at her, and tackled her to the ground. They rolled over the snow, laughing and screaming in an entirely unskilled and undignified wrestling match.

Kirsty stuffed snow up Frej's jumper, followed by a series of hot kisses over his chest. He flipped her over to nibble his way over her hip and slip a shard of ice under her bra. It was early enough that the streets of the East End were quiet, but they were going to get done for indecent exposure if they weren't careful. Kirsty reluctantly pulled away.

'Breakfast rolls,' she said firmly.

Frej kissed the tip of her nose, and she smiled as shivers rippled through her. 'First,' she whispered.

'Just, eh—haud on a wee minute, Kirsty,' said a voice.

Kirsty froze.

She turned around, horror curdling in her as she took in the sight of Kenny standing over them, silhouetted by the morning sun. Big Mad Kenny. Kirsty's old pal from the gym.

'Hurricane Kirsty,' Kirsty said slowly. 'You've always called me that.'

'The Great Storm of 1968 was a belter, doll,' Kenny chuckled, shaking his head. 'Always said you were trouble.'

'You -- knew? All that stuff about stars and Sauchiehall Street being sacred, you've known about it all the whole time?'

'Ach aye, I was a trader, once upon a time,' Kenny chuckled. 'I started that rumour about the willow forest being sacred to get more foot traffic. Worked a treat till bloody Ninian came along an' filled folks' heads with nonsense.'

'Kirsty!'

Nathan, Morag and Solveig were making their way up the hill towards them.

'No—stay back—' Kirsty shouted.

'Did you do it? Is he trapped?'

'Please—stay where you are —'

Kirsty had known Kenny for most of her life, yet terror slithered in her guts as she saw his expression shift. Kenny raised a hand slowly over his face. His body simultaneously grew and crumpled in on itself, his cheeks becoming hollow, his skin papery thin and translucent. Eye sockets gaped as though too big for his shrunken skull, and long fingers became spindly and skeletal. His hair turned pure white and soft. He shimmered in the morning sun, ancient, inhuman and terrifying.

Solveig broke into a run, shouting something in another language as she belted up the hill. Kirsty looked to Frej, but he shook his head. He didn't understand either.

'Lailoken!' Solveig shouted joyfully.

Lailoken? Kirsty shook her head, terror stabbing at her. Frej's hand slid into hers, but even that didn't provide its usual comfort.

'You're—you're Merlin the Magician? What the fuck, Kenny?'

'I've never wore a pokey hat.'

Horror pooled in Kirsty's stomach. The night before

Kirsty had found Owen leaving the disused building above Kenny's gym. She'd tried to tell herself it meant nothing, that it was a coincidence—but she'd known it wasn't good news.

Solveig stopped just before she reached Kenny, staring uncertainly as she took in his appearance. 'What are you doing?' she whispered. 'Anyone could see.'

Sure enough, a wee white van came tearing down the street, careened wildly as the driver evidently spotted Kenny and crashed into a bus stop.

'We need tae have a wee word before anyone's getting rolls,' Kenny said softly, his eyes never leaving Kirsty's.

'You've been lying to me all my life,' Kirsty spat. 'I don't need a wee word wi' you about anything.'

'We're having a word if I say we're having a word.'

'Are we fuck, old man. I've had it up to here with all this magic pish the night. I'm getting rolls with Frej and you can just bloody lump—'

Kenny casually flicked his hand, and Kirsty's arm nearly jerked off as Frej slammed several feet backwards into a shop window. The window shattered and Frej winced with pain, blood running down his face. He raised a weak hand to reassure Kirsty as she lunged towards him.

'I wouldn't move if I were you, doll.'

It was then Kirsty realised Kenny wasn't alone. He nodded to someone behind him. Kirsty got a flash of white hair.

Mrs McCafferty.

But it was Agnes.

And with her was Martin Finnegan.

Thank you so much for reading *Before Again*. As you could maybe tell, it's a story I am very passionate about - and there is lots more where it came from!

The second book, *Days Gone Next*, will be out early 2023, and is currently being serialised for **free** in my newsletter.

Even you prefer to binge your books in one go, my newsletter is the place to be to find out the release date before anyone else — and also the chance to get hold of pre-release copies before anyone else!

You can sign up right here:

Fikabooks.com/newsletter

Thanks again!

Claire xxx

Printed in Great Britain
by Amazon

16346948R00171